A Murder of Convenience

by

Kathleen Buckley

Publishing History
First Edition, 2025
Trade Paperback ISBN 978-1-5092-6028-7
Digital ISBN 978-1-5092-6029-4

Published in the United States of America

Dedication

To Christopher N. Roybal, MD, ophthalmologist par excellence, and the helpful ladies of Facebook's 18th Century Sewing group, Laura Kalnaja, Kelli Wilkinson, Josefina DelTorre, LK Scott, Diana Lynn Stevens, and Melissa Ennis

Prologue

Early September, 1740, Cuthbert Hall, Cumberland

"You look a veritable dowdy, Ellen," Randolph Cuthbert said, not for the first time since escorting her from her home in Durham to his uncle's estate in Cumberland. "I would think at least you could be ready on time to spare me embarrassment." He had come to her chamber to take her down to supper.

Why would I wish to do that? She preferred to avoid an acrimonious exchange lest some servant hear and report it to Randolph's—known as Randy to his friends—uncle, the Earl of Keswick. "Living in the country I would be ridiculous, dressing à la mode." But he had flustered her by crowding into her room and standing where she had to brush by him to get to the chest of drawers to find her string of amber beads.

The house party was a small one, almost a family affair. They had been given separate bedchambers as Randolph was very clever at getting his own way. He could not count on doing so with his uncle. Considering the earl's observation on their arrival several hours earlier—"I see you still cannot expect an heir yet"—his success this time was remarkable.

"Even so, you might have thought how odd we would look with you dressed like a rustic. I had to tell my uncle you thought such unfashionable dress suitable for the wilds of Cumberland."

His uncle must have commented upon her simple gowns and petticoats. Perhaps they had come as a surprise, as the last time they had visited Earl Keswick she still had the elegant clothing bought on her betrothal. The Cuthberts were not a particularly close or fond family.

She and Randolph would not be present now, if the earl's remaining child had not died six months ago, leaving no living son. Randolph was now Keswick's heir, to his carefully concealed jubilation.

They had only been at Cuthbert Hall for hours, after spending the previous two days in Randolph's traveling coach. If that had been the equivalent of Hell, the next nineteen days were likely no worse than the Papists' purgatory. She and Randolph would spend little time in each other's company. He and the men would amuse themselves with cards, riding, coursing hares, and fishing in the river. The women would stroll or ride, play loo, sit with their needlework, and chatter.

She would play her part, less out of fear of embarrassing her husband and the earl than to avoid revealing herself as an object of pity or contempt. Only nineteen days to endure and then two more in the coach with her husband.

As it fell out, her husband's presence was not the worst trial of the gathering.

Chapter 1

September 30, 1740, Cumberland: The First Day Following the Michaelmas Rent Day and Harvest Festival

Ellen woke earlier than usual to a conviction that she had heard something. Snug under her blankets and coverlet, she lay listening. Faint sounds in the passage near her door had roused her. Nothing more than the housemaid going about her work, which no one of the late-rising fashionable set even noticed. The girl must have dropped something. Nothing for Ellen to worry about. A cheering thought occurred to her: today and tomorrow to be got through, and the following day she would be on her way home. That meant two days trapped in the coach with her husband, but sometimes he would choose to ride instead. Then Cuthbert would leave her to her peaceful life in Durham, well away from him.

A sudden urgent whisper in the passage broke into these happy reflections. She rose and padded to the door, wondering if she should open it and see what the disturbance was. No. Embarrassing for all concerned, especially if 'twere a guest, fallen asleep over brandy downstairs, trying now to creep to his chamber and lost, or someone's lover taking his leave of her surreptitiously but not silently enough. The only occupied rooms at this end of the wing were her own and Lydia Forsyth's.

Her door did not fit quite tightly. Standing so near, she was able to make out murmurs, though not words. Servants from the intonation. A domestic crisis, then, not an assignation. A sense of movement followed a silence. She waited to hear anything else, but the difficulty must have been resolved. She could put on her *robe de chambre*, light a candle, and settle down to read by the fire. Whatever the problem, it had taken place after the girl had laid her fire, fortunately. But it was still far too early to rise. Even if she did not fall asleep, she could still drowse until a reasonable hour.

Climbing into bed, she turned on her side and pulled the covers up over her head. Four more days to the end of purgatory, then she need not see him again for months. In Durham, she would take up her usual activities. The man who came to tidy the garden every week would have sown the seeds of poppies, cornflower, and larkspur, but he would have done so in geometric beds. He did not approve of flowers rioting at will. She would add some to grow in drifts, softening the straight lines. The carpets should be beaten and the chimneys swept before the cold weather set in. *Ask what fruit Cook had preserved...*

When the girl came with her wash water, she had little to say, a change from her usual cheerful prattle. She laid out the plain green riding habit without comment instead of suggesting the more elegant London-made habit. Ellen would have asked if she were unwell or unhappy but did not feel she knew Kitty sufficiently to do so. Her own maid, left behind in Durham, was subject to moods, which Ellen ignored as she did not really care if the woman was distressed. On their marriage, Randolph had insisted Ellen needed a maid able to dress a lady of the beau monde and had selected Manon Allard himself. She was wasted in Durham and on Ellen. They both knew it.

She went down to breakfast despite the custom of most ladies of taking their morning meal in bed. Ellen wanted more than a bun and chocolate. Downstairs one was not constrained by what the kitchen or one's maid considered a lady should eat and in what amounts. Besides, it made less work for the servants.

The footmen Ellen passed on her way were expressionless, but their eyes were restless. The disturbance she had sensed upstairs was rippling through the house.

Perhaps no one else noticed. People of her own class seldom paid attention to the men and women who served them unless they were old family retainers or else gave cause for offense. She had known and valued all her family's longtime servants. Since her marriage, watchfulness had become a matter of self-defense. Randolph's servants tended not to stay long, except for his butler, housekeeper, and valet, all of whom had been not quite openly contemptuous of her during the time they had lived together in London. They had undermined her authority whenever possible. Now, that was a problem only on her occasional brief visits to London. All but one of her Durham servants were loyal to her.

Lord Keswick's seat at the head of the table was empty. She was surprised as he usually breakfasted early. She respected him except for his unvoiced but obvious assumption that she did not try hard enough to become pregnant. It would have been amusing if only he had believed the same of Randolph.

Only Stephen Cuthbert and Cornelius Wilmot, the earl's other nephews, and his distant cousin, Ismay Tate, were present when Ellen entered. The others were either breakfasting in their chambers or had not risen yet. Randolph clung to London ways even in the country. All the better. His remarks about her unladylike appetite were not a good beginning for the day. She was not the one who had gained weight since they married.

Stephen and Cornelius were discussing today's riding expedition. Cornelius favored Penrith Beacon as a destination. Stephen maintained that Brougham Castle, a picturesque ruin at which three Roman roads met, was both more impressive and older.

The young men usually rode out in the morning, though often Ellen was the only female present. Ismay Tate, an accomplished horsewoman, did so when her duties as the earl's hostess permitted. She was in habit and boots today, so she meant to join them. Georgina Hodge sometimes rode, too, when she could drag herself out of bed; she was not a lark. She probably went for the chance to speak in some privacy with Cornelius and without her mama, an eagle-eyed chaperon. Ellen avoided inflicting herself on them, gaining an opportunity to canter or even gallop; Georgina was a timid rider. As long as Georgina and Cornelius did not stray far from the others, a duenna was scarcely necessary: the idea of a seduction on horseback by so well-conducted a young man as Cornelius made her want to laugh.

Neither Caleb Hodge nor his wife came of the

gentry class though they were not coarse, and the girl had been brought up with the advantages of a governess and lessons in music, dance, and drawing. She was indistinguishable from any number of girls of the landed gentry or nobility. Still, Georgina's remarkable dowry was the reason for her presence at Cuthbert Hall.

Those who advocated marriages made solely for money or position were quick to assert the couple would soon learn to rub along together. Perhaps some did.

Cornelius was a pleasant young man, though "young" was his most relevant characteristic. He and Georgina might do very well for each other if Lydia Forsyth did not continue to toy with Cornelius for sport. He was too inexperienced to appeal to her, though perhaps she was simply unable to refrain from flirtation with any man. She had not used her tricks with Keswick, but mayhap she was wary of him.

Ismay pointed out several advantages and disadvantages of the proposed destinations: length of ride, terrain, and presence or absence of some inn where they could find refreshment. Ellen had no opinion as her only desire was to get out of the house and ride. The young men had almost decided on Brougham Castle when Caleb Hodge bustled in.

His sharp eyes darted around the room. His greeting, "Good! No servants," captured their attention. Savoring the moment, he continued. "The earl has brought in a magistrate."

"A magistrate?" Ismay repeated. "Whatever for?"

Hodge puffed up, great with news. "I overheard one of the footmen tell the butler the magistrate had arrived. The butler warned him there was to be no talk among the servants about the death on pain of dismissal."

Ismay opened her mouth and closed it again, compressing her lips on some question she realized was best unasked, a feeling Ellen knew well.

Stephen spoke quietly in Cornelius's ear. The latter nodded, stood and strode to the door. Opening it, he raised his voice to speak to the footman on duty halfway down the passage. "Send a message to the stable. We will not ride this morning after all."

Ismay had finished her meal and now drank the last of her chocolate, her brow furrowed. After a moment she rose. "I will change out of my habit and go to the family parlor. "

"A good idea," Stephen said.

Cornelius had not resumed his place at the table. "So will I. I believe I saw the most recent issue of *The Gentleman's Magazine* there."

Ellen was not immune from the instinct to huddle like sheep or cattle in the face of a storm. They left Hodge to eat his breakfast, the attraction of food being stronger at the moment than his desire to be with his fellow kind. Perhaps he did not feel threatened. For that matter, why did she and the others? Someone was dead, but although it might be cause for pity and sorrow, it could have little to do with them.

Hodge did not fail to pass on his tidbit of gossip to those who had broken their fast in their chambers and wandered into the parlor. This ended any discussion of today's possible amusements. A subdued gathering settled to read, do needlework, or talk quietly while waiting to learn more. The butler's warning to the servants must mean there was some odd or scandalous circumstance about the death. If the earl had hoped to keep the matter private, he would be disappointed.

Although Ismay had suggested the parlor, she did not linger there but begged their pardon and went off to speak to the butler about some sort of arrangements. She had put on a plain brown mantua, as Ellen had abandoned riding clothes for her comfortable old green sacque.

Cornelius Wilmot said, "Now I think on it, I may have seen the magistrate ride up, mayhap with a constable or a doctor. There were two men, anyway."

Stephen Cuthbert suggested they not speak more about the crime. "If Lord Keswick finds out we know, the servants will get the blame for letting it slip."

Hodge agreed. "Mayhap I shouldn't have spoken. I'm close-mouthed about business matters, but hearing what the butler said set me right back upon my heels."

Studying the group, a book unread in her lap, Ellen wondered. The only ones not present were Randolph, Mistress Hodge and her daughter, and Lydia Forsyth. She doubted either of the Hodge ladies was dead as Mr. Hodge would have known. Neither Cuthbert nor Lydia were early risers. They might still be sleeping.

The victim need not be a guest, of course. Perhaps some servant? Of all the possibilities, who would be missed the least? As she mused over this question, memory struck her with the force of a blow: the stir and voices outside her door in the early hours. The parlor was pleasantly warm, but Ellen suddenly felt as chilled as if she had been drenched in cold water.

****

Watching his cousin sip distastefully at his breakfast, a caudle of green tea, white wine, egg yolks, and sugar, Sir Hugh Montgomery began to think the doctor was correct. Wallace Seaton might really be dying. He had always been a hearty trencherman, in despite of which he had been so active he had not developed a paunch though he was in the middle of his fifth decade. Now his eating habits were those of a frail, toothless old lady: soft foods only.

"I can't easily swallow solid food. It often sticks part way down. Sometimes it makes me cough, and I vomit it up. At least now that I eat pap and soft-cooked eggs, I seldom have indigestion. But you see why I summoned you. I need to have my affairs in order before…" He grimaced. "My son is sixteen. Too young to deal with the aftermath, even if I were to live several more years."

As Sir Hugh did not know how to respond, he welcomed the entrance of the butler.

"Sir, his lordship, the Earl of Keswick, requests your presence most urgently, relating to a crime."

"What is it? Poaching?"

"The groom who brought the message did not know, only that he was told the matter was urgent."

"One of his guests has misplaced a piece of jewelry, I suppose. Well, then, Hugh, would you like to accompany me? This may be the best amusement I can offer you."

"And two magistrates are better than one? I look forward to it. The coach?" Wallace tired easily.

Seaton sighed. "Too slow. We will ride."

Seeing this part of Cumberland again from horseback woke memories of the summers he had spent with his uncle's family during his school years.

Their nearest neighbors had been the Hamiltons,

whose only son was some years older than Hugh and Wallace. They had never got to know him well. Instead Eilidh, several years younger than Hugh, became their favorite playmate. Unlike his own sisters, or any other girl he'd known, she didn't care a straw for dolls or ribbons. Her tomboyish ways were sighed or tutted over, but even her mama saw no point in trying to reform her. If they played marbles, she won. When they scavenged planks to build a fort in an oak tree, she helped and proved better at planning its construction than they. He cherished a memory of her kilting up her petticoats, shoeless and stockingless, to ford a stream with them. She had been seventeen at the time.

On his last visit a year later, before he began his five years' training as an articled clerk to an attorney, she had changed. She was no longer permitted to run as free as a stray cat; her mother would scarce let her outdoors and never unchaperoned. Lady Hamilton was waging war against her freckles with parasols, broad-brimmed hats, and a variety of lotions meant to preserve the complexion. Previously the baroness had spent all her efforts on Eilidh's older sister. Now she was preparing for Eilidh's eventual marriage.

He had regretted her transformation from tomboy to young lady. In a rare moment when they could speak freely, she explained that circumstances required it now her brother was dead.

"I must make a good marriage, and soon. Andrew's death brought home to my father and mother that life is uncertain. We have no male relative who could inherit when Papa dies, so the manor will be lost to the Crown. My mother has her jointure, but it is not large enough to support herself, Grace, and me, and to move in the kind of society where we might make suitable marriages. Mary and her husband live in Bristol and are not in circumstances to take us all in. They are comfortable and his prospects are excellent, but he is in commerce." She smiled wryly. "My parents let my older sister marry for love and now are set upon us making marriages suitable to a baron's daughters. Papa will contrive to betroth me to someone who moves in higher circles than ours. Grace is so beautiful finding a suitable husband for her will be easy, but she is too young to marry yet or for the next half dozen years."

"How difficult can it be to find you a good marriage, with your papa being a baron?" Too late it occurred to Hugh that it might be a question of coin, or its lack. Did the girls not have dowries?

Eilidh grinned in that unrestrained way he remembered from earlier summers. "You have forgotten. My grandpapa on my mother's side made his fortune in trade, though we never speak of that," she said primly. "Grace and I have excellent dowries. Mine will make up for my red hair, freckles, and height. The difficulty is, Papa's family never moved in society— empty pockets—so he never made more than acquaintances in the beau monde. He did not set out to marry a merchant's daughter, but he met Alexander Argent in Carlisle and Argent saw the chance of getting his daughter a title. My father saw the opportunity to mend the family fortune. I am named for my maternal grandmother. Now we face a similar problem. Our family still does not possess sufficient connections to men of our own class. Andrew seldom brought his friends from school and university here. The distance was too far or the neighborhood not interesting enough."

"Will you to go to London or Bath to meet suitable men?"

"A betrothal is already being discussed."

"Who is he? Do you like him?"

"He's the nephew of a nobleman." She gave a little shrug which would have drawn her mother's wrath down upon her. He would never have guessed Lady Hamilton had come from mercantile origins. "I haven't met him. I don't even know the family's name as my father wanted no gossip in case it came to nothing."

"Then how did your father find him?"

The humor drained from her face. "Father merely had to hint in letters to friends who have at least one foot in the beau monde that he had a marriageable daughter with a dowry of such-and-such pounds."

The idea of Eilidh marrying a fortune hunter saddened him. She was one of his best friends, after all, and as dear as a sister. No, more dear, and in a different way. But he would have no means of supporting a wife until he finished his legal training. Even then, his father's baronetcy was nothing compared to a higher title.

She saw it. " 'Tis not what I would have chosen, to marry a man I have never met and about whom I know nothing except that he is no more than nine or ten years older than I. However, I have a duty to my family. Perhaps I may like him very well."

"I hope you will." He already knew marriages and one's place in life, in fact most choices, were made according to one's circumstances. As he was not his father's heir, he needed a profession. In September, he would begin training in the law. He counted himself fortunate his father had not insisted on his entering the military or the church.

Not long after he left his uncle's home for London, he heard the betrothal was a fact. Hugh did not know whether he regretted he could not attend the wedding or not.

He and Wallace had been young men taken up with their futures. They corresponded but only about their own interests and activities. His cousin had not mentioned Eilidh or her family, and Hugh had not thought to do so. Reflecting that he'd been a careless young ass to forget one of his best friends, he was about to ask what had become of her when Wallace spoke.

"Whatever caused Keswick to summon me, I fear it must be serious." He fell silent.

"I don't recall meeting any of their family the times I was here. I may have seen them at church."

"Not likely, as they have always attended St. Cuthbert's in Clifton. The Hamiltons lived farther from Cuthbert Hall than my family and neither her family nor mine had any truck with the current earl's father, or more to the point, he with us. I doubt he ever gave a thought to anyone below the rank of earl until he needed brides with large dowries for his sons. He got a duke's girl for his first-born and another earl's for the second, our current Lord Keswick. The third and fourth got the heiresses of a banker and an importer respectively. I hope 'tis not another Cuthbert dead."

Hugh turned his head to stare at his cousin. "Another Cuthbert?"

Wallace shrugged. "The family has been unlucky. The old earl's heir lived long enough to marry and sire a daughter, though she died a few years later. Abel, the current earl, was the second son. Neither of his boys survived. The third fathered Randolph, who is now heir presumptive to Abel, Lord Keswick, and Eilidh's husband. He has two more nephews, neither married, and only one is a Cuthbert. That's cutting it pretty fine, given the Cuthbert males' propensity for dying young."

"I see." He could not stop himself from asking, "How is Eilidh?"

"She is known as Ellen now, so don't use her old name at Cuthbert Hall. Too Scottish. It is my understanding she has not been blessed with children. I suppose Stephen's son, when he gets one, will inherit the title."

Poor Eilidh. He could not think of her as Ellen.

"Keswick's well respected, but I don't doubt this matter will be delicate, as he has gathered most of his family and a few others, and the rumor is that he means to arrange marriages for his unmarried nephews."

"I thought 'twas the ladies who took care of such matters."

"His wife is dead. According to my manservant, who heard it from my housekeeper, who heard it from her niece, whose cousin works at Cuthbert Hall, he's worried for the succession. As well he might be."

"Unfortunate."

"Indeed, and what will make this worse, unless it is only a tempest in a milk jug, is that I know little about the guests, and almost my only acquaintance with the earl is from dealing with poaching on his land or property line disputes with a neighbor whose property marches with his." A faint smile. "Usually I know something of the parties if only by repute, which makes finding the truth easier. I am relying upon your

15

assistance, Hugh."

****

Hugh retained a vague memory of having ridden past Keswick's estate once as a boy during some summer's forgotten excursion with Wallace. He recalled it chiefly for its medieval appearance.

The butler, rigid-faced, led them to the study, where the earl stalked back and forth before the fireplace though a cup of coffee and a tumbler of brandy sat on his desk.

"Seaton." The earl, a thick-set man in his late sixties, shifted his gaze to Montgomery. "Who's this?"

"My cousin, Sir Hugh Montgomery, who is staying with me. He is a magistrate from Rochester in Northumberland. Why did you summon me, Lord Keswick?"

Keswick huffed. "This is a damnable situation, and I want no idle talk about it. I trust I need not say more?"

This could not be a matter of poaching or theft. "Neither Sir Hugh nor I are loose-tongued. What crime has been committed?"

"One of my guests is dead."

"Presumably not of obviously natural causes as you've requested my presence, my lord. Let me begin by seeing the body."

The earl's lips compressed. "There are features that need some explanation first. Will you be seated?"

Wallace waited a moment for Keswick to sit. The nobleman waved an impatient hand and remained on his feet. Hugh's cousin dropped into the nearest armchair, and he took another.

"The housemaid couldn't get into the woman's room to sweep out the ashes and lay a new fire. She

16

could not open the door. She told the footman on duty that she would do the rest of her rooms first." The earl raised his hand as if to run his fingers through his hair, then remembered he was wearing a wig and dropped it. "She didn't want to wake Mistress Forsyth or, ah…"

"Wake whoever was sleeping there."

"Just so. The maid assumed that by the time she finished the other hearths, the door would be unlocked. It wasn't. She asked the footman on duty in the passage to report it to the housekeeper in case of a complaint later by the guest. Then the girl went on with the rest of her duties. When she finished them, she went back to Lydia Forsyth's chamber. It was still latched, and this time she informed the housekeeper who told the butler. They decided between them that there was nothing more to be done until the sleeper woke."

An awkward situation but most easily dealt with by ignoring it.

"When breakfast was set out, Carson, the butler, began to be concerned. Mistress Forsyth was not in the habit of leaving her chamber until eleven but she expected her chocolate at nine, followed by a tray. He asked the housekeeper to find out if the lady's door was now able to be opened. It was not. She rapped on the door, hard enough to wake someone sleeping, and called out to ask if she was well. When there was no response, the butler came to me, and I sent for the estate carpenter."

"Was there no access from a dressing room, or perhaps from a servant's stair?"

"No. The dressing room is between the bedchamber and a linen closet. The stair is after that. There was no possibility of breaking down the door. It's oak, and the hinges and latch are strong. I did not wish it cut except as a last resort. He had his assistant go up a ladder to see if he could lift the window latch with a thin blade." The earl drank off the last of his brandy.

"He was able to raise the latch on the window and then on the shutter—thank God the wood has shrunk over the years, leaving a little space for a blade—and open the casement. He pushed the curtain aside but wasn't able to see much. I told him to get himself in and raise the door latch. The fool let out a yell when he climbed through the window and found the body almost at his feet. When I saw how matters were, I posted a footman at the door and sent for you."

"Then if you'll have us shown to the room, I'll begin my investigation."

"I'll take you there myself, Seaton."

He led them to a door at the end of the north wing's first story, and a nervous footman opened it for them.

"We'll need more light," Wallace said after surveying what was visible by the light from the one window with its shutters opened. The meager illumination showed little beyond what appeared to be a dressing table and stool against the right wall.

"Hugh, will you open the shutters on the other windows? I trust you have no objection, my lord?"

"Not at all. I thought it best to permit nothing to be disturbed after the boy got in."

Hugh opened the shutters on the other window in the west wall and on the one in the north wall. His cousin strode across the room. By the dressing table, he stumbled.

"Wallace? Are you—? " Hugh had seen that his

cousin tired easily but not that he was significantly weakened.

"I tripped. 'Twas the cushion from the window seat. Dislodged by the carpenter's assistant during his scramble into the room, I suppose, though we should verify…" Seaton stood by the dressing table staring down at something on the other side of the cushion. "Will you send for candles, my lord?" The chamber was no longer dark, but they would need better light to examine the room and its contents.

Keswick strode to the door and spoke sharply to the footman who hurried away to return in a matter of minutes with two candlesticks holding tapers.

"Hold the candle for me, Hugh."

Wallace knelt by the heap, which had been a woman. She lay on her left side, swathed in a night rail, its white linen embellished around its low neck and cuffs with white silk embroidery. The cushioned stool lay on its side at her feet. She must have been sitting there, ready to retire, when someone struck at least one hard blow. That much was obvious from the blood matting the side of her head, horribly visible against hair as pale as flax.

"You see the problem, Seaton."

"Apart from the murder?" his cousin asked.

The earl gave an irritable grunt. "The scandal, man. No one in attendance at this affair is titled but myself, and all but she"—he jerked his chin at the corpse—"and a family of Cits are related to me in some degree. I can control them. The servants are another matter. Threaten as I may, keeping this quiet may be impossible. The best solution I can hope for is that the inquest finds she fainted or had drunk to excess and hit her head on the table."

This was clearly a suggestion that Seaton should endorse one of these explanations. Hugh managed not to reveal his opinion of such fiddling with facts and legal procedure.

Wallace's attention wandered the room. Without answering he moved away from the body, toward the other side of the toilet table, then stopped and bent to inspect something in its shadow. He straightened, a heavy candlestick in hand. "I sympathize with your concern, Lord Keswick, but murder cannot be tidied away." He set it on the dressing table. In the light, traces of blood in the candlestick's ornate moldings stood out against the silver. A broken candle, its wick unburnt, lay on the floor.

Wallace knelt to touch the woman's hand. "The body is cold, so she has been dead some time." Wallace scribbled a few lines in his pocketbook, turned the page and wrote on the next, then tore out both pages. "Please have this one delivered to Dr. Lockhart and the other to the coroner. Both are urgent."

"The woman's obviously dead."

"Nevertheless, she must be examined and the inquest arranged. By law, it must be held within forty-eight hours."

Lips compressed, Keswick went to the door to issue orders to the waiting footman.

Hugh murmured, "There is something I wonder about."

"What have you noticed?"

"She was sitting at the table, but the candle had not been lit. What was she doing?"

"Very good, Hugh. I was too intent upon the means

of murder." He stood pondering. "At this date, with no candle alight, I think she would have had too little illumination to do anything more than comb or brush her hair by early evening, and hers is not yet braided for the night." He made another note. "Which gives us an idea of when she died."

The earl rejoined them.

"Lord Keswick, would you see to it your guests are occupied, please? They may wonder about your absence if you are not seen to be about this morning. And, er, none of them must leave here, as I will need to question them in case any of them saw or heard something."

That shook his lordship's composure. After a moment, he gave a curt nod and left them.

"We'll do better without him. Start from the door." With no further consultation necessary, Hugh and Wallace began to work their way around the chamber. Wallace went right, opening the tall clothes press immediately to the right of the door. He did not go through the contents, a task for later.

Hugh went left to examine the hearth which yielded nothing but ashes. He poked through them in case anything other than wood had been thrown on the fire and failed to burn completely: a forlorn hope.

Next came the dressing room door. He found nothing unexpected, only a narrow cot, shelves and pegs on the walls for hanging clothing, and two empty trunks, valises on top. He emerged, and in the corner a screen concealed the wash stand and close stool. Against the south wall, the bed stood, the bedclothes turned down as the maid would have left them, undisturbed. A small cabinet on its other side held another unlit candle and a handkerchief. The drawer was empty.

Wallace returned to the toilet table which had received short shrift when they had viewed the corpse.

Hugh moved on to the west wall, pausing to examine the first window seat recessed in the wall with its thick cushion to pad the sitter's backside. There was a small table and two armchairs between it and the next window. An open wine bottle was almost full beside one glass still containing a drop or two and another which had not been used. A spot of candle wax marred the polished wood, as if a lit candle had been picked up or set down carelessly. He joined his cousin, who had completed his own search and returned to the clothes press to go through it. "Nothing but garments here and nothing in the dressing table but what one would expect. What did you discover?"

Hugh reported. "Where did the candle wax come from when there were no candles burning?"

"A question, indeed. Make a note to ask the servants when we learn who waited upon her. The thing that troubles me is the latched door. That introduces a twist, and one I don't care to become common knowledge."

Hugh's dry "I think we can rule out witches and murderous ghosts, though as the boy had to get in through the window, I imagine the locked door is no secret," earned a grunted laugh from his cousin before he said, "It's time to interview the guests and servants, though I suppose first we must speak with Keswick."

They could not have avoided speaking with the earl if they had wished to, as the footman outside the late Lydia Forsyth's chamber informed them the man in the downstairs hall would lead them to the earl, who wished to hear their findings.

In the estate office in the other wing, Keswick deigned to explain the choice as being the least likely place to encounter guests. "I suppose a servant killed and robbed her. I've given orders none of the male servants is to leave the house."

Wallace Seaton had had a trick even as a boy of staring unblinkingly at someone he wished to disconcert. He employed it now to good effect. One might have supposed a man like the earl would be proof against the tactic or at least would resist longer than most. Instead he reddened with embarrassment rather than rage, muttering, "What else could it be?"

"It cannot have been robbery as I found a locked jewel case in the dressing table along with a purse of coin. And you have forgotten the door was locked."

He had. The color drained from the earl's face. "Impossible. The murderer must have escaped the room somehow. By the window, perhaps."

"The windows were latched and shuttered. If he could somehow have closed and latched them, the wall is sheer. A fly or a spider could have climbed down. A human would have fallen, and there was no body on the ground."

Keswick bit his lip in vexation at his lapse of memory. "Of course, Seaton. Then he slipped out after the carpenter's boy unlatched the door."

"Was the door left unguarded between the lad opening it and your arrival?"

An uncomfortable pause. "I told him to remain there until I came. I'll soon have the truth out of him."

Wallace said, "The greater objection to that

argument is, why would the murderer not have let himself out? He had only to lift the latch."

The earl went as red as a chicken's comb. "My wits have gone begging, for which I can only blame the day's stress. I am not accustomed to such untoward occurrences."

I would hope not was Hugh's unvoiced thought.

"Is it possible she battered herself to death?" The man was snatching at straws.

"The doctor may be able to tell us." The colorless statement suggested Seaton thought it quite unlikely.

"Sir Hugh and I will need a room or preferably two, in which to question everyone. With two rooms we can complete the questioning more quickly."

"Everyone? Not my guests, surely."

"Everyone, my lord."

"But that will cause talk and the most pernicious rumors. I cannot think it possible any of my guests can be guilty. Most are related to me. Surely there is a way to, to…"

"Pretend the decedent died of natural causes? By now, most of your servants know she was murdered. Hang an innocent man? I won't be part of it."

To spare his cousin future awkwardness with Keswick, Hugh said, "Although my magistracy is in Northumberland rather than Cumberland, I would have no choice but to refer any attempt to pervert justice to the Lord Lieutenant of this county."

After a tense moment during which the earl made no rejoinder, Wallace said, "I will start by questioning the maid who attended Mistress Forsyth last night."

"I will send for her."

"As I mentioned, we will need rooms for

interviewing all who may know anything about the lady's movements and activities yesterday. I trust there are two available? With both myself and Sir Hugh, we will be able to get through with the interviews with less inconvenience to your guests."

Keswick might still have hoped the matter could be cleared up by speaking with the servant. However, after a pause in which he may have been thinking of Hugh's reference to the Lord Lieutenant, he replied, "The Yellow Parlor in the western end of the north wing should suit your needs. It's small and seldom used. Montgomery, you may use the room in the north wing directly by the staircase behind the Great Hall. Is there anything else you require, Seaton?"

"There is. Please inform your guests and family I will wish to talk to each of them beginning in half an hour."

Chapter 2

"This is a devilish difficult thing," Wallace Seaton said grimly as they waited in the Yellow Parlor. "If you think of any question for our witnesses, either ask it or tell me."

"I will."

"I've never had to inquire into a murder before, more's the pity." After a reflective pause, Wallace went on, "I don't mean that, precisely, only that my lack of experience hinders me somewhat."

By the time the maid appeared, a footman had kindled a fire to take the chill off a room long unused. The Yellow Parlor was a better choice than either of them had anticipated or hoped. From its cheerful informality, Hugh suspected it had been the late Lady Keswick's personal parlor. The furniture was worn but comfortable and included a little desk where Hugh could take notes while Wallace spoke with Kitty, who had helped the Forsyth woman prepare for bed the previous night.

In one of the armchairs by the fire, Kitty sat bolt upright, wide-eyed, hands clenched in her lap. She expected to be blamed, as any servant would in such circumstances. She told them her name, how long she had worked at Cuthbert Hall, and how she had come to be assigned to the ladies who had brought no maid: Mistress Cuthbert, Lydia Forsyth, and Ismay Tate.

"I'm the newest, Your Worship, sir."

"I suppose it must have caused some inconvenience, them not bringing their own women."

"Mrs. Dankworth was right put about at first, until Mistress Forsyth told her she didn't need me underfoot all the time, only to dress and undress her, put up her hair, and bring her chocolate and breakfast. The laundry maid could see to having her clothing pressed or laundered or mayhap a spot cleaned away. So I was still able to do most of my usual duties."

The lady's own maid had fallen ill before they were to set out, and there hadn't been another female servant suitable. "She wasn't no trouble to maid for, which I'd feared she might be, as fashionable and beautiful as she was, if she was a mite short-tempered at times, not like Mistress Cuthbert who is a pleasure to maid for, and Mistress Tate who's used to doing for herself and no trouble at all. I was happy to get the experience of doing for the ladies, and maybe it's as well Mistress Cuthbert's maid didn't come, for seemingly she's little use. O' course, if a lady will choose colors and gowns that don't suit her, there's nothing her maid can do to stop her, but I don't reckon as she tries. Mistress Cuthbert's new gowns don't do her any favors, though she doesn't wear them as a rule. Wrong colors, wrong styles, too much…just too much, if you take my meaning, sir. I like lace, ribbons, ruffles, and bows, but not so many. Her old gowns suit her far better." Apparently feeling she had said too much, she ended, "Not that I should speak ill of my betters, not that I'm saying it of her, for I'm sure it's all her maid's fault."

"We'll forget we heard anything you regret

saying," Wallace assured her mendaciously. "Now, what time were you summoned to attend Mistress Forsyth last night?"

"Maybe sometime after five?"

She sounded doubtful. Wallace said, "It's hard to recall such a busy day, isn't it? What time was supper in the servants' hall?"

"We was to have our meal at five, the supper for the quality folk having been set back because of the festival, and the lady sent down to ask for her meal a little before that, when Cook was busy with ours."

Hugh wrote *L.F. asked for supper a few minutes before five. Ask footman that floor.*

"That must have been vexing for Cook, having to cook a separate meal for Mistress Forsyth and make your supper late." His cousin smiled in sympathy.

"Oh, no, sir. She wanted something light that could be served quick, as she was not feeling well. Our soup was already done and hot, and Cook sent me up to the lady with a bowl of that, bread and butter, a tart, a custard, and wine, which Mistress Forsyth asked for particular."

"Was your own meal on time, then?"

"A'most, sir. The others sat down to eat as I started up with the tray."

"Hard luck, to have your meal interrupted," Hugh remarked. "So you went up to Mistress Forsyth at about five or ten minutes after five?"

"I reckon that's about right, sir."

"Then you went down to your meal?"

"Ay, that I did."

"Kitty, when you returned to the kitchen, what were the others doing?"

"The others hadn't been eating more than a few minutes. It was lucky Aaron, the footman who came down to ask for Mistress Forsyth's meal, took a cloth and napkin up with him and covered the table. She was in a fidget to have me put everything down and go."

"My folk have half an hour for their meals. Is that true here?"

"Yes." She smiled shyly. "At supper we might linger a while, just talking and maybe drinking another cup of tea. We couldn't do that last night; we were still so busy."

"My people do the same. Were you upstairs about twenty minutes?"

"Less, I'd say. I set down the tray on the table, arranged the dishes, and uncorked the wine. Before I could ask was there anything else, she dismissed me. Downstairs the others' half hour wasn't up yet when Aaron was back with her tray and said she wanted me to make her ready for bed."

"Did you notice what time that was?" Hugh interposed. There was certain to be a clock in the kitchen.

"I didn't, but Mr. Carson did. He give a cluck and said, 'You've another ten minutes when you get back, Kitty.' And Cook says, 'She hasn't eaten the custard nor the tart, and I'll put them aside for you, seeing as your supper's interrupted. Your plate and bowl will be by the hearth to keep warm.' "

"So the time then was…?" Wallace prompted.

"It lacked five-and-twenty minutes to six, Your Worship."

"Surely that was very early for the lady to be retiring?"

"It was, sir, but she had the headache. That's why she wanted to go to bed."

"How long did the lady keep you from finishing your meal, Kitty?"

"Not long at all, sir. I'd have brushed her gown, but she said I could do that in the morning."

Hugh, out of the girl's line of sight, made a staying gesture to his cousin, who gave him a slight nod.

"Tell us about preparing Mistress Forsyth for bed. I am a bachelor and know nothing of what is involved."

"I unpinned her gown and helped her out of it and all her petticoats and the like." Kitty blushed and went on. "And took off her shoes and stockings, unlaced her, and took off her smock. She washed while I set aside her stockings and the other things to be laundered and hung her mantua in the dressing room to brush. I'd have done it then and cleaned her shoes, but she was done washing and was ready for her night rail and for me to take the pins out of her hair. She sat at the toilet table and rubbed some cream onto her hands while I brushed her hair. I'd have given it a hundred strokes if she'd let me, but she was fidgety."

"Her hair was loose when she was found," Wallace said. "Did you not braid it?"

"No, sir, she didn't want her hair plaited. She said as 'twould make her head hurt the worse. She told me to close the shutters excepting for the ones on the second window in the north wall."

"Did you light a candle for her?"

"No, sir, 'twas still light enough, and she said she did not mean to sit up long."

"The bottle of wine and the glasses were still there," Hugh said.

"She told me to leave them as she might drink a little more to ease her head, sir."

"Do you know why there were two glasses?"

"She asked for two, saying she might want a sip of water as well as the wine."

"Did you see her into her bed?" Wallace knew the bed had not been disturbed so his question must be a test of the chambermaid's truthfulness.

Kitty twisted a corner of her apron. "No, Your Worship. She meant to read a sermon first to put her in the right frame of mind, which she needed for she was almost beside herself by then. I started to go to the dressing room to bundle up the laundry, but she told me to go, she couldn't bear to have me fussing around. She was sitting at the dressing table with her little book, but when I was pulling the door shut, I saw she had stood up and started to follow me. I stopped, thinking there was something more she wanted, but she told me to go."

Hugh glanced at his cousin, who had drawn the same conclusion: Lydia had latched the door behind Kitty.

"So you returned to the kitchen and your well-earned supper," Hugh began. "I suppose you noticed what time it was, to know when your meal time would end."

"I forgot. I'd just got my plate that was keeping warm on the hearth and sat down when Cook told Sukey to make sure there was oil in the betty lamps and then to begin lighting them. I looked at the clock then and 'twas just six. I'd been hardly any time at all with the lady."

"Does the kitchen have many windows, Kitty?"

"More than some kitchens, sir, but most face north, which isn't much help. There's not as many in the south wall and when the sun gets low, the other wing is in the way."

"And you finished your meal and had a cup of tea, I hope?"

"I did and ate my custard and tart that Cook kept for me."

"Were the lamps lit by the time you finished?"

"Sukey was lighting them as I scraped my dishes into the pigs' bucket."

"Do you know how long you had been at your supper then?"

She looked down guiltily. "A little more than ten minutes. I begged Cook's pardon, hoping she wouldn't tell Mistress Dankworth, the housekeeper, or Carson, but she just said, 'Pish, girl. Never mind about that this time.' There was no one else in the kitchen then that might tell on me."

In his pocketbook, Hugh wrote: *kit. lamps lit about ten or fifteen minutes after six. Go down to kitchen to confirm.* He believed the maid, however. By a few minutes after six, a kitchen without west-facing windows would probably need some light for preparing food, as they would be doing for the guests' supper soon if not at once.

Wallace raised his eyebrows to ask if Hugh had any more questions. He did not.

After a few more questions, Wallace let her go.

"She was truthful, I think," Wallace said.

"And we've learned a great deal. Lydia latched the door as soon as Kitty was out of the room, although from her description of Lydia's wanting to be rid of her, she may have been expecting a visitor."

"I am sure you are correct, Hugh. By my calculation, Kitty was with her for no more than twenty minutes. My late wife could not have completed her evening beauty ritual so quickly, and she was not a fashionable lady with drawers full of paint, lotions, salves, and such things."

"At least we now have a fair notion that she was probably killed between six and perhaps half six at the latest," Hugh said. "She was still sitting at the toilet table, and I don't think she could have seen to read by then without a candle."

Wallace acknowledged that remark with a grunt before saying, "I wonder who was in the house then apart from servants?"

He sent for the footman who had been on duty at the door into the south wing. "According to Keswick, that was the only one available to those in the garden. The french windows between the wings were blocked by the refreshment tables, and a man was at the kitchen door to keep people out, except the servants bringing out food or returning empty trays."

The man reported to the Yellow Parlor, wooden expression in place. Hugh was not deceived: no one who was not rich or titled could fail to worry when questioned by a magistrate. Wallace would ask the questions while Hugh sat apart and out of the man's sight, taking down his answers.

"Rent day and the harvest celebration coming together made a busy day for you, I imagine." Wallace was enough older to play the affable uncle. Seaton employed a member of the butler's family, which meant those employed here knew something of

Seaton's easy-going ways through servants' gossip.

"Ay, Your Worship."

He had been posted at the door for several hours, until the last of the guests came in and he was dismissed to have his supper.

"I think most of the ladies and gentlemen went in and out, one time or t'other."

Wallace waited, brows raised inquiringly.

"Ahhh...because of the drinking, you see, sir."

"So they all went up to their rooms?"

"No, indeed, sir. There were two rooms set aside not far from the door with, ummm, chamber crockery. Bowls and pitchers of warm water for washing and so forth."

The "so forth" referred to chamber pots and close stools. Most were in and out again quickly.

"...except the ladies took longer, as they'd want to tidy their hair and the like."

Wallace stalked information like a Scottish ghillie after a deer. "Hard to keep the guests all straight, I suppose, with so many."

"No, sir. The only ones as used my door was the guests and the gentry who'd come for the festival. We've seen them all aforetime. There wasn't a one I didn't know."

"I suppose you'll not recall if any went in and did not come out or took longer about their business than most."

"I do, Your Worship. The poor lady that died come in with her hand pressed to her forehead and went straight up the stairs."

His estimate of the time Lydia Forsyth entered was consistent with the time Kitty said she had requested her supper.

"Was she the only one who did not come out again?"

"Mistress Ellen Cuthbert didn't, neither. The front of her gown was wet, so I thought she'd go up to have it sponged and to put on something dry and then come down, though she never did. She did look mifty, so mayhap she didn't care to stay until the end."

"Out of humor at the damage to her dress, perhaps."

The footman agreed. "Belike Mr. Cuthbert wheedled her out of her temper, for she was herself again by supper."

"Oh, did he go in with her, then?"

The man hesitated before replying, "Not with her, exactly, sir. He was behind her."

"By how much?"

"Maybe thirty feet or a bit more."

"Did he follow her upstairs or did he come in only to use the jakes? If you noticed," Wallace added.

"Happen I did, there being another gent close behind him. Mr. Simmons, the parson, that was." A shadow of perplexity passed over his face. "Parson went to the gentlemen's retiring room, as the ladies call it. Mr. Cuthbert was in the passage beyond him when Parson turned into the jakes, so he can't have gone in. Now, that's an odd thing as he didn't go upstairs. Or if he did, he used the stair at the other end."

Mighty odd in Hugh's opinion. He jotted a marginal note to map the south wing.

"Do you recall when Mr. Cuthbert came out?"

"Not rightly, sir, no. There was so many coming and going and some of the guests asked me questions."

They would need to establish the guests' whereabouts through questioning each about whom they had seen and when.

Chapter 3

Keswick opened the parlor door himself and strode in to stand in front of the hearth, his face grim.

Without greeting them, he said, "Pray, silence." Keswick seemed almost insignificant with the mantel on a level with his head and the ornately carved stone overmantel reaching the ceiling. Nevertheless, the words cut off all discussion.

"I must request that you not go out today. Overnight, there has been an unfortunate occurrence."

The expressions of some of Ellen's fellow guests reflected no surprise. Fortunately for the servants, the earl did not notice.

"It has necessitated the presence of a magistrate."

Mistress Hodge, placidly setting stitches in a piece of petit point, looked up at that. "Why, whatever for, my lord?"

Georgina bounced in her place on a settee and gave a little squeal. Neither she nor her mother had been at the breakfast table.

"A theft?" Stephen Cuthbert inquired artlessly. "What's missing?"

"Nothing was stolen, as far as I am aware." His hearers waited for a further explanation which did not come. "I hope that by your answers you may be able to cast some light upon the incident. "

Ellen's stomach roiled. The others stared in silence

at the earl.

"An investigation is being conducted." Before anyone could ask another question, he stalked out.

"Strike me dead." Joseph Wilmot's comment was the more surprising because he was such a soft-spoken, scholarly man. Mistress Wilmot who was sharing a window seat with him in an unfashionable display of wifely fondness, edged closer. He patted her hand.

Randolph lolled in an armchair, legs stretched out and ankles crossed. He was dressed for riding. "How tiresome. I do hope we will not be kept waiting all day."

Ellen looked around to see who was not present. Ismay was doing the same.

Chapter 4

The earl had provided them with a list of guests with a few notes about each as well as a list of the servants on duty in the two wings and any who might have had reason to be there. Hugh made a copy while they waited. The guest list was short.

Randolph Cuthbert, my eldest nephew and heir presumptive

Ellen Cuthbert, his wife

Mrs. Dorothy Wilmot, my half sister

Mr. Joseph Wilmot, her husband

Cornelius Wilmot, my nephew

Stephen Cuthbert, son of my youngest brother, currently after Randolph Cuthbert in line of succession

Mr. Caleb Hodge, commercial interests, and Mrs. Joan Hodge, his wife

Wealthy Cits, Hugh thought.

Georgina Hodge, their daughter

"Meant for one or the other of the nephews, probably," Wallace said.

Lydia Forsyth, widow

Ismay Tate, my cousin, spinster, acting as my hostess on this occasion

"How do we plan to proceed, Wallace?"

"We have an embarrassment of riches," his cousin said obscurely.

"Er…what?"

"It's from a French play I heard of the last time I was in London. Plenty of potential witnesses when you take into account the neighbors, tenants, and laborers who came for the day. Fortunately for us, the laborers wouldn't have gone farther from the home farm than the field where the sport and contests were held. They'd have been noticed if they came as close as the garden between the wings. As we know when the murder must have taken place, we'll start with the guests and those who were in the house shortly before and during that time."

"Then we will have to add questions about who was seen entering or leaving."

A nod from Wallace. "There are the servants, of course, but most of them were surely too busy to take time from their duties to murder a guest. Still, we'll bear them in mind. Here, I've marked the ones for you to question. We had best begin with Randolph and Ellen Cuthbert, as the highest ranking after the earl. I haven't met him before, but he might take it as a slight if we ignored his position as the heir. You'll speak with him, being titled yourself."

"A baronet is unlikely to impress an earl's heir."

"He's been Keswick's heir presumptive no more than six months. Until then, you had the advantage of him."

A pair of footmen opened the double doors into the parlor with the precision of well-drilled troops. Wallace entered a step or two ahead of Hugh and stopped short. Every eye in the chamber was fixed upon them. His cousin must feel as he did, that they had made their entrance onto the Drury Lane stage. At least the audience was not armed with oranges to throw at them.

In the earl's absence, Wallace cleared his throat, intending to introduce himself and Hugh.

Instead, the older footman announced, "His Worship, Wallace Seaton, magistrate, and Sir Hugh Montgomery—" a momentary hesitation "—magistrate, Northumberland, assisting his Worship."

"I trust you mean to inform us why we are gathered here." The speaker, a tall man in riding dress, slumped in his seat as if weary. About forty years of age, he carried some extra flesh as sedentary middle-aged men often did. Too much food and drink, too little exercise.

The older footman spoke again. "Your Worship, may I make known to you Mr. Randolph Cuthbert, Lord Keswick's heir."

This drawling, fleshy fellow was Randolph Cuthbert?

Introductions continued. With the guest list in mind, Hugh had no difficulty identifying the Hodges before the servant named them.

His attention faltered, caught by a lady's uneasy movement. Her height and extreme thinness were the first things he noticed. Her collarbones stood out in sharp relief. A few tendrils of red-gold hair had escaped her linen and lace cap. His eyes came to rest upon her dear face. "Eilidh is here?" he whispered to his cousin.

Wallace replied sotto voce, "Of course she is. Don't call her Eilidh." Wallace had told him she was the heir's wife. Somehow it had not sunk into his brain.

The servant said, "Mistress Ellen Cuthbert, wife of Mr. Randolph Cuthbert."

That was the match her father made for her?

Eilidh, no, Ellen, acknowledged them with a dip of her head.

The door opened again, and Keswick entered. "Seaton, Sir Hugh, I apologize for my tardiness. You've met my guests?"

"We have, my lord," Wallace said.

"Good. Mr. Seaton will be assisted by Sir Hugh, a relation of his, another magistrate, who providentially happened to be visiting him. All to the good, I say, if it enables him to complete this business sooner."

Ismay Tate peered around. "My lord, Mistress Forsyth is not here. Perhaps a servant should be sent for her?"

"There is no need, madam. She has suffered a mishap and is dead. As it is not clear how she died, they will be questioning all of you as well as the servants."

Feminine gasps from the Hodge ladies, a stifled "Hades!" from Stephen Cuthbert, and restive shifting met this pronouncement.

"You will each be summoned to one or the other to speak with them privately, and I ask that you give any assistance you can. Seaton will use the Yellow Parlor, and Sir Hugh the room located beside the northwest staircase."

"Your lordship, I do beg your pardon, but I can't let my daughter be questioned by a man without my presence," Joan Hodge protested. Something about the way she inflected her words, though not her dress, identified the speaker as not having been born to the gentry class.

Keswick raised his grizzled brows at Wallace.

"I must insist that the young lady be chaperoned by someone other than a member of this group."

"And not from outside this house," the earl said. Not unreasonable, as an outsider however well-intentioned, could let some word slip. Even so, one of the servants would confide in some friend or relative, no matter what the earl might threaten.

"Would my family's old nurse be acceptable, Mistress Hodge? There are no children here now, but she remains to do some of the mending, and to give the maidservants good advice. She is somewhat hard of hearing," his lordship concluded with mordant humor.

This was agreed to by the Hodges. The earl excused himself, saying he would give orders for refreshments to be made available for any who wished them and for Hugh's assigned room to be furnished with a table and chairs. The footman outside the parlor would supply any amusements or pastimes the guests wanted while waiting. Mistress Hodge immediately asked for her daughter's needlework to be sent for, and Ismay Tate wanted paper, ink, and a quill in order to catch up on her correspondence. The gentlemen were provided with newssheets and the latest *Gentleman's Magazine*.

Wallace said, "We'll go down the list in order. You take Cuthbert while I speak with Mistress Cuthbert. She may have noticed something."

Hugh agreed, wishing he were to be the one to talk to her. However, he might have found it difficult to focus on the death of the Forsyth woman when he was so curious about his old friend's life.

****

Lydia Forsyth is dead. Judging from the others' stunned or blank faces, Ellen was not alone in struggling to grasp the news. Perhaps they should have guessed by her absence, but the Forsyth woman had been a law unto herself. While she was still trying to absorb what it meant, they heard the earl's gruff voice in the passage demanding, "Well, who the devil does know?" presumably of either the butler or a footman. A murmur, and Keswick reappeared and approached Wallace Seaton and Hugh on the other side of the room. She did not catch his quiet words to Seaton.

Wallace's response to whatever news her husband's uncle had imparted carried. "Good! You can supply a wagon or cart and driver to take it to Penrith?" Another few words, apparent agreement, and he sketched a bow to the earl. Had they been talking about the body? Randolph's face revealed nothing.

"My lord, ladies, gentlemen, I must beg your indulgence. There is someone Sir Hugh and I must speak with immediately," Wallace said. "We will begin your interviews as soon as we can."

The earl nodded curtly and departed.

Sir Hugh, now; his father and his older brother must have died.

Cuthbert drawled, "Need we be confined here while you take some servant or menial out of order?"

"Yes, I fear you must, as Lord Keswick wishes this matter dealt with in the most expeditious manner. To do so, my colleague and I must attend upon the doctor—"

"Why, if she's dead?"

Wallace replied more peaceably than Ellen would have managed, but then, she had had years of Cuthbert's ways. "So that we can get his immediate impressions, which may help us direct our investigation. And our work will be needlessly slowed if we have to have you and his lordship's other guests sent for."

He turned to approach Ellen, who prayed he would

not address her informally.

"Mistress Cuthbert, I must beg your patience and ask you to wait for me in the Yellow Parlor. I do not expect to be long. A footman will escort you there."

"Certainly, sir." She curtsied and started for the door. Randolph continued to sprawl in his chair.

Hugh addressed him, apologizing for the delay. "Mr. Cuthbert, you are welcome to remain here until I return, rather than waiting in the room Lord Keswick mentioned."

From her two visits long ago, she knew he meant the one from which servants served the courses and to which they removed the dishes when the Great Hall was used as a banqueting room for the most consequential occasions. She doubted there had been such an event in the Great Hall since the dinner in honor of their marriage.

Cuthbert grunted irritably, as expected. The house was amply provided with better rooms. Allotting that windowless closet to Hugh might seem an insult although Keswick could have chosen it because it was near the Yellow Parlor. Randolph would take it as a slight, however.

She did wonder why Wallace had directed her to go to the Yellow Parlor at once, though she was glad of it. She could not bear the thought of listening to the others' exclamations and speculation about the death. The discovery of the body must have been the reason for the stir outside her chamber this morning. Lydia was in the large bedroom next to her own smaller one.

The shabby Yellow Parlor was comfortable, unchanged since the late countess had used it as her own little retreat, and near enough to the kitchen, housekeeper's and butler's offices to be convenient for consultations. She had done needlework by the hour, most of it to give as gifts: embroidered book covers, handkerchiefs, scarves, night caps, slippers. Had Lady Keswick needed her pastime as a retreat from her marriage? As her own retreat from life was to read, it was fortunate Durham possessed a circulating library. Ellen found the earl austere, but then, she did not know him well; this was only her third visit to Cuthbert Hall. He was certainly more courteous than Randolph.

In London, she was considered a model of deportment which earned her no close friends. Instead she was thought cold and distant, having lost the ability to reveal her emotions within a year of her marriage. She had believed lack of response to Randolph's remarks would end his making them. Not revealing hurt did at least salvage her pride.

She chose a book of poetry from several volumes stacked on a side table with all their edges aligned. Everything was dusted, swept, or polished, though the air was stale from having been confined in an unused room. On her earlier visits, it had been scented with flowers. She doubted anyone had used it since its mistress died.

It fell open to Andrew Marvell's poem, "To His Coy Mistress," perhaps a favorite of the late Lady Keswick. The line "The grave's a fine and private place" gave her a qualm today.

She flinched on hearing Wallace Seaton's voice. "Mistress Cuthbert, I'm sorry to have kept you waiting. It has been a very long time, ma'am." He bowed.

Setting the book aside, she rose and curtsied. Alas, still as awkward as a badly managed puppet. "It has, sir." They would keep the meeting formal, far easier with Wallace than it would have been with Hugh.

"Do you know why we are talking to Lord Keswick's guests?"

"From what his lordship told us, Lydia Forsyth suffered an accident, and there is some question about how it occurred."

He nodded. "When did you last see Mistress Forsyth?"

"At the harvest festival yesterday. The tenant farmers paid their rent at the home farm's barn, and there were amusements for them and their families and Lord Keswick's guests. Not all the same, of course. The tenants and laborers had their games in a field near the barn while we were in the garden and on the lawn behind the house, though there were some events in which both groups participated. There was something to entertain everyone."

"Did you happen to notice who went into the house in the late afternoon and early evening?"

"The family, guests, and servants came and went to use the retiring rooms or to replenish the food and drink. Ismay Tate, as the earl's hostess, was everywhere. An entertainment like that needs a good deal of management, and it can't all be left to servants. I did not notice anyone else in particular."

"What time did the festival end?"

"The earl's neighbors and guests began to leave or return to the house by about seven, I think. Some stayed on longer to enjoy the bonfire and dancing."

"You say you think it broke up. What time did you go in?"

"About half five, I think. The afternoon was

growing cool, and I was a little tired." Weary of making superficial conversation with people she did not know or had met only once or twice before, but mostly annoyed with her husband.

"What did you do there?"

"I went up to my chamber where I washed my face and hands and applied a lotion to discourage freckling, not that it's ever done much good," she added wryly. "I had not been able to keep the sun entirely from my face even with a wide-brimmed hat."

"And then?"

"I changed my gown, took my shoes off, and put my feet up until it was time to go down to supper. That was served later than usual, as food and drink had been available outdoors all day."

He made a notation in his notebook.

"Do you recall Lydia Forsyth's presence?"

When had she seen the woman? "Stephen Cuthbert brought her a glass of lemonade while she watched some of the young men playing at bowls. That was at midafternoon. After that, I can't recall seeing her." *I preferred not to notice her.*

"Did you see Mistress Forsyth at supper?"

"No. Someone said she had gone up to bed with a megrim brought on by the sun." *More likely some man failed to be enthralled by her wiles.* "But a number of the party were not present. Some were still outside. There was food and drink out on trestle tables both near the house and out by the bonfire where the tenants and farm workers were dancing." In her youth she would have been there, too, and she would have danced.

"Do you recall who was at supper?"

"All three of the Hodges, Mr. and Mistress Wilmot,

Keswick, Randolph, and me." Seaton made notes as she spoke.

"Mistress Forsyth is not a connection of the earl, is she? Do you know why she was invited?"

Ellen's face flushed. What would it be like to tell her old playmate the truth? She would dearly love to do so. On the other hand, she would humiliate herself and embarrass the earl. Discretion forced her to say, "I believe she may have been meant for Stephen Cuthbert as Georgina Hodge was intended for Cornelius Wilmot."

"I can understand his lordship tolerating the Hodge family for the sake of his half sister's son. Hodge's fortune is enormous, and it's not as if Cornelius is a Cuthbert. On the other hand, Stephen is the son of the earl's youngest brother. Forgive me for bringing this up, but he would be the heir after Randolph Cuthbert, wouldn't he?"

His tone was apologetic, and bless him for that.

"He is. Cuthbert and I have no children."

"Then I would expect Keswick to want more than just a fortune for him. Is—was she connected to a titled family or an influential one?"

She was certainly connected in one sense, Eilidh reflected, though it was not a thought she could utter. "Her people were county gentry without much property or any connections to titled or wealthy relatives." She smiled, hoping she seemed merely amused. "Families, and men, will tolerate a great deal when a fortune is involved. Lydia's Cit husband left her the bulk of his fortune."

Seaton laughed. "I'm surprised you didn't use a cant term like 'well inlaid.' As I recall, your brother taught you a choice vocabulary."

"In those days, I was little more than a child and wild as one of the natives of the New World."

"We had some adventures, didn't we? Remember the bull?"

"And running for our lives? We can laugh now, but at the time I was sure one of us would die. You or Hugh, as you both were trying to keep the beast from chasing me."

Wallace's lips turned up. Her old friend still possessed a cherubic smile. She managed a faint reflection of it. In Durham, such chill composure held at a distance those whose company she would have enjoyed. Wallace's merriment faded.

"Did you know her well? What can you tell me about her?"

While she was attempting to frame a noncommittal reply, he said, "The convention that one does not speak ill of the dead, no matter how much they deserve it, is not helpful when investigating a crime."

"A crime?"

"Ay."

"Not an accident?" A foolish question when he had confirmed it was a crime, but the idea was so startling she could not immediately comprehend it.

"She was murdered, Eilidh. Can you think of any reason someone would kill Mistress Forsyth?"

Ellen could. "I don't like to say it, but in London or mayhap Bath, she was not universally popular." Wallace and Hugh and she had been good friends and stood on no ceremony, and her ease with Wallace at least had come back unbidden. "She can no more resist exercising her wiles on men than she could go without breathing. Coy glances, fluttering eyelashes, and a pretense of being fascinated by whatever the man spoke of or else a sort of cool appearance of being unattainable, like a goddess. Which she employed depended upon the man. She also contrives to look as if she were about to fall out of her bodice without ever actually doing so." That revelation slipped out. Heaven help her, what might she say to Hugh if she were alone with him? Seeing Wallace's surprise, she bit her lip. "I am sorry. It's hard to think of her being no more when she was so vivid. How did it happen?"

"That is what we are trying to determine."

The parlor now felt confining rather than snug. He was no longer her old friend from childhood; this grave-faced man was investigating a murder. She must remember that.

"Thank you, Mistress Cuthbert. I have no more questions. If you should think of anything you heard or observed of Mistress Forsyth or anyone else, however trivial it may seem, please inform me at once. Or Sir Hugh, if I am not available."

The fact she had withheld loomed like towering clouds that portended thunder and lightning.

****

Five minutes into his interview with Randolph Cuthbert, Hugh decided he disliked the man intensely. Despite his gracefully expressed concern over the death, nothing showed in his pale blue eyes. Cuthbert's flashing smile was much in evidence, too. Hugh distrusted his facile charm and its contrast to his surliness in the drawing room. Besides, he was too handsome despite his fleshiness, which admittedly was far less extreme than that of many gentlemen his age, and too sleek. He was also Eilidh's husband, and Hugh added that to his list of reasons to detest the man.

Yes, Cuthbert had seen Lydia Forsyth at the festival and had spoken with her briefly.

About what?

Oh, the clownish sport on the estate's home farm. Lydia was not fond of the country or rustic pastimes. Yes, he knew her quite well; they moved in the same circles and attended many of the same entertainments.

If she did not care for the country, why had she accepted the earl's invitation?

The lady was a widow. She may have hoped Keswick wanted to marry again and get another son or two, his children by his first wife having died young, except for his oldest son who had survived to marry and beget a daughter and then died. His smug contempt was unmistakable. "Or else she was invited because my cousin Stephen should marry, and a rich widow would be a good choice."

Had he noticed anyone going into the house between about half five and eight? Or coming out between those same hours?

Cuthbert laughed. "Whyever should I? We were milling around, talking, watching the activities or taking part in them. I suppose most of us made use of the necessary at some point, certainly those of us who had been drinking ale."

He did not know when Lydia Forsyth had slipped away. He had lingered outside, watching the peasants at their games and went in sometime before supper to make himself tidy. The meal was to be served at eight. As an afterthought he added, "Mistress Cuthbert went in a little earlier. After the quoits competition, I think."

Was it possible he had failed to notice his own wife so short a distance ahead of him, Hugh wondered. "What time did you go inside?"

"I did not notice."

"But after the quoits match?"

"Yes, definitely."

"Ah, well, I expect your valet can give us a more exact time."

"Unfortunately, I did not bring my man. I made do without assistance, the footmen all being occupied."

"Did you go out again?"

"What, after removing all traces of dust and straw from my person? Hardly."

Two and one-half hours between the time he entered the house and supper. Could he have spent so long washing his face and hands and changing his suit?

"There was some time between the quoits match and supper. Did it take you so long to make ready for the meal?"

Cuthbert's airy reply, "I took my time and a glass or two of brandy," came a heartbeat slow. Note: *find out who saw him between going in and supper.*

The next on his list was Joseph Wilmot, the earl's brother-in-law.

Wilmot was thin, vague, and squinted. Bad eyesight, no doubt. He had met Lydia Forsyth here for the first time. Very fashionable, he thought, or so his wife said. She was not easy to talk to, being clever, flippant, and full of quips, which he confessed he did not always understand. "Not a comfortable female," he judged her. He had no idea who might have gone in or come out, except for his wife, whom he recognized by the color of her gown and her general shape, and his son for the same reason, and one or two others who wore coats or gowns he recalled from seeing them earlier. "My eyes are not strong. I would probably know a deer from a horse at that distance," he said apologetically.

After Wilmot, Hugh made his way to the Yellow Parlor, hoping to catch Wallace between witnesses. The nearest footman confirmed that he was still speaking with Mistress Cuthbert. Hugh idled nearby. When she emerged and saw him, she froze.

"E—Mistress Cuthbert." To address her as he always had, where he might be overheard by a servant, would cause talk.

"Sir Hugh, good day. Please accept my condolences on your father's death, and your brother's too, as evidently you succeeded to the title since you were last in this neighborhood."

"I did. My older brother died before my father, of a swollen organ in his gut."

"I'm sorry. But you no longer live in your family home, if you now reside in Northumberland."

He acknowledged the first sentence with a dip of his head. "Our manor is not large. My mother still lives, and my brother's widow and his daughters live there as well, as does my younger brother, who acts as steward. I inherited the property of my paternal uncle."

"And you are also a magistrate."

"My uncle had served in that office, and as I'd been trained in the law, an advantage most magistrates do not have, when it was put to me that I should take the position, I could hardly refuse." Their conversation was as stiff as if they were the merest acquaintances when he wanted to speak with Eilidh freely. Now there seemed to be nothing more to say that could be said. "I need a word or two with my cousin and should not detain you."

She curtsied and whisked away.

Wallace greeted him with "I'm glad you're here. We should compare notes as we go, while our impressions are fresh in our minds. What did you think of Cuthbert?"

Hugh related the baron's few useful remarks. He did not express his own opinion of the fellow, trying not to let his personal reaction color his report of Cuthbert's responses. "Have you heard any rumors about their marriage?"

"They have come to stay with the earl only twice that I can recall, once for the wedding and the last time was about seven years ago, I think. I saw her in Penrith then, coming out of the saddler's shop whence she had gone to ask them to cut replacements for the soles of her boots, there being no cobbler in the town. The people hereabout hardly know them." Wallace twisted his signet ring. "I am not quite happy about Eilidh. Ellen. She is older, which might explain it. I'm not the same man I was at eighteen. You remember what she was, Hugh. She has become a marble statue."

Hugh could not disagree, based on his observations thus far.

"Now I will send for Mistress Wilmot, and I want you to take the Hodge girl out of order before she can be schooled to say nothing to the point. I wish I'd thought of it when we made our lists. You may as well question Ismay Tate after the girl. I'll take Stephen Cuthbert from your list."

While waiting for Georgina Hodge and the old

family nurse, Hugh copied out his notes from Cuthbert and Wilmot for Wallace's reference. He expected little from Georgina. In his experience, young persons of either sex were too wrapped up in their own concerns to pay much attention to others.

When Nurse Kettlewell herded Georgina bashful and blushing into his makeshift office, he had no reason to change his opinion. She stammered a greeting and peeked up at him. She would take gentle handling in a purely avuncular way.

"Now, then, Mistress Georgina, what do you think of Cuthbert Hall?" No point in asking if she were enjoying her stay for how could she reply except by exclaiming in horror over the sudden death?

" 'Tis very old and grand, sir."

Of course. Hugh resigned himself to prying out answers bit by bit. Instead, she surprised him.

"I do wonder there is no fashionable furniture and no Chinese furnishings. Perhaps it would be too costly to change the old furniture. My mama favors the Chinese style though Papa will not let her decorate his study or bedchamber. But the silver and Meissen porcelain in the dining room are very fine, she says."

Kettlewell might not be as deaf as the earl believed or else she could follow conversation by watching the speaker's lips. She was clearly suppressing amusement at these artless confidences. *Come, this is promising.*

"I hope you do not find the party boring with so few young people for your amusement."

"Oh, no, Sir Hugh. Mama says I am to find a husband here, and though she was thinking of Cornelius Wilmot, Stephen Cuthbert is not too old and will likely inherit the earldom unless Mistress Cuthbert dies and

Mr. Randolph Cuthbert's second wife bears a son. Mistress Cuthbert is surely too elderly to conceive, and besides, she is not beautiful and wears such antiquated gowns."

His composure slipped for a moment though Georgina was oblivious. Nurse Kettlewell frowned, her lips turned down. Hugh gave her a slight head shake, hoping she would not rebuke the chit. The old woman stared back blandly.

"He's handsomer than Stephen," the Hodges' daughter prattled on, "and pays such pretty compliments."

She had not known Lydia had gone upstairs early "though she was not at supper, but no one was really hungry anyway because of all the food at the harvest festival." Afterwards some played cards. She herself had been at a table with Stephen, Cornelius, and Ellen Cuthbert, who had changed her gown, having spilled ale on it. The older men had talked politics, she supposed, because she heard the words "parliament" and "food riots"—whatever they might be—and her mother and Mistress Wilmot sat discussing remedies. Mistress Tate might have been speaking with Lord Keswick.

"Mistress Forsyth's death must have come as a shock."

"It did throw the household into confusion, and we could not ride today, which I only discovered when I came down to meet the riding party after I ate in my chamber, which I prefer because gentlemen at the breakfast table are so grumbly if one talks to them. We can go tomorrow or the next day. Was it female troubles? Older women have them though I don't really understand what they consist of."

Hugh's eyes met the nurse's, willing himself not to let a chuckle escape at her expression. She would not have let one of her charges speak so freely.

After a few more questions which only proved Georgina Hodge knew nothing else, he bade her good afternoon and thanked Nurse Kettlewell for chaperoning them. The latter gave him a sharp-eyed glance over her shoulder as she followed the girl out. It troubled him as he made notes of Georgina's artless disclosures. Nothing of interest there, but he would like to speak with the nurse. Old family retainers likely knew more about their masters' families than those families would like. She was kept on to do mending, according to Keswick, and perhaps because he was fond of the woman who likely knew him better than his own mother. He would bear that in mind. Hugh asked the footman in the passage to summon Ismay Tate, a rather plain spinster of about thirty, the earl's hostess for the occasion.

He began with a few questions about her to get a sense of where she fitted in the Cuthbert family. She was the granddaughter of the earl's granduncle. "I can never keep straight in my mind what sort of cousin that makes me." She was a spinster possessed of a cottage in Kent and a competence sufficient to her needs. Cousin-of-whatever-degree-he-was Abel had asked her to act as his hostess for the house party and she had been happy to oblige. She had no other demands on her time, and the journey, though long, had been comfortable, as he had sent his traveling coach for her.

She was enjoying the gathering as it was mostly family. The Hodges were pleasant people even if they were rather common. A pity Georgina could not govern her tongue or even realize she should. "Keswick hopes to match her with Cornelius Wilmot, so her tendency to run at the mouth does not signify as he is not in the line of succession. Though it may give him some uncomfortable moments."

She liked Joseph Wilmot, who was bookish, and considered Dorothy Wilmot a good wife and mother, but her head was stuffed with recipes, remedies, and babies. All important things, of course, but limited conversational fodder.

"Do you think Lydia Forsyth was invited for Stephen Cuthbert?" He would have preferred not to ask directly, but Mistress Tate had not broached the subject as he would have expected her to do after talking about Georgina and Cornelius.

She gazed at the sideboard which took up the opposite wall of the little room. Finally: "Please forgive me for falling into a brown study, Sir Hugh. I really do not know the answer. One would assume that the only unmarried female, apart from Georgina, who is as good as spoken for, and the only other unmarried male were intended for each other."

"How did she come to be invited? As you are acting as Lord Keswick's hostess, I believe you sent the invitations." No need to speculate why his lordship had not asked his half sister to act as hostess. Dorothy Wilmot, despite having been brought up in an earl's household, lacked the force of character to organize more than a gentleman's home.

She hesitated, and he read doubt in her carnelian brown eyes. "Lord Keswick requested she be added to the guest list because Stephen should marry. Perhaps he thought Stephen might court her. Sometimes these pairings proposed by others work out, and sometimes they don't. In this case, I cannot imagine why anyone would think they might suit."

"Why do you think them ill-matched, ma'am? I am at a disadvantage here, never having met the parties."

"On the surface, such an alliance might appear to make sense. Stephen has a comfortable income, but more wealth is always desirable, isn't it? Lydia was lovely, not stupid, and had a sizable fortune. Not that she boasted of it, which would be vulgar, but she arrived in her own travelling coach. Her garments are in the latest fashion and her jewelry is exquisite and genuine, not paste. Her house is on Grosvenor Square. My old friends who live in town keep me informed of the news and gossip from our circle. It is a most desirable neighborhood."

"Could she not be a family connection of someone who lives there and lent the coach to her?"

"No, it really is hers. She is, was, very fond of crimson. Two or three of her gowns are of that color, and her cloak is lined with crimson silk. The upholstery in the coach is crimson as well. One of the maids heard it from the coachman, and it was plain from other bits of servants' hall discussion that the coachman and groom were employed by her. Only the outriders were hired for the occasion."

"She sounds like a matrimonial prize."

"Financially, that is true," she admitted.

"You have some doubt about her, Mistress Tate?"

"Not precisely, sir. She was intelligent, or maybe clever would be a better description, and she could be very amusing, though her wit was not always kind.

Stephen is a man of intelligence and sound principles. Most men are easily beguiled by beauty and an excessive display of femininity. You must know what I mean, Sir Hugh, being a sensible man yourself."

"Thank you." The two most attractive women Hugh could think of were Eilidh, whose greatest charm was her liveliness and her unconventional mind, or had been in their youth, and a lady in Northumberland who shot better than most men. Mistress Tate's forthright speech also appealed. "By excessive femininity, do you mean a pretense of needing male approval in all things?"

She chuckled. "Exactly!"

He waited, sensing another revelation was coming.

"She also radiated a sensuality which must have drawn men as flowers draw bees, even more so than the rest of her charms. Not that I think there is anything wrong with that. I'm sure it's a desirable quality in marriage. But its blatancy struck me as being in questionable taste. I believe I'd be sorry for any man caught in her toils. Any decent man, I mean."

Did that imply Lydia might deserve a scoundrel? Perhaps. However, Lydia did not sound like a woman who would be taken in by such a man. He would have liked to delve into her relationship with the earl.

Ismay Tate might not have revealed everything she knew or suspected, but she had nothing more she was willing to share with him at the moment. He thanked her and escorted her to the passage, where the footman informed him that Mr. Seaton requested his presence in the Yellow Parlor immediately.

****

"Dr. Lockhart has escorted the corpse to the

Crossed Keys to examine it. He is qualified as a surgeon as well as a physician," Wallace said.

"Edinburgh?"

"Ay. A good thing we have him. My second choice would have been a military surgeon if one were to hand. I am going to the Crossed Keys now to learn what else he may have discovered, as I do not care to be surprised at the crowner's court. Come with me, and we'll talk to Lockhart. I've informed the other guests that we'll continue later and asked Keswick to make sure none of them decides to end their stay here prematurely."

They described their respective gleanings during their ride to Penrith.

"Mistress Wilmot twittered a good deal, but it all amounted to this: she and Mistress Hodge were acquainted from their work with a charity that clothes the deserving poor. A marriage between their respective children would be beneficial to both families, so she asked Keswick to invite them. Not a straw there to help us. Stephen Cuthbert added one useful bit. I am quoting him here as it gives a flavor of his mind. 'There is a female like Lydia Forsyth at every house party, though one doesn't anticipate their murder. Usually, being English, the guests don't murder them.' "

"Not a ringing endorsement of the victim, Wallace."

At the inn, they found the doctor had confiscated the landlord's keys to the unused cellar storeroom "by order of the magistrate." His sharp eyes twinkled as Seaton had given no such order.

"Otherwise the servants would be taking the customers down for a look at the poor lass at a penny a head, no doubt." He had sent for his oil lamp to give enough light.

"I will do surgery by candle if I must, but for something like this, there's nothing to match whale oil."

"Excellent, Doctor, when even a small detail may matter."

On a long table, wide enough to allow the oil lamp to be moved around Lydia Forsyth's remains, the body lay curled in the same posture in which she had been found. Hugh and his cousin stood on either side of Lockhart. The woman might have been vivacious in life. Death had wiped away every sign of intelligence, wit, and kindness.

The doctor ran his fingers over the right side of her skull. He took longer about it than many would have thought necessary, given that the blow had clearly been fatal. Hugh needed no medical training to know that.

"She was struck at least several times with the candlestick, the blows not having fallen all in the same place. The murderer meant to make sure of her."

"Do you mean to perform an autopsy?" The foreboding in Wallace's voice made it plain he hoped the answer would be negative.

"There is an obvious cause of death," the doctor allowed. "However, given that the victim is a female of child-bearing age, we should determine whether she was with child."

Wallace was tiring, his expression losing its habitual keenness.

"Because it might provide the motive?" Hugh inquired.

"Ay. Question her maid. I'd rather not perform an autopsy if it's not necessary."

"She did not bring a maid with her," Wallace said.

"I wonder why she did not? I would expect one when a lady is so particular about her grooming and clothes. That much was evident from her dressing table." Lockhart wiped his hands on a cloth. "One of the household's maids served her, surely? She'll be able to tell you what I need to know."

"The girl will not have been in her confidence as her own maid would."

Lockhart gave him sardonic look. "I imagine she will. Mistress Forsyth was at Cuthbert Hall for near three weeks, wasn't she? If she sent rags from her courses to be washed, that would indicate she was not with child. Even if she did not, the maid who empties and washes the chamber pots would notice if she had been sick of a morning or if she had been urinating frequently. I don't like to cut a body up if it's not necessary. The family is always troubled by it."

"Would you be able to do an autopsy before the coroner's inquest?"

"I believe so, Sir Hugh. When I saw her, her body was beginning to lose the stiffness that comes on after death. From prior experience, I can hazard a guess she probably died at least twelve hours before. The muscles may take another twelve to loosen fully, or they may take longer. This postmortem stiffening is not well understood. In any event, I will wait until the stiffness passes off as it will do in time. By then, you should be able to tell me if it's possible she was pregnant."

"Is there anything else you can tell us?"

"If she was with child and far enough along to suspect it, the father was likely someone she knew in the biblical sense at least six weeks ago or thereabout,"

Lockhart said. "Which of the men here have been in London in that period?"

Wallace was still slightly red and perhaps speechless from the doctor's casual mention of the victim's menses. Hugh cleared his throat. "Finding out which of the men were in town before coming here should be a simple matter. We will also question the maid who attended her again and any others who may have served her and cleaned the room."

Recovered from his embarrassment, Wallace said, "We do have some information for you, Doctor. We believe she was killed between six o'clock last evening and half after the hour at the latest, the maid having left Mistress Forsyth by six. The candles had not been lighted, and she would have lit at least one if she intended to read, as she told the maid she meant to do."

There was that spot of wax, Hugh thought. *That needs explanation*. He believed Kitty had been truthful, but they should take nothing for granted without some evidence. Reluctantly he asked, "Could a maidservant have done this? Standing behind her at the dressing table would not be unusual for a lady's maid, or indeed a female friend."

Wallace protested. "Surely a woman could hardly have struck such blows?"

"Oh, certainly. Servants have to be strong, even maidservants. Have you ever carried a laden tea tray, Seaton? Or kneaded dough made from a stone of flour?"

"No. I take your point, Doctor."

"But I would not swear a lady could not strike such blows. They are not all frail, and strong emotion may give anyone greater strength than one would expect."

"Why would the girl do such a thing?"

"That's for you to determine, Seaton. I can only tell you how the decedent died."

Hugh replied, "Maybe to rob her, though if she were killed for her money or jewels, they should be missing. The jewel case was still in the drawer, locked and quite heavy, and there was a purse of money as well. There are other possibilities, too. But we can talk about them later instead of wasting your time, Dr. Lockhart."

"Thank you, Sir Hugh. I will say, however, you will most likely be looking for a man. When I was walking the wards of the Royal Infirmary at Edinburgh, the women being treated for injuries had almost always suffered them at the hands of a husband or lover. Some patients refused to say or claimed to have been attacked by a stranger, but they were often trying to protect the man who supported them. So all things being equal, I would say that you should inquire into the men with whom she was either intimate or by whom she was being courted."

He paused, to be sure of their attention before continuing.

"However, when the body was raised, a bit of evidence came to light." He turned to the bench against the wall and took something from his instrument case. Holding a stained piece of fabric by one unblemished corner, he spread it out on the table near the lamp. "This was under an edge of her smock or night rail. Not being a married man, I am not schooled in the difference, if there is one." A brown stain striped the center of the handkerchief, a dainty bit of linen edged with lace with an embroidered design in one corner.

Hugh mimed holding a candlestick near its base and ran his closed hand up its length. "The candlestick was wiped with it, leaving a band of blood across the middle and two edges mostly unstained?"

"So I surmise."

Wallace took it and held it up. "You found this under the body?"

"Ay."

"Dr. Lockhart," Hugh ventured, "under what part?"

The doctor approached the body on the table and pulled the smock up a few inches so it no longer covered the right ankle. "This is as close as I can recall to how she lay when I saw her in her chamber. The handkerchief was just out of sight under her night rail about a handbreadth up from the hem."

"Will you draw it for me, please? It may be useful in our inquiry." Wallace passed the doctor his pocketbook and a stub of pencil.

In a few strokes, the doctor outlined the body lying on its left side, knees bent.

"The handkerchief was several inches down from her patella. The whirl-bone of the knee, we call it. But it was not under her leg, you'll ken, only under the smock."

Wallace pulled up the edge of the linen gown as far as he could to peer at it. "There's no stain I can see, and yet the center of the handkerchief is stiff with the dried blood."

"Sir Hugh, if you'll assist me, we'll raise the body a bit to see more of the garment?" The doctor took the shoulders and Hugh the lower legs and lifted it slightly.

Wallace pursed his lips. "There's no stain on the gown. Is it likely, Doctor?"

"From the amount of blood on this piece, I would have expected at least a bit to be transferred to the shift. Smock. Whatever this garment is. However, when I examine a patient or a body, I often find things I do not expect. Perhaps the smock did not press hard enough to take a stain. But what I would not expect is for the handkerchief to be under her."

Hugh eyed the doctor. "You have a flair for the dramatic, sir."

"Alas, 'tis so. I indulged myself a bit because a physician seldom is able to impart startling news."

His cousin's brows shot up. "That is a point. I had not thought of how the handkerchief could have come to be under the body. That is what you are suggesting, Doctor Lockhart? That it was placed there?"

"The thought occurred to me. If I had killed the poor woman and wiped the candlestick, I would have dropped the cloth. It would likely fall by my feet or on the stool. Unless he held the body in place to keep it from falling while he was striking the blows, thinking the sound of it hitting the floor might attract attention."

Trying to visualize that sequence of events, Hugh shook his head. "He'd need three hands unless he set the candle down on the table, picked up the handkerchief, wiped the candlestick, dropped that on the floor, then reached across his body and his victim's body to drop the cloth to the left of the dressing table while steadying Lydia's body with his left hand. He would need both hands to lower her to the floor. What would be the point in concealing the clout?"

Wallace shook his head. "In theft, burglary and brawls that end in a death, there are often inconsistencies that make no sense."

"Still, the handkerchief being where Dr. Lockhart found it needs explaining." Now that he knew of it, that problem perplexed Hugh as much as the latched door.

"It does, but it's time we returned to the Hall. We have the rest of the guests and servants to question."

"When is the inquest to be held?" Lockhart inquired, covering the body with a sheet.

"I asked the coroner to schedule it for nine in the morning the day after tomorrow. It will be held in the assembly room upstairs."

"Good. I should be able to complete an autopsy by then if necessary. Let me know as soon as you can if you learn she may have been pregnant."

"I hope the assembly room is large enough." Hugh had never set foot in it during his boyhood visits.

"It is, and enough for any spectators who may come out of curiosity."

"Which they undoubtedly will." He remembered the last inquest he had attended. With a noble family involved, the room had been packed.

"On the whole, the less secrecy, the better. Besides, someone who has little direct knowledge of the matter may catch a lie in someone else's testimony. I want to examine the dressing table again, and we must complete our interviews tonight." As an afterthought, he said, "As you sketch well, Doctor, will you draw the design on the handkerchief and bring both to the inquest?"

"Certainly."

They left Dr. Lockhart packing up his box of instruments in the chilly little room.

Chapter 5

They had missed dinner at two but had eaten a quick meal before leaving the Crossed Keys. They went over their next steps as they rode back to Cuthbert Hall.

"One of us must question the housemaid or the chambermaid, whichever dealt with the chamber pot, and the laundry maid so we can apprise Lockhart of any evidence of pregnancy or the reverse."

"We should also make a chart of who went into the house and when," Hugh added. "There's probably some foolscap in the house. That ought to be big enough to use."

"A good thought. Also of anyone during that period who was not seen outside by at least one person."

During a lapse in their discussion, Hugh said, "I suppose the killer must have snatched up the handkerchief from the dressing table rather than use his own."

Wallace said reluctantly, "Unless the murderer was a lady."

"True, but I incline to Lockhart's opinion that it's more likely a man's crime."

As they left their horses with the grooms in the stable yard, Wallace said, "I would like to look at the chamber again before we question the others."

The air was close and faintly scented with

chamber-lye, the chamber pot having gone unemptied and only the one window opened that morning, then closed again. Nothing else had changed, except that the estate carpenter had put a lock on the door and given both keys to Keswick. Wallace appropriated them and assured himself there were no others.

"I missed something," his cousin said grimly, surveying the room. "I did not pay enough attention to the dressing table. My wife's used to tell me a good deal about her mood and her day."

Hugh, a bachelor, stood beside him. The linen cloth covering the top bore a few traces of blood and held a daunting assortment of aids to beauty. "Patch box, box with a bottle of rouge and applicator, a pot of lip salve, comb, brush, etui holding tweezers, pomatum…scent bottle with no stopper. I'm wrong: there it is behind the pomade pot." He sniffed the air. "I can just smell a trace of scent. Can you?" Raising the bottle to his nose, he found the heavy, musky scent overpowering. "Ugh."

Wallace's nose wrinkled. "Too strong. Reminds me of, er, civet cats."

"I know what you mean, and I agree, though I am not in the habit of patronizing, er, civet cats."

Wallace barked a laugh. He began to make some rejoinder when Hugh said, "Where is the book she intended to read? Alleged to be intending to read, rather. Though I can't imagine Kitty inventing that, can you?"

Wallace chewed his lower lip. "No. I don't recall seeing any book, not that I was looking for one." He opened the table's drawer.

Hugh continued around the room. She had drunk a glass of wine with her supper and presumably meant to drink another for her head. Why not request a ptisan? The cook must know of some herbal drink for the megrim.

After repeating their earlier search, neither had found a book or any other thing which might be a clue. As they left the room, Wallace said, "The chief problem is still how the murderer made his exit."

After brushing his riding clothes and washing his face and hands, Hugh sought out Polly, the housemaid, who denied there was anything in the lady's chamber pot " 'cept what should be there." The laundry maid denied there were any blood-stained cloths to be washed for Lydia Forsyth. That proved nothing.

"She might be with child or it might be too early for her courses this month," Wallace summed up. "I'll send a note to Lockhart to use his own discretion regarding an autopsy. I'm more concerned about the latch."

By six o'clock, they had completed questioning the guests without gleaning much more information and compared notes.

Hugh's questioning of Mistress Joan Hodge agreed with Dorothy Wilmot's account. She had not seen or else not remembered who had gone into the house, though she herself had had to do so once. She had been too enthralled by the harvest festival for she had never attended one before, having been born and brought up in Manchester.

Wallace had better luck. During the archery contest, Caleb Hodge had been describing to Randolph Cuthbert the business opportunities available to a gentleman without sullying himself by a connection to trade. Hodge had had to excuse himself, pleading an urgent need for the jakes, but they'd finished their discussion of investments by then. That was not quite half after the hour of five. He often checked his pocket watch: a man in business had to mind his use of time. When he came back, the contest was over and the watchers were gone, including Cuthbert.

Wallace added, "Stephen Cuthbert was one of the participants in the match and confirmed when Hodge left and that Randolph Cuthbert departed soon after."

"I wish Cornelius Wilmot had paid more attention to the other guests," Hugh said. Cornelius had noticed Georgina enter the house sometime in the late afternoon. While he did not admit it, he had paid little or no attention to anyone else. "He unburdened himself of much that's of no use but a little that is."

He had confided he did not think the wished-for match with Georgina would come to anything. "Mistress Georgina is a delightful girl, but I can never think what to say to her."

"Not that he'd have a chance to speak," Hugh observed, having interviewed the chit.

He continued, reconstructing Wilmot's statement from his notes, less complete than Wallace's but still adequate to aid his memory, " 'Stephen is older and taller than I am and has such confidence and polished manners. Even Randolph Cuthbert, who is too old for her and married besides, throws me into the shade. I suppose Stephen will get her.' "

"He was vague as to the time," Hugh admitted, "but perhaps between a little before six and half six. Georgina came out again after about twenty minutes. I suppose she did a good deal of tidying of her hair and neckerchief and whatever."

"That's one entry for the chart, at least. I don't see her as a murderess, do you?"

"No. Though I'm often surprised at what a man or woman will do at need, Wallace."

Stephen Cuthbert also had been forthcoming. Wallace quoted from his extensive notes, " 'I have never been in such ill-assorted company, which is odd considering so many of them are related to me. Most of us aren't really to Keswick's taste. Mr. Wilmot is intelligent but colorless. Mr. Hodge is a Cit and a necessary evil when the earl has a nephew who needs to marry a fortune but not a bad fellow otherwise. Both Mistress Hodge and my aunt, Mistress Wilmot, are good women who talk too much and lack education and worldliness. Heaven help us, I have never met a sillier female than Georgina Hodge. Even the silliness isn't the worst of it. She speaks any thought that comes into her head. Mayhap that won't bother Cornelius. I'd be driven mad in a week. For serious conversation, I'd choose Mistress Tate or Mistress Cuthbert. When Randolph is present, she fades into the background, but in other company she shines.' "

Hugh remembered her warmth and eccentric charm. Her husband had suppressed it, curse him.

Stephen had seen a number of people enter or leave the house. " 'The servants were in and out, fetching and carrying, and the guests to use the necessary, given the quantities of ale some had been drinking. Not the ladies, of course.' "

"You did not see any ladies go in?" Wallace had inquired.

" 'I did. I suppose both for reasons of comfort and to make repairs to their gowns or hats. I didn't mean they'd been swilling anything. Not even lemonade. Awkward for them, you know, with their panniers and petticoats.' "

"Could he recall anyone who went in during that time?"

Wallace looked up from his notes. "Stephen Cuthbert is not the frivolous fellow he sounds. He saw both Georgina Hodge and Mistress Cuthbert go in and noticed that Cornelius watched the former like a love-sick puppy. Stephen saw Ismay Tate go in several times, but usually through the north wing, the kitchen being there. That might have made it possible for her to kill Lydia; she would at least have been in the correct part of the house. He saw her enter by the south door once. I believe he noticed her comings and goings in particular because he is attracted to her." Wallace cleared his throat. "He saw Randolph go in by the south wing, as did the earl also."

"All within the same period?"

"He did not look at his pocket watch but thought they all were around that time," his cousin concluded. He sighed heavily. "There is no more we can do tonight. We'll resume in the morning. Let us take our leave of his lordship now."

There proved to be no need. The earl said, "It's near time for supper. I'll have bedchambers readied for you and send a groom to request your servants pack valises for you. To ride back and forth between your home and mine makes no sense. I do not want uncertainty over the murder to linger, and I have little doubt you will soon be able to send the killer to Carlisle to be held for the assizes."

"That is kind of you and will save Sir Hugh and me

a great deal of time."

His cousin tired easily. Being spared the ride each day would preserve Wallace's strength.

****

The Second Day

Their chart of the guests', family's, and servants' whereabouts and the times thereof had grown, although not all of the statements had been confirmed by a second party. Some they could dismiss as unlikely suspects, like Georgina Hodge. If she had killed the woman, she would have let the fact slip the first day.

Wallace observed, "Joan Hodge is not accounted for."

He had spoken hesitantly. His cousin might fear Hugh would laugh at the suggestion.

"No, she isn't. She might think she had reason to dispatch Lydia, too. If the Hodges wanted Georgina for Cornelius, she could have misunderstood Lydia's manner toward him and believed she would snatch him from under Georgina's nose."

"That occurred to me, Hugh, but is Mistress Hodge clever enough to have carried out the murder?"

"I grant you that from her conversation she sounds like a goosecap unless she is speaking of everyday matters. Many excellent housewives are not educated or particularly intelligent and yet manage a household well. Murder being a practical matter, it might not be beyond her capabilities. She would have the advantage also of seeming harmless. She might have simply been lucky enough to have gone to Lydia's room while whatever footman who might have seen her was away or busy. But luck would not account for the door being latched, which is true of everyone else, too."

Wallace brought his fist down sharply on the table, then massaged it ruefully. "How in the name of all that's holy did he or she get out of the room? I do not want my investigation to end in a verdict of murder by a person or persons unknown. That would leave a cloud of suspicion over at least several here. I confess I am out of my depth, Hugh."

"So am I."

"Well, put aside the problem of the locked room for the moment. Who would want to murder Mistress Forsyth? If she were pregnant, that might be a reason to kill her."

"A wealthy widow could take an inconvenient pregnancy to some obscure place under another name or even go to the Continent to give birth if the man already had a wife or he refused to wed her. These things happen. She could then return from her travels without the child," Hugh objected.

"I don't think we can assume she would go away quietly. Joseph Wilmot found her uncomfortable, and I think she was also described as a coquette. Would such a woman steal away without making a scene? I have never counted a female of that sort among my acquaintances," his cousin confessed.

"I have known of one or two. A man who might lose some more desirable prize if his name was linked to hers or whom she tried to force into marriage has a potential motive. Any man here with whom she had contact of that sort within the last month or two should be considered a suspect."

Wallace made another note. "The earl hasn't been away since returning from town in May. Stephen Cuthbert, the Wilmots, and the Hodges live in London.

So does Randolph Cuthbert, though I suppose he may have been visiting friends in the country. If she was with child, that does not narrow our field of suspects."

"If she was not, there are other reasons to kill. She had coin enough to make it worthwhile to rob her, and jewelry as well, but she was not robbed. He might have panicked after killing her and fled without taking them. Ordinarily I would consider that the killer had gone to her chamber, they argued, she said something that enraged him, and he grabbed up the candlestick and killed her," Hugh said. "But wiping the candlestick and then hiding the kerchief is not the action of a panicked villain. Nor does it explain why he had the handkerchief and how he escaped from the room."

"No, but the handkerchief may have been Lydia's, and he might have known of some way of getting out of the room," Wallace suggested.

"One coincidence I might believe in, but not two. Here's another motive: what if she threatened to expose someone's guilty secret?"

Wallace's eyebrows shot up. "Do you have reason to think she might have been extorting money or trying to?"

"No, but I have no reason not to suspect it, either. Ismay Tate had no very high opinion of Lydia and her ways. I would not rule it out until we know more of Mistress Forsyth."

Wallace frowned over that before agreeing. "She might be blackmailing either a woman or a man, and whatever proof she was holding would be gone, I suppose."

"Unless she was brandishing the letters or other evidence, the killer would have needed time to find them. That would mean before twilight was so far advanced Lydia or the killer would have had to light a candle."

"As someone did, judging from the drop of wax you found."

"Yes, but what a careful murderer it was, to search for the incriminating letters or whatever and leave no sign of disturbance and only that drop of wax." Hugh cocked a satiric eyebrow.

"He would know that leaving signs of having rummaged through her possessions would indicate he was looking for something other than her jewels or money. If he killed her almost as soon as Kitty left, he might have had as much as half an hour to search. If the candle wax came from one he lit and took away with him, he could have searched longer and neatly because with Lydia retired to her room with a megrim, he would not expect anyone to come to her."

"That is true," Hugh agreed, "and with a guest bedroom having few places to hide something, he could still have gone to supper at eight. And not everyone was present at that meal anyway. But what of the chance of meeting someone in the passage? The guests began to trickle into the house at twilight when the contests and games ended. He would run the risk of being seen."

Wallace tutted. "Unless the killer dressed as a maidservant or in livery? Someone who had been here often and knew the servants as individuals might recognize him, but even then, we tend not to see someone in livery or cap and apron as a person, any more than we really observe the furniture. I admit I do not believe most men would be able to pass as a woman however briefly."

"Whether he did or not, use of a disguise means the killer made his plan in advance and that proves the killing was done with malice aforethought as Sir Edward Coke would have said."

"Which I think we already know. Whether the killer is male or female, he or she knew how to latch the door on the way out or how to escape by some other means."

Keeping his voice level, Hugh said, "I don't think our murderer was female, based on Lockhart's remarks. Do we not agree the murderer must be male?"

"It's likely but not certain. We have to keep open minds and not say, as many do, that a crime must have been committed by a servant or laborer."

Hugh nodded reluctantly. He did not like the idea of any woman hanging, but his aversion to considering a female killer here was more personal. He could not believe Eilidh guilty, but she was not happy in her marriage. There were other women here. They had already eliminated Georgina Hodge as too talkative, and she was also too silly and seldom far from her mother or her maid. Mistress Hodge or Mistress Wilmot? Unlikely, even if they were practical in housekeeping matters. Ismay Tate? She was intelligent, and she had been busy supervising the servants so she was in and out of the house. He did not like to think she might be guilty, though she would have had the opportunity. "Mistress Tate could have done it."

He did not need to explain his reasoning. "She could. No one would wonder at her bustling about the house. What would her motive be?"

"Blackmail."

"Hard to imagine how the Forsyth woman would

have discovered anything about her. Ismay lives in the country and has no connections to the beau monde and not much money. She would scarcely be worth blackmailing. How would their paths have crossed except right here?" his cousin inquired.

"Someone among her friends might live in London. Many keep up close friendships by letter. That friend might inhabit Lydia's circle, or they might have a friend in common."

"It's something to look into. Kitty had the best opportunity, of course, and a female's own maid might kill her mistress in a blind rage if she were threatened with being turned off with no character. That's unlikely when she was being attended by someone else's servant, however. I'll write to Lydia's butler, enclosing a letter to her man of business, and to a magistrate I know in London, in case it's necessary to obtain a search warrant. Then we'll know more about her."

"Like who in this house benefits from her death or has a grudge against her?" Hugh asked. "What about Hodge? Caleb Hodge has been successful in business, which suggests he's clever and may be ruthless."

"Why would he kill the woman?"

"She might know something discreditable about him and try to squeeze him."

Wallace perked up. "How would she be aware of Hodge's existence before this gathering, let alone of some secret of his?"

"A widow left her Cit husband's fortune and in control of it? I'll hazard a guess she knew a bit about his business."

"A knowing one," Wallace muttered. He countered, "How would he have known about a secret entrance? If there is one."

"Mayhap there isn't. What if Lydia still lived when her attacker left her? She might have regained consciousness, risen and locked the door before returning to the dressing table and collapsing."

His cousin snorted. "Can you imagine Lockhart's pithy comment if he were asked about such a possibility? 'Only in a play of the most ridiculous sort, man,' that's what he'd say. The body was lying as if she had fallen off the stool after those savage blows to the right side of her head. That is a fact."

Hugh's face heated. "I am a fool and clutching at straws."

His cousin studied his face, an uncomfortable scrutiny that hinted he understood. Instead of broaching a conversation neither of them wanted, Wallace said pacifically, "I have been trying to avoid the question of how the killer escaped, hoping we could easily determine a suspect and discover from him how he did it. All I can think of is a secret entrance. That has complications of its own."

No need to spell them out. Who except a member of the family would know of such a thing? The idea of arresting an earl for the crime made Hugh's head ache. They could not contemplate doing so unless they had an irrefutable motive and proof. Even then, he would never be punished for it. He pointed this out to Wallace.

"Any one of the Cuthberts might know of a concealed entrance. It's hard to keep secrets in a family." His cousin took a pinch of snuff and sneezed mightily.

Perhaps it depended on the family, Hugh thought.

"Or it might be no more than a concealed servants'

door."

"If so, many would know of it. The family, the servants, mayhap someone who had visited before and had that bedroom. Wouldn't the earl have thought of it?"

Lydia's room shared its south wall with the Long Gallery. That would be an odd place for a servants' entrance to the suite. They could ignore the exterior walls on the north and west. Lydia's own dressing room, the passage, and Eilidh's chamber adjoined the east wall.

Wallace responded, "Indeed, as he's urgent to have this murder solved, you'd think so, but relevant details are sometimes not thought of in the midst of a crisis. There's little point in speculating. We'll ask him."

Not thought of. "Wallace," Hugh began.

"Ay?"

"What became of Lydia's book? That's the one thing we know is missing."

His cousin straightened up. "A good question. That slipped my mind."

"And mine. The room being locked has distracted us."

"Another thing, Hugh. Why did Lydia go to her chamber so early? I don't believe she had a megrim. Have you known a sufferer from severe headaches?"

Hugh shook his head. "Not to my knowledge."

"A fellow in my college had them. All he could do was lie down in a darkened room until it passed. Would anyone in such a condition eat a meal, drink wine, and then spend time prinking herself up for bed before reading? She'd be more likely to ask the cook to send up something for it, as she had no maid to mix a headache powder for her. I do not recall seeing any headache powders among her belongings. Of course, she may have lied because she did not care for country frolics and wanted an excuse to go inside."

Hugh tapped one forefinger on the table. "I agree, and I wonder about the perfume bottle. It was not knocked over when she fell. It was open and the scent was a heavy one. Would a woman put on perfume before retiring? By herself, that is."

Wallace harrumphed. "I believe ladies often do go to bed sweetly scented, but my own dear wife did not care for strong scents."

"If Lydia were expecting someone, she might put on scent. We should ask Kitty about that."

****

The maid arrived still tying the strings of a clean apron, summoned from some messy char.

"We have another question for you about Mistress Forsyth's preparations for bed. I hope you can help us, if you remember."

The girl nodded mutely. Belatedly she added, "Ay, sir, if I can."

"There was a scent bottle on the table. Do you recall it?"

"I'm sure there wasn't one there when I left Mistress Forsyth. She had a box with little spaces for four bottles, but she kept it in the drawer."

Hugh glanced at his cousin and raised his eyebrows. His cousin nodded. "I saw it. The bottles matched except that the glass was different colors. Did she put on a bit of perfume before bed as a rule?"

"She often did, Your Worship."

"Was it always the same one?"

"No, sir."

Seeing Wallace at a standstill, Hugh asked, "Did she use them in a particular order?"

"No, 'twas always just whatever she happened to fancy."

"Did she often use the red one, Kitty?"

The girl puzzled over the question. "Since she came, near three weeks ago, I don't recollect her ever using it while I was there. Though there was times I thought I smelled it upon her night rail in the morning."

Wallace asked sharply, "How did you know it was from the red flask?"

"I didn't, Your Worship, but I know the scents of the three she used when I was there. They wasn't near so strong."

He nodded, satisfied. "Now tell me, did you see the book Mistress Forsyth mentioned she would read?"

"Ay, 'twas a red one bound in leather with gold stamping."

"Did you notice the title, by any chance?"

His cousin did not sound optimistic, with cause.

"There was writing," the girl said, "but I couldn't read it, o' course."

Even some ladies never learned to read. A country girl employed as a maid did not need to be literate. Reading might make her dissatisfied with her station.

"How big was it?"

Wallace nodded approvingly at Hugh's question.

She mimed dimensions with her hands. A small book, then.

"Its thickness?"

Her thumb and forefinger indicated a thin one.

After dismissing her, Wallace said, "I've never

seen such a small book of sermons, have you?"

"In my experience, they're quite thick as a rule."

"If it was inscribed with the killer's name, that would account for its disappearance."

"Which brings us back to why someone would kill her, Wallace."

His cousin relaxed into the wing chair's embrace and stretched his legs toward the glowing coals in the grate. "A point. From Ismay Tate, we know she was a coquette, and that is supported obliquely by Stephen Cuthbert. Ellen did not like her although she did not say so."

"I suspect women who throw out lures to every man they meet are not popular with their own sex."

"Just so, Hugh. The Wilmots and presumably the earl hope Cornelius and Georgina will make a match. To ensure it occurred, would one of the parties do away with someone who seemed likely to lead Cornelius astray?"

"Would any of them consider Lydia a serious threat to their plan? She must be eight or ten years older than young Wilmot and more than that in worldliness. Why would she be interested?"

"Merely to make trouble, perhaps, or it may be her habit to try to charm any male she meets. I admit I can't imagine any of the Wilmots being our murderer. Keswick might…" Wallace shrugged.

"Or he might not care. Cornelius is not in the line of succession. What would it matter if Cornelius married an older widow who may not be able to breed. At least she was rich." They should verify the woman actually was wealthy and would not lose her fortune by remarrying.

"We can't disregard the earl as a suspect, however. She might have tried to blackmail him." Wallace sipped from his glass of small beer. With little alcohol and plenty of sustenance, it was almost all he drank. "If he is the killer, we may have to leave the murder unsolved. The Lords would never convict one of their own."

Hugh grunted. He had no argument with noblemen who valued their country's and their tenants' good as much as their own. The other sort deserved no privileges, in his opinion. To say so would be sedition, for which one might be imprisoned.

"What reasons drive men to murder? Or women," Wallace amended. "The fair sex does occasionally stoop to kill. We've discussed blackmail, but a desire to inherit can be a cause of murder. So can love, when someone kills a rival for a loved one's affections. Revenge is another reason, though I think it's not very common except among felons. Then there's fear, if the killer believed the victim possessed proof he had committed a crime. Those would all apply equally to either sex."

"And I believe women consider us generally annoying, Wallace. However, I'm tolerably familiar with the *Newgate Calendar* and recall very few examples of murder by females compared to the number committed by men."

"Women are generally weaker. That's probably why they are the gentler sex."

That view seemed unusually cynical for his cousin. Or it might simply be realistic. "I have noticed that when they slay, it is usually their babies in order to preserve their own reputation or mayhap a very sick or elderly relation from whom they will inherit. A woman may feel injured or furious at her man who strays to another, but have you ever heard of one killing her rival? I thought we had concluded this was not a woman's crime."

"I don't think it is, given the means. I think a woman might kill, but she would probably use poison or some other subtle means rather than bashing. According to my housekeeper, there are things growing in most gardens that will drop you like a stone, though I imagine one would need to know which could be put in food or drink and not be detected by the taste. A clever woman could likely learn what she needed from an apothecary's text."

Hugh said, "But Lydia was not poisoned, and I want to know why she was invited. Apart from the Hodges, whose reason for being here is understandable, she was the only one not related to Keswick. Was she really present for Stephen Cuthbert's benefit? From your interview notes, he was not interested in her. Mistress Tate only surmised the woman might have been invited in the hope she and Stephen would marry, though she thought them ill-matched."

Wallace shifted his wig in order to scratch his head. "Being the nearest magistrate, I've come to know Keswick a bit. He might attempt to bring about a good marriage for Stephen. After Randolph, Stephen is next in the line of succession, and Randolph has no sons. Nor daughters, neither."

Randolph Cuthbert was a few years older than Eilidh. Had Eilidh had miscarriages or failed to breed at all? Either way, Hugh pitied her, because the woman was always blamed for not being able to produce children and because she would have wanted sons and daughters to love. Was lack of an heir the reason her husband appeared not to value her and her glow had dimmed? All Cuthbert's fault, he was sure of it.

Wallace went on. "At the same time, he's a great believer in propriety, and I can't quite believe he would consider the widow of a Cit a suitable wife for someone who might inherit his title, no matter how rich she was. Unless the earldom's finances are shakier than I'm aware."

"That's two reasons against the matchmaking suggestion," Hugh pointed out. "From Wilmot's description, Lydia sounded too lively to devote herself to good works and a countess's duties. She sounds like a female with considerable worldly wisdom as well as money, which might equal no desire to give up her freedom for a second marriage. Could Keswick have hoped to make her his mistress?"

"The earl has kept the same woman in a cottage near Penrith for years. She's a quiet female, moderately well-bred, and by all accounts makes him comfortable when he is present and does not trouble him with questions or requests. I can't imagine him enjoying a frivolous or demanding mistress."

"Have you questioned him?"

"Not yet. I was hoping not to have to do so."

"Awkward when you have to deal with him regularly. Would you mind if I did? As you will be taken up pursuing other possibilities?"

With a sigh, Wallace agreed. "You always were more tactful than I. I wish you will also ask Eilidh if she recalls who went inside during the relevant time. She was needle-witted and more likely than most to be a good witness. That won't have changed."

****

Maneuvering a conversation with the earl out of hearing of others, Hugh praised the Keswick who had enlarged the house and increased its comfort without sacrificing its exterior appearance of great antiquity. Wallace had primed him with the knowledge the earl was as proud of the house as of his title.

"Ours is an old family, and we do not run mad for novelty and change, Montgomery. You won't find me pasting a Palladian front over these walls that have seen so much of our history and all of it fortunate. We changed our religion under King Henry, changed it back under Queen Mary, then changed it again for Queen Bess. Neither Cavalier nor Parliamentarian cannon balls ever touched the Hall." He laughed ruefully. "I value the house and land the more as I never expected to inherit the title. I was only the second son and intended for the church."

"A great deal of history and an honorable heritage, my lord." After they had sipped their Madeira in silence for a few moments, Hugh ventured, "If I may ask something relating to the unfortunate incident here as it may come up at the inquest?"

Still basking in memories of his family's glory, the earl assured Hugh he was happy to cooperate.

"As the group here is almost all related to you, how did Mistress Forsyth come to be invited?"

Keswick studied the amber wine in his glass. "Randolph hinted that my nephew Stephen was interested in her as a mistress and that throwing them together here would be a kindness."

"A mistress rather than a wife?"

"Stephen is certainly of an age to marry, but

Randolph assured me he had no thought of offering for her. He knows he will inherit my title if Randolph fails to get an heir, as seems all too likely now. I have no objection to his amusing himself with a willing widow. He'll court an appropriate young lady when he's ready. I married young at my father's direction and would not demand that a potential heir of mine do the same."

That sparked an idea. "I wonder who her heir is, my lord?"

"I must write to her household to inform them. Or mayhap Seaton should inform them and ask about her family, man of business, and heirs, and I will write a letter of condolence."

"Seaton means to write to Lydia's home, having learned her address and her butler's name from her coachman. He hoped her driver might know who handled her legal business, but he was an empty well. The mail to London goes out three times a week, but given the unreliability of the postboys, it might or might not reach London in a week or ten days. Then after the Forsyth butler conveys the enclosed letter to her man of business or attorney, his reply may take as long." He chose not to mention his cousin's letter to a London magistrate.

"Damme, why entrust so important a matter to a postboy? They're not only unreliable, they're a scoundrelly lot as well and are often robbed of the mail. Tell Seaton I'll send his letter and mine by one of my grooms with the coin to change horses as often as he thinks fit. He can bring the reply back."

"Thank you, my lord. That will be helpful."

He also inquired whether Keswick had paid any attention to who went in the late afternoon and evening.

He had not: he had been talking with his neighbors, from those with titles down to the gentry and farmers large and small, and his own tenants.

Chapter 6

Uneasy in mind, Ellen made her way to the little room in the passage to the kitchen offices. Why did Hugh need to question her? What had he learned?

When the footman opened the door and she beheld Hugh studying a sheet of paper on the sideboard, her mind went blank. Could a heart both rise and fall at the same time? Years of practice helped her curtsy and bid him good day without showing anything of her thoughts.

"Eilidh—may I still call you that? Or should I be formal and correct and address you as 'Mistress Cuthbert'?"

How she had missed him. "In the presence of others, please be formal. My husband dislikes the name with which I was christened."

"So I understood from something Wallace told me. Please sit down. I apologize for the less than comfortable chair."

"I believe this room gets little use except when the Great Hall is used for some gathering." She waited, hands folded in her lap.

He seated himself in the other chair but did not speak at once. Eilidh wished they could simply talk as they had when she was a carefree girl: about what they'd been doing or wanted to do, or about some book or piece of news. Impossible now, with Hugh here in his official capacity as Wallace's assistant. Perhaps he was thinking the same thing.

"Since you and my cousin spoke, we've learned something. We know to within about half an hour when Lydia Forsyth was killed. We need to identify the people who were inside the house in that period."

"And therefore might have had the opportunity to kill her?"

"Some of them. We know some were within too briefly to have done so. As I remember, you were very observant, inconveniently so on a few occasions."

"Oh, dear. You mean like the time I remarked I could smell the Williams girl's perfume in the parlor when only my mother, the curate, and you and I were present?"

"You were sitting nearest the poor fellow. I don't know how I kept from laughing. Did he marry her?"

"Yes. I think my mother had a word with hers. She also spoke to me about thinking before speaking."

"The memory of his expression has often given me a smile. Ah, well." The humor left his face. "Did you see anyone go into the house between half four and half six? And who did not come out again quite soon?"

"Before I went in myself at about half five, people came and went, to the retiring rooms, most likely. Ismay had been back and forth all afternoon, making sure the tables both by the house and by the home farm barn were well supplied with food and drink, though she went by way of the kitchen door in the north wing."

Fourteen years ago, she could have told Hugh almost anything. Since then, there had been no one she could confide in.

"Have I changed, Eilidh?"

Had she spoken aloud or had he divined her thought?

As she sat dumbstruck, he said, "We've both grown up. I'm not the boy I used to be, but I would not have expected you to lose your joy."

"I was a girl when you knew me."

"Please tell me. What happened to you?"

If he had not asked that question…but he had. Fourteen years of pain and anger burst out as if an abscess had been lanced.

"I had to change to be a suitable wife for a fashionable man. We 'rub along' well enough when we aren't in the same room. Or the same county." She should not have let that slip out. Hugh's wits were as sharp as ever, unfortunately.

"You live separately?"

"We do, except when I visit London."

His brow furrowed. Keswick was sufficiently courteous not to air his dissatisfaction at her childlessness in public, but anyone would understand that with Stephen Cuthbert the only heir after Randolph Cuthbert, Stephen's marriage at least must be soon and fruitful.

"I've been told by more than one person that Lydia was invited as a possible bride for Stephen Cuthbert. I am surprised the earl would consider a childless widow of her age as a suitable choice, unless the earldom's finances are in disarray."

Ellen compressed her lips on an inconvenient truth.

"Even then," he continued, "I think Keswick could find several ladies without the drawbacks that came with Lydia Forsyth."

"More than several, I am sure."

"Eilidh, how did the notion that she was intended for Stephen Cuthbert spread?"

"If there are two unattached ladies at a house party and two unattached men, assumptions will be made. As Dorothy Wilmot and Joan Hodge had already settled it between themselves that Georgina would do for Cornelius, anyone might conclude that Lydia and Stephen would make a pair."

"No one has claimed that Cuthbert was attracted by her, and in fact she seems to have impressed some as a minx."

"She was not well suited to Stephen, who is a serious man." She knew that expression and braced herself. Hugh was going to broach some delicate subject.

"An intelligent man does not always insist on a sensible mistress."

"No. I saw no sign he showed any partiality for her, however."

"The reverse, in fact, according to one or two I spoke with."

Lydia Forsyth had been a gillflirt, a match for—

"The earl says Cuthbert asked him to invite Lydia because Stephen wanted to make her his mistress and throwing them together would provide him an opportunity."

Eilidh bit her lip. Lydia's presence had surprised her, but she had not had the least doubt that Randolph had arranged it. Her husband had not been doing a kindness for Stephen Cuthbert.

"How thoughtful of him," she said. Perhaps instead she should have limited her remark to "Really?" She had forgotten how perceptive Hugh could be.

Brows drawn together, her old friend asked, "Is Keswick aware of how matters stand between you?"

He had not lost his ability to piece together seemingly unrelated facts and words. She took a deep breath and told the truth.

"I didn't think so. Cuthbert did not want him to know, but it's possible some friend or correspondent of his may have commented on my never being in London with Cuthbert except briefly. It's really only possible to get a good riding habit and boots in London, and my maid insists upon it for new gowns. If he heard of my absence, Randolph would have explained it as my being unable to support London's smoke, dust, noise, and endless entertainments. Cuthbert prefers town life and leaves London only during the summer."

"Which he spends in Durham?"

"No."

"Where does he go? To house parties?"

"I suppose so. Those whose host and guests do not move in the same circles as the earl, I assume, and Keswick is not a sociable man anyway. He does his duty in Parliament and while in town meets with his friends at their homes or in coffee or chocolate houses. I don't think he ever sought out my husband in town, not to my knowledge, anyway, so he would not necessarily know I wasn't in London. He did not go to town for Parliament, either, during his son's illness or after his death. Now because we will not be able to hide our separate living arrangements, Randolph has informed me I must spend more time in town. I am to see some physician who is said to have had good success with females whose health is not robust. I suppose that was Keswick's suggestion. I'm sure he blames me for not breeding."

"Forgive me for being blunt, but if Cuthbert fails to do his marital duty, no dosing by some fashionable quack will produce offspring. The earl will eventually give up and you can return to Durham."

"I fear that will not be possible, as Randolph intends to give up the lease on the house there. He says there is no point in spending money on it and on a caretaker if I am to live at Keswick House." She swallowed a lump in her throat. "He actually suggested that I should find some man to oblige me by getting me with child, as long as the fellow resembled him."

Hugh was silent so long and with such an abstracted gaze that she wanted to flee the room. Did he believe she had acquiesced? "Need I say I ignored his advice?"

"No. Your demeanor may have changed, and damn him for that, but your heart and mind have not. I wish you might have been spared a lout of a husband, my girl."

So did she. But Hugh's family was mere gentry, and he had had only the limited prospects of a second son and a future in the law, whereas Randolph Cuthbert was the nephew of an earl. To her father's mind, there was no question which was the more suitable to provide her with comfort and security. Papa would have been mad as fire if he had ever learned how her prudent marriage with the charming Randolph turned out.

Chapter 7

The Third Day

Wallace spoke with him privately before they left for the inquest as they would be travelling in the earl's carriage. "I asked the coroner to suppress the detail about the room being locked if he could, but there may be no way to conceal it."

"Even if he tried, the Cuthbert Hall servants know and will speak of it to their families and friends."

Wallace rasped out a laugh. "What a gift for understatement you have, Hugh. I fully expect someone, or perhaps several persons, to come before me claiming the Cuthbert Witch has sickened their child or killed their cow or caused their wife to miscarry."

"Then you will charge those persons to up to a year's imprisonment under the Witchcraft Act of 1735. Is it not convenient when miscreants report themselves to you?"

"How many of the common people do you suppose have heard of the Act, Hugh? Even if some have, they may think it a foolish error on the part of Parliament and thus best ignored. Well, well, wait and we'll see."

The inquest's findings should have been limited to the identity of the decedent, the place and approximate time of her death, and the verdict predicted by Wallace

Seaton: murder by a person or persons unknown. However, though they could not suppress the fact of the door being locked, all but the coroner and those present at Cuthbert Hall were left to assume it had been locked from the outside or else the decedent had locked it after regaining consciousness briefly. The coroner, a wizened elf of a man, had agreed that revealing the mystery of the locked room would not serve the public interest.

"Talk of witchcraft and demons," he grunted. "Half will panic and accuse the other half of summoning devils or riding on broomsticks. Ha! They'd claim that was how the murderer escaped. No, no. We'll have no talk of someone able to walk through walls or fly."

All proceeded as planned until Dr. Lockhart testified. There was a murmur when he described the several blows to the victim's skull, any one of which would have rendered her unconscious and at least two of which might have killed her. The statement she was not believed to be pregnant, based upon the usual early signs of pregnancy and no external indications, was met with disapproving silence. No decent woman who was unmarried and a widow of several years' standing should be with child. That she might be suspected of it marked her as a loose woman.

The blood-stained handkerchief elicited no surprise when it was displayed to the jury. It was a lady's and had been found in a lady's chamber. The jury doubtless assumed it belonged to the victim. Lockhart explained he believed it had been used to wipe the blood from the candlestick. Then the coroner asked, "Where was it found?"

Wallace would be thinking as Hugh was, that the location of the handkerchief was another riddle best left unspoken. From the doctor's reply, he agreed.

"The handkerchief had apparently been dropped after its use."

The handkerchief was then given to the jury to inspect. They examined it with more interest than they had shown when taken down to the cellar to view the body, now supine, the limbs straightened.

After they had all seen it, one of the men inquired, "Who does this belong to?"

The coroner, who clearly had heard foolish questions from juries before, gazed at Wallace wearily. "Mr. Seaton?"

Wallace frowned. "Presumably it belonged to the decedent."

The man who had posed the question said, "Then why isn't the embroidered initial an L or mayhap an F for her last name?"

Another juryman muttered, "I didn't see a letter there anyplace. Calvert, you must be seeing things."

"Here, let me look at that," the coroner said. He stared at it, then beckoned Wallace and the doctor forward, and added, "You, as well, Sir Hugh, as you've been assisting Seaton." Three pairs of eyes fixed on the thickly embroidered square in one corner of the linen.

"I sketched this," Lockhart remarked irritably, "and saw no initial of any sort. I still don't. It's just a design of flowers and vines and leaves."

Hugh stole a glance at his cousin to see if he recognized it as he himself now did. From his wooden expression, he saw it, too.

"I was an engraver and a printer before I retired here," Calvert volunteered. "The design is skillfully done, but I'll swear those vines form an E."

After a frowning scrutiny, the coroner observed, "The embroidery is very fine and so dense with vines and flowers that the letter is not easy to read, but after studying it, I believe you are correct." The exhibit was passed around the jury a second time.

To Hugh's relief, Calvert did not renew his question as to whom it belonged, and he thanked God for the day's chill and pouring rain. Only the earl, Cuthbert, and the several servants who were to testify were present from Cuthbert Hall. Some of the male guests might have attended if the weather had been fit for riding. The earl's coach was full with Keswick, Cuthbert, Seaton, and himself, as was the old coach carrying the servant witnesses. The merely curious had mostly stayed home with warm fires and hot punch.

Had the weather been fair, any ladies who expressed an interest in attending would have been dissuaded in the strongest terms. Most people felt females had no business being at an inquest unless they were witnesses or the decedent. While the attitude might often be reasonable, Hugh no longer agreed with it wholeheartedly. The testimony of Margaret MacGavin at the last coroner's court he had attended persuaded him that women's courage was often underrated. From having known Eilidh, he had already known their wits were as keen as men's.

Eilidh. What were they to do with this new information?

When the inquest adjourned, Wallace reclaimed the handkerchief. Neither of them commented on the initial as they lingered waiting for the earl and Cuthbert who were speaking quietly in one corner of the assembly room. Many of the spectators had dispersed to refresh themselves downstairs with punch or coffee and to chew over the fascinating revelations. The servants had already been sent back to the Hall.

When Keswick rejoined them, he said, "Seaton, I trust you will remain at my home until you have taken the murderer into custody, and Sir Hugh as well, of course. Now that you have a clue, you should be able to wrap the matter up without difficulty."

"I'll have the coach brought around from the stable yard." Cuthbert left the room, bland-faced.

"I'm sure we will all be glad to find the malefactor, my lord. Once we know how he escaped from the bedchamber, we may know his identity," Wallace said. Hugh hoped he was correct.

"You discount the possibility the killer was female?"

"We rule nothing out, but battering someone to death is an uncommon method for a woman to use. As a magistrate, I take an interest in the trials and reports of murders. Women are far more likely to kill by poison, or if their victim is elderly, weak, or a baby, by smothering, though unwanted babies are most often thrown into a privy." Amused Wallace had made use of Hugh's own argument against a female killer, Hugh kept his face void of expression.

The last detail ruffled the man's composure. "You know your business best, I suppose," he grumbled. "I only know I wish for the matter to be decided as quickly as possible."

"Then we should be on our way, Lord Keswick."

****

By the time they were relieved of their greatcoats, hats, and gloves, many if not all of the guests had assembled in the drawing room. The servants who had been summoned to give evidence had related all they knew to their fellows on their return, and the knowledge had passed from the servants' hall to the butler, housekeeper, valet, or lady's maid. Others, including some of the guests, heard it from them.

Ismay Tate was pouring tea as Hugh followed the earl, his heir, and Seaton into the room. Randolph Cuthbert blurted out, "Ellen, your handkerchief was used to wipe the candlestick that struck down Mistress Forsyth."

She had just accepted a cup of tea. Her eyes widened although the face he had seen her wear in company since he arrived at the Hall did not change. But the pretty tea bowl and its saucer fell from her hand, the Bohea splashing her petticoat.

"Was it?" she inquired after a moment. She ignored the stain on her petticoat. A maid hastened to pick up the pieces of china and wipe the floor with a rag.

Cuthbert's utterance struck the other guests like a lightning bolt. Glances flickered back and forth: at each other, at Cuthbert and the earl and Ellen, and last, at Wallace Seaton and Hugh.

"How could it have got there?"

"I have no idea, Cuthbert."

Mistress Tate said, "You should go up so Kitty can have that stain treated as soon as possible. The laundry maid will know how."

"I suppose I should." She stood for a moment more, oblivious of the maid at her feet and everyone else, before walking out.

Georgina Hodge whispered to her mother, audible in the silence, "She is very clumsy. She spilled ale on herself at the harvest festival."

Hugh's opinion of the girl fell yet farther. Poor Cornelius Wilmot, if he married her.

Icy-voiced and ignoring the chit's remark, the earl said, "I have no doubt the magistrate will determine how it came there. Seaton?"

"We will ask Mistress Cuthbert about her handkerchiefs. If you will have her sent for to the Yellow Parlor as soon as she is able, my lord?"

A footman standing like a statue to await the earl's orders went to fetch Eilidh. Ellen. Hugh struggled to remember his and Wallace's old playmate must now be called by a name that conjured up a frail, milk-and-water miss with neither wit nor spirit. Imagine an Ellen cooking a fish she had caught over a fire she had made? Impossible.

As they waited in Wallace's temporary office, his cousin asked, "How did Lydia do without her own maid for three weeks at a house party? From all I have heard and observed of her belongings, she was a lady who required a great deal of care and attendance."

"I don't know much about such things, but I agree that a chambermaid hardly seems an adequate substitute for a lady's maid."

Wallace pursed his lips. "Her maid being too ill to travel might be true, but she could probably have found a lady's maid at an information office. They list available positions and those looking for work, lost goods, found goods, and I don't know what else. They'd be bound to have some female who'd be more suitable and willing to take a month's employment."

Eilidh entered without hesitation. Studying her serene face, Hugh knew it for a mask.

When his cousin produced the handkerchief, her composure shattered. She swallowed and raised her eyes from the linen to meet first Wallace's and then Hugh's gaze. "That is mine."

There was no mistaking her shock. Something tight unwound inside Hugh.

"This is one of a set my mother made for me when I married. Do you remember how beautiful her embroidery was, Wallace?"

"I do. Was there a piece of fabric in your home that was not monogrammed or decorated with some floral or geometrical design? Lady Hamilton made me a set of handkerchiefs before I went off to school." Wallace grinned reminiscently. "Considerably less ornate than that one."

Hugh said, "I asked the laundry maid if she knew whose this was. She did not recall seeing it."

"I use some that bear only a simple monogram. I keep these"—touching a forefinger to the unstained edge of the linen—"put away in my sewing box."

"You never used to sew." Wallace was not alone in his surprise. Hugh remembered Lady Hamilton's chagrin at her daughter's clumsy stitchery, less ineptitude than lack of interest.

"I still don't, but every lady has one with all the tools necessary at least to repair a split seam or sagging hem."

He and Wallace exchanged a glance.

"Then Kitty might have seen it?" His cousin's suggestion was tentative.

Eilidh, or Ellen, shook her head. "She would not find my mother's handkerchiefs. My box has a false bottom. I keep them there with a few letters from my parents and a trinket or two. Do you wish to see it?"

How vexing that Cuthbert had announced to all that the handkerchief was hers. How had he even remembered she had a set like that? She had never made a habit of using them: they were too precious to her.

In her chamber, Eilidh emptied the box of pin-pillow, needle case, thread winders, shears, embroidery scissors, and buttons, and pulled out the drawer that held skeins of thread, bits of ribbon, trim, and lace that might someday be needed. Slipping her open hand as far as it would go into the space that had held the drawer, she poked her fingers into the slot in the top. The bottom of the main compartment rose, and she pried it up with the deftness of long practice.

The shallow recess under it held a packet of letters, a necklet of beads, a ring with a roughly cut Cairngorm stone, a pretty pebble Hugh had given her when she was a child, and the handkerchiefs. She studied the contents for a long moment before taking them out and offering them to Wallace.

"There are six here, and they match that one," he said after looking at each and comparing it to the blood-stained one on the bedside table.

Hugh said, "Who had access to your chamber?" as Wallace asked, "When did you last open this?"

Eilidh frowned a little, trying to remember. "I read over the letters from my mother and father a few days or a week after I received Cuthbert's letter telling me we would be coming here. That would have been about the end of July." She had needed the comfort of her parents' love showing in every line.

"Did you notice if any of the handkerchiefs were

missing then?"

"They were all present. They lay on top as you saw. I smoothed each one as I put them back." Touching them was a connection to her mother who had never once voiced concern over her freckles, height, ungraceful bearing, unattractive thinness, or occasional impulsiveness.

"There must have been a month or more after you looked at your letters before you arrived here. Did anyone have reason to open your box that whole time?"

"Yes, of course. I did, to fetch out the shears to trim the frayed ends of the ribbons on the hat I wear in the garden."

"I'd think your maid would do that for you," Hugh remarked.

"I don't like to bother Manon. When we married, Cuthbert hired her to be my maid, or my 'dresser,' as he called it. He said Isobel wasn't suitable. I sent her back home and asked my father to keep her employed until I could find a situation for her. I would have dismissed Manon as soon as I moved to Durham, but Cuthbert would only support me there if I kept her on. She's his spy in my home." God alone knew what her old friends would think of that. Neither commented on her humiliating revelation.

Wallace frowned. "Did Manon not have occasion to mend something or whatever it is tirewomen do to fill their time?"

"I suppose she must have, but she would probably use her own sewing chest, a pretty one inlaid with ivory. I suppose it must have been a gift from a former mistress. It is far better supplied than mine. But if she did use this one, what of it, Wallace?"

He raised his brows. "Eilidh, you have just told us that she is your husband's spy. Do you think she does not prowl through your belongings in search of something to report to Cuthbert?"

Eilidh knew she did but had given up thinking about it. Manon would be looking for love letters or some proof she was unfaithful to Cuthbert so he could divorce her. "I imagine she does but why—oh, are you thinking she took it to incriminate me?" Cuthbert would likely divorce her if he could, though how he would get the money to bring a divorce bill before Parliament was a mystery.

If I were hanged for murder, he would not need to divorce me. "In any case, she is not here."

Neither man answered her question.

Wallace went on, "I suppose Cuthbert broke his journey at Durham. He would have had an opportunity to take it."

"No, he would not. Cuthbert stayed overnight at the best inn in Durham where he could be assured of a meal and service up to his standard."

A prickly silence followed.

"I doubt he would have been able to suborn one of your servants by post." That was Hugh, sounding regretful.

"It was always more likely the theft happened here." Wallace chewed his lip. "He or someone must have known about the secret compartment in the sewing box."

"Why not simply take a handkerchief from the chest of drawers?" Hugh asked.

"Oh!"

When their heads swung to stare at her, faces full

of concern, Eilidh realized her unintended exclamation had come out as a wail. "I'm sorry! But I just remembered that I took one of them out the day we arrived." Tears stung her eyes. "I was going to put it in my left pocket, with the one I'd use in my right. I-I needed it for reassurance," after two days in Cuthbert's company. "Then before I did, Cuthbert came to my chamber to tell me I was late in going down to the drawing room before supper which put me in a fluster." He had also been in the way as she hurried to her jewel case for her favorite jewelry, amber beads and a topaz ring flanked on either side by a diamond with asymmetrical, unevenly cut facets. "He hurried me out and I was so afraid of offending his uncle, I must have left it on the bed."

"When you returned to your bedchamber, was it not on the bed?"

"If it had been, I would not have forgotten the whole incident. Supper was difficult as his lordship was irritable." Her continuing failure to breed was no reason for the degree of annoyance she had sensed; someone else must have incurred his ire. In the drawing room after supper, Lydia Forsyth had managed to pay her an acid-laced compliment or two and exchanged glances with Cuthbert. No surprises there though those incidents had kept her seething.

"There's no way to lock the bedchamber doors from the outside," Wallace said slowly. "Anyone lodged in that wing or with a reason to be there could get in. When you went to your room, did you notice anything different?"

"Nothing I saw. Though I suppose I might have missed something between being tired from travel and troubled by the earl's bad temper," and her anger at Cuthbert's and the Forsyth woman's barbs.

"Nothing had changed? Had the fire not been laid and new candles put in the candlesticks?"

"Why, yes, of course, Hugh. Sir Hugh. I thought you meant something out of the ordinary."

Wallace went to the door to call down the passage for the footman to summon whichever maid attended the north wing to come to the Yellow Parlor. Turning back to Eilidh, he thanked her and made his bow. Hugh did the same, though with a look that seemed to convey sympathy. How humiliating that he now knew so much of her disaster of a marriage.

Alone, trying to puzzle out why anyone would wish to murder Lydia in fact rather than in daydreams, the danger of her position was borne in upon her. The handkerchief was hers, and the victim was her husband's mistress. Many might suppose she would resent the trollop. She had not liked Lydia Forsyth, and not because Cuthbert warmed her bed; she didn't want him herself. No, her dislike sprang from Lydia's parading her *affaire* with Cuthbert. It was an on-dit in London. She must have infuriated many others, both wives and her own lovers or would-be lovers, but who would kill her here? Did Hugh think her likely to be charged with Lydia's murder?

But Cuthbert evidently thought Eilidh had cared enough about the embarrassment of being a scorned wife to kill his paramour. How typically arrogant of him to think so.

Chapter 8

Polly Holliday hesitated at the door, twisting the corner of her apron in her hands. She dropped it when they looked at her. Bidden to sit, she tried to smooth the tortured linen.

On hearing her last name, Wallace said, "Related to the innkeeper in Penrith?"

"Ay, sir. My dad." She relaxed under his avuncular manner.

Admitting she was one of the housemaids for the north wing, she grew timid again until he asked her to describe her duties. She rattled them off as briskly as a well-drilled boy reciting his multiplication tables. The amount of work she had to do in each room morning and night seemed impossible. Did Hugh's chambermaid do so much, if only in his chamber? He supposed she must.

"Do you have a good memory, Polly?"

"I think so, Your Worship. I was always good at learning songs and Bible verses. I used to win a little prize every year for the most verses got by heart. Ay, and I always knew anyone who'd stayed at our inn, if he came for another visit."

"Do you know which guest is in which room in the north wing?"

She listed them in order from the first room from the stair on the south side of the wing back along its north side, ending with Lydia's suite. Wallace, his eyes on the sketch he had made, nodded. "Exactly right. Very good. Now, you'll have to think back a bit farther to answer this: do you recall the day Mr. and Mistress Cuthbert arrived?"

"Ay, they were the last to come, and I noticed because…" Her cheeks flushed. Hugh guessed she was chagrined because she had been about to say something indiscreet about her betters.

"You must tell the truth, Polly, and whatever it is, no matter if it is embarrassing to you or someone else. It may help to discover who murdered Mistress Forsyth."

She twisted her fingers together. "I'd never lie, sir, but I don't want to be turned off with no character, either, if his lordship comes to hear of it."

"Don't worry about that. He'll be glad for the murderer to be known, and I needn't tell him how I discovered the information."

"Mayhap 'tis just the way lords and ladies are, but I wondered that Mr. and Mistress Randolph Cuthbert didn't share a room like as Mr. and Mistress Wilmot and Mr. and Mistress Hodge do. Mr. Cuthbert has the suite in t'other wing. Mistress Cuthbert's chamber is in this wing, instead o' being t'one next door. And hers is the smallest in t'north wing." She stole a glance at Wallace's face.

"Ah, well, fine folk sometimes have their own ways. You'll have had a great deal to do with so many rooms to attend to. I suppose Kitty had unpacked all of Mistress Cuthbert's things by the time you reached her room to lay the fire?"

"She had, for they'd arrived in the middle of the

afternoon. Not many keeps late hours in the country. As soon as they'd gone in to supper, I started my rounds."

Wallace asked a few more questions, none of them important. Then, "Did you do anything else in Mistress Cuthbert's bedchamber that first night, besides your usual tasks?"

"No, sir. I made sure there was new candles in the candlesticks, dusted what needed it, there being a bit o' rice powder on the wash stand where the lady fixed her face, emptied the chamber pot, and laid the fire. Kitty would close the windows and latch the shutters when she made Mistress Cuthbert ready for bed."

"Was there anything on the bed?"

The girl's eyes went wide, and her mouth dropped open. "There was a kerchief a-lying on the coverlet. However did you know that, Your Worship? I'd forgot until you asked."

"I am a magistrate. I am supposed to know things." The pompous statement was belied by the twinkle in his eyes. "What did you do, seeing it there?"

"I thought to myself, the coverlet being white, when the covers was turned back, it might end on the floor. Maybe I shouldn't have opened the chest o' drawers, but I put it away with t'others. I hope that was all right."

"Anyone might have done the same. You're in no trouble for it," Wallace said. "One more question before you go. The night of the quarter day and harvest festival, how did you ready Mistress Forsyth's chamber in the evening?"

"I'd have done it just the ordinary way, sir, 'cept that I started early as the gentlefolk were all outside, though I knocked at each door first. 'Twas that lucky

Kitty told me Mistress Forsyth was going to bed early, so Kitty had done my job and I needn't bother her."

They sent the girl off much relieved.

"Anyone could have taken it from the drawer at any time Eilidh's chamber was empty," Hugh said.

Wallace sighed, leaning back in his armchair. While his cousin was physically exhausted, his brain was wide awake. "Not quite anyone, perhaps, and only when there was little likelihood of others coming and going in that wing. Though it is true that anyone whose room was in the north wing, or any of their servants or most of Cuthbert Hall's servants could have done it. Almost all of the servants could have found a credible reason to enter on some excuse: bringing wood or peat for the fireplace or delivering fresh linens or clothing that had been washed, or tidying. With guests in the house, some of the usual tasks may have been delayed. However, we do know one more thing."

With the maid gone, Hugh had risen from his own chair to stand by the mantel, too tense to sit. "What?"

"In my drawer at home, my clouts are kept in a stack. Are yours?"

"Yes."

"The girl put the handkerchief in the drawer with the others. We'll ask Eilidh, but I'll hazard a guess hers are also stacked. Young Polly would have placed the one she found on top, wouldn't she?"

Hugh followed that hint. "Of course. She wouldn't have moved anything around when she was hesitant even to open the drawer. So it would be the next one Eilidh or Kitty took out, whether before she went to bed or else in the morning. Eilidh would have noticed it at once."

"And she would have mentioned it to us, which strongly suggests that between Polly finishing her work in that bedchamber and Eilidh returning to it, someone took it."

"He or she would have to avoid running into Polly," Wallace mused. "Would she have told us if she'd seen someone?"

"She was quite forthcoming. I think she would, as she would be expected to do her work out of sight of the guests. But she would be in the rooms more than in the hall."

"Or the person may have waited until they'd finished supper and slipped upstairs on some pretext. Three weeks have passed. How likely are we to find someone else who's a Bible verse champion?"

****

Hugh sat up writing out everything he or Wallace had discovered which seemed incontrovertible, together with further questions to be answered. At last he completed his notes, capped the ink bottle, wiped his pen, and sought his bed.

Perhaps because he was worried about his cousin's health as well as the murder, sleep did not come at once even in the warm embrace of the bedcovers and the embers' glow. He could do nothing about Wallace except try to spare him as much work as possible. On the theory of counting sheep, he began to review what they had learned or thought they knew about Lydia Forsyth's murder, reminding himself that a fact had to be provable.

They knew the bedchamber door had been latched from within, so the murderer must have escaped some other way.

116

The carpenter's lad had got in by slipping some sort of tool with a thin blade between the two halves of the window to raise the catch, then using the same method with the drop bar securing the interior shutters. Would that work in reverse if you held the bar up as you shut the door and let the bar drop when you pulled out the blade?

Hugh threw the bed clothes back, lit his candle from the embers in the hearth and took up his pocket knife from the chest of drawers. The blade was tolerable thin. Would it pass between the door and the door jamb?

It did. He used it to raise the latch. He would have to test it from the outside…only perhaps not in the middle of the night when he might be shut out of his chamber in his shirt, or in shirt and banyan if he took the time to put it on. Better to try it in the Forsyth chamber with Wallace's assistance.

****

The Fourth Day

When he opened his door to go down to breakfast, the morning's light showed that one's imaginings of the night before were nonsense. Raising the latch from the inside with a blade was possible. Lifting it from the outside was not. He did not even need to test his theory. A wooden strip on the jamb prevented the door from opening outward rather than into the chamber, rendering it impossible for the thinnest knife to reach the latch from the passage side. He would inspect Lydia Forsyth's door to be sure but expected it too possessed a stop.

He gave Wallace his notes when they had a quiet word after breakfast and confessed the failure of what he had thought a brilliant idea.

"Huh." His cousin stood there, miles away in mind, until Hugh feared he had suffered some kind of a brain fit.

"Wallace?"

"Hmmm? I was wondering if your idea might have been worked another way. Do you think Nurse Kettlewell would let us have a length of thread? I would like to speak with her anyway."

They found the old woman sewing a shift by a window in the sewing room. At Hugh's introduction, she said, "I know who Mr. Seaton is, having seen him now and again."

"Mistress, to help me would you give me a length or two of thread?"

"How long, sir? And what kind?"

"A foot would be enough. I think silk would be best but being only a man, I'm not familiar with the thickness of thread. Do they come in more than one?"

With a look that confirmed he was, indeed, only a man, she said, "They do," and commenced to burrow in her sewing box.

"Here's some silk." She held up a bit of thread in a trying shade of pink wound on a slip of heavy paper and set it on the table beside her.

"Thank you, Nurse. We'll let you—"

"And this is finer, as you can see." Another few twists of white on a cylinder of paper. "Then there's linen thread. Here's some for sewing stays, and another I'd use for sewing smocks or the like."

"Can you spare them all?" Hugh asked.

"Ay, Sir Hugh, they're only short lengths left from skeins and might never be used."

Wallace pocketed the four samples and thanked her.

She chewed her lower lip. "Your Worship, you might ask yourself why Mistress Cuthbert wears gowns that are old or else are new but not right for her. No use asking her. She won't say. Them being wrong, that's her maid's doing, I'll swear on a Bible. Not in the latest fashion, that's something else."

In the passage, Wallace murmured, "Did you think her gowns were not in the mode?"

"Georgina Hodge said something of the sort."

"She was probably correct. Ellen's, or Eilidh's if you will, don't look quite like what the other women here wear. Even I can see that. I wonder Cuthbert doesn't object. He is finickal in his dress, especially for someone in the country."

"He insisted she have a dresser, too, rather than just any maid skillful with hairdressing and keeping clothing."

At the guest chamber, they conducted their experiments under the fascinated gaze of the footman on duty halfway down the passage. Inside the chamber, Wallace looped the thread around the little bar. In the passage, Hugh held the free ends high to keep the latch-arm up while gently pulling the door closed with his other hand. He kept the line taut and the bar up until the door was fully shut.

Wallace's "Curse it!" was audible, though muffled by the door. He opened it and said, "The loop slipped off before the latch-arm dropped into the staple. Try holding the thread off to your right."

By the eighth attempt, they had succeeded in latching the door twice.

"The trick could have been worked this way, Hugh." His cousin sounded dubious, as well he might.

"That assumes the killer was willing to make however many attempts it took to succeed, when someone might have entered the passage at any time. He might have been lucky, but who would trust the odds? And he must have known them because he must have tried it in advance."

"He might have practiced until he could reliably drop the bar. It's what I could imagine a child doing, but that would mean he'd lived here, wouldn't it?"

Like the earl, or maybe Cornelius, Stephen, or Randolph, if they had visited often as children.

They tried knotting a thread around the bar. Success!

"Now pull the thread free," his cousin ordered.

A sharp jerk and a strand of pink silk dangled from his fingers. Wallace opened the door and stood aside. A short length of the fiber was still knotted around the latch-arm.

"Send for the carpenter's boy," Seaton told the footman. "Quick as you can." To Hugh he said, "I suppose we should have anticipated this. I'm hoping the lad took it off not realizing its significance."

"The murderer must possess a degree of mechanical ingenuity and have practiced this."

"Agreed."

Their footman returned, breathing hard, with a tow-headed boy about fifteen.

Aaron Tompkins touched his forelock on being introduced, but his eyes were steady, not intimidated to be summoned by a magistrate. Wallace took him through his actions from the moment he climbed in through the window. His recital did not vary from his previous description of what he'd seen and done.

"Did you notice anything about the latch?" Seaton asked.

"Only that 'twas down, Your Worship, just as everyone knew it must be."

Wallace led him to the door. "What do you see now?"

"There's been something tied around the bar," Aaron said. His surprise was impossible to miss.

"Was there when you unlatched the door that morning?"

"No, sir."

"Are you sure?"

"I'd've noticed when I lifted it. I was shook at being in a lady's bedroom and her lying dead, but not so's I could miss a knot like that."

He was thanked and dismissed. "He wasn't uneasy or hesitant, was he?"

"No. I think he was telling the truth, Wallace."

Wallace scowled at the latch. "You are correct, much as I hoped this explained the locked room. The trick wasn't worked this way."

They stood in the room, assessing the possibilities. Wallace spoke first. "Let us banish from our minds the notion that 'twas impossible to get out of that room, because obviously he did. Every room has six sides and thus far we have only considered the door and the windows."

"I'd be inclined to suppose no one could get out through the ceiling, given its height," Hugh said, "except for two things. As it's coffered, the design lends itself to a concealed hatch, and an agile man might reach it from the bed's canopy. Or from the top of the wardrobe. That might be tall enough."

Wallace tilted his head back and stared at the tester bed with its ornately carved wooden canopy, then at the ceiling. "Huh. There's only about two feet of clearance between the top and the ceiling. Mayhap only eighteen inches. I can't see how anyone but a child would have enough room to get into a hatch above the bed."

"I suppose a very athletic man might manage it."

"But he had to enter the room as well, Hugh, unless Lydia unlatched the door for him."

"Maybe she wouldn't. But I agree with you about the difficulty. He couldn't have got in through the ceiling without her noticing, and if he wasn't welcome, would she sit there at the dressing table while he was wriggling through the hatch and off the tester? The same is true of entering from above the wardrobe."

"Considering the perfume and that second wine glass, what if she arranged a liaison with one of the men? The locked door is the problem. Why lock it? To leave it unlatched would be more discreet: he wouldn't have to knock and wait where someone might see him. We established there was a footman on this floor, because Lydia sent him down to request her supper, again to take away her dishes and to summon Kitty."

"She might have planned with her hypothetical lover to do so at such-and-such a time."

"Ay, but their timing would have to be precise and there was no clock in her chamber," Hugh said.

Wallace grunted. "That's true. Well, the fellow dodged him or got in somehow, because he killed Lydia. Then he got out by some means."

"Which leaves access by a concealed door." Hugh

ran a finger over the linenfold paneling that covered the walls. It might not be to the modern taste which ran to wallpaper or paint, but he liked it and the dark oak suited Cuthbert Hall's antique architecture.

But the minutest examination of the walls yielded no sign of a means of egress. They rapped from floor level to head height on the walls between Lydia's suite and Eilidh's smaller bedroom, the Long Gallery and the little windowless room in which Lydia Forsyth's maid would have slept. Wallace observed, "That was worth doing if only to prove the walls are solid."

The other side of the dressing room backed upon a large closet with shelves for bedlinens, spare chamber pots, and cleaning supplies. The filled shelves would prevent any access to a hidden panel.

Beyond the storeroom was a staircase containing a double set of stairs: a narrow one down to the ground floor and up to the second floor, with a wall separating it from the wider stair for the guests, which did not go past the first floor. The servants' stair ended by the servants' door into the Great Hall, at the end of the passage to the kitchen and its offices. The other stair terminated at an anteroom to the Hall. He had high hopes of this unusual arrangement until the most cursory examination proved there was no room for a passage of any sort.

Hugh said grimly, "He got in, so there is a way to do it. We know that much. Do we agree his arrival was no surprise to Lydia?"

"Yes, I believe so, or at least she was not alarmed because she seems to have continued to sit at the dressing table or else returned to it and sat down after she had let him in."

"As she permitted a man into her chamber while clad in her night rail, we can assume they were already intimate or she hoped they would be...probably." He qualified the statement, not entirely sure what a lady of the beau monde might do, though he felt quite sure no respectable woman entertained any man except her husband while only half clothed.

"I agree that sounds like a lover, Hugh, unless we're wrong and a woman did kill her. She wouldn't hesitate to admit a female. And she might seat herself and continue her preparations for bed either because they were friends or as a gesture of contempt." He sat down heavily on one of the two chairs by the table. "We know one fact. Somehow the murderer escaped from a room almost as secure as the Tower of London."

"We also have a collection of bits that make no sense by themselves but surely cannot all be coincidences, and I don't like coincidences." Hugh steepled his fingers. "Three of the guests who might have brought their personal servants did not do so. Lydia Forsyth did not bring her maid, even though she was given a chamber with a dressing room where her maid would probably have slept. Two, Cuthbert also occupies a suite but did not bring his valet. Eilidh is not in a chamber with a dressing room and did not bring her maid. Mistress Tate has no personal maid at home, so there's nothing strange about her not having brought one."

Hugh went up to the attic to inspect the floor and walls of the servants' rooms above Lydia's chamber. Having asked the butler and housekeeper what servants were lodged in the north wing, he learned that the kitchen servants and half the footmen had rooms at the east end of the wing over the kitchen, pantry, stillroom, and related offices. The Hodge ladies' maid slept on a truckle bed in Miss Georgina's room.

The rest of the footmen and the personal servants of family members were in the south wing where the Wilmots, Stephen Cuthbert, the earl, and Randolph Cuthbert had rooms. Of them, only the earl and Joseph Wilmot had valets; Stephen had not brought his man, and Cornelius shared his father's servant. The earl and Randolph Cuthbert occupied suites identical to Lydia Forsyth's and the Hodges' in the other wing.

The rooms above Lydia's and Eilidh's accommodations were empty. The floor was bare and the walls paneled with less expensive wood than the oak used downstairs. The windows were identical to those on the first floor, however, with the same wide window seats built into the thick wall.

He returned from examining the other unoccupied rooms to find his cousin seated in one of the deep window seats, frowning.

"Nothing to find up here, Wallace."

A sigh. "Then we must hope my friend in London can discover what motivated the killing, and work at the 'how' from that end."

"Do you think a jury will convict based on motive without any explanation of how it was accomplished?"

"I don't know. I've never dealt with a case where there was no indication of the method, and I should be extremely reluctant to charge anyone with the crime when I have no idea of how it was done."

Hugh agreed.

"However, once we have a suspect, he may let something slip during close questioning."

He hoped Wallace was correct. Whoever had bludgeoned Lydia Forsyth to death and left behind a locked room bore no resemblance to the petty thieves, brawlers, poachers, and stealers of sheep and poultry he usually dealt with. He had never had even a highwayman before him.

They had not yet reached the Yellow Parlor when a footman intercepted them with a request that they attend his lordship in his study.

Keswick was not behind his desk when the footman outside the door admitted them. He was pacing before the hearth, grim as bull beef: less the stately peer and more like his border lord ancestors.

"Sit," he commanded, throwing himself into the chair behind his desk. Its high back and carved frame featured heraldic elements from the family's coat of arms, giving it the appearance of a throne.

"My lord," Wallace began.

"Have you determined how the murderer escaped?"

"Not yet, your lordship."

"Good God, you've spent all morning in and about the bedchamber. You must have found how he got out. I do not believe in witchcraft as some do."

After Wallace described all they had done, the earl muttered a curse. "There must be some way." The statement sounded more like a hope than conviction.

"Once we know more about the victim and who gains by her death, we should have a motive that will lead to a suspect. When confronted, his nerve may fail him, leading to some damaging disclosure."

Certainly that would be true for a petty criminal if not for their murderer. Just as well to reassure the earl, however. It worked.

Keswick heaved a breath. "I heard from the coroner this morning, asking how the woman was to be buried. Given the wait to hear from her relatives or attorney, the decision falls to me. The funeral takes place tomorrow. I dare say the innkeeper will be relieved to have the body out of his cellar."

Released from his lordship's study, Wallace said, "I am going to my chamber to ponder such evidence as we possess," which Hugh took as meaning a nap. He went outdoors to walk around the house and imagine what it had been like the day of the harvest festival.

Cuthbert Hall had begun as a simple medieval house, no more than a rectangle consisting of a kitchen and its associated offices at one end adjoining a great hall in the center, and a private living area for the family at the other end. Thick walls and small windows made it defensible. He stood back some way to view the entire front. It appeared to be all of a piece with no clue that any addition had been made to the original house. The two wings added at right angles to the medieval hall were built of the same roughly cut blocks of the local red sandstone, forming a *U*.

Nobles and wealthy commoners in the days of Henry VIII and Good Queen Bess had built lavishly ornamented homes. If they did not build a new house, they built on a wing or two or added a façade in the current style. The owner of Cuthbert Hall in those days might have been thought eccentric for not aping the latest fashion in architecture. Hugh admired the consistency of appearance, which deviated from the older construction only in having more and larger windows and, he supposed, walls less thick than the old hall. Other improvements had been made inside: the quantities of wooden paneling, much of it finely carved.

Hugh turned the corner and stared up at the second window on the north side of Lydia Forsyth's bedchamber, the one the carpenter's boy had climbed through. Wallace was correct: the wall was impossible to scale on either the west-facing façade or the north wall. There was no projecting stonework, no ancient, thick-trunked climbing plants, standing drainpipe, and no trees nearby to which even a gymnast might have jumped.

Could he have got onto the roof, secured a rope around one of the chimney stacks and dropped a rope beside one of the windows, re-entered the house, been admitted to Lydia's suite in the normal way, killed her, then climbed the rope? The stone blocks were irregular enough that a daring man might have been able to brace his feet against them as he climbed. Not something Hugh would care to try. Nor could he imagine how the climber would be able to refasten the window and shutters. No. Utter nonsense. Besides, why take such chances of being seen or falling when he could simply go to her door and ask to be admitted for some plausible reason?

He walked on and turned the corner at the end of the addition. The guests and genteel sort had congregated on the parterre and lawn between the wings where tables of food and drink had been set up. The tenants, laborers, and the like had their own refreshments on the part of the home farm nearest the house, with the intervening space being used for sport.

He paused by the end of the south wing and rested his hand on one of the quoins that wove together the building's corner. Clouds like gray fleece hung over the low hills. Taking out his notebook and pencil he sketched the manor's floor plan, both ground floor and first floor, side by side. Something niggled at him. Whatever it was, it would not come to him.

Chapter 9

When they gathered in the drawing room before supper, Keswick asked for their attention.

"The funeral service will be held in the Great Hall tomorrow. I don't want it to become a spectacle for the vulgarly curious for miles around, as the inquest was," the earl said, tight-lipped. "You need not attend unless you wish to do so. However, I must ask you all to remain until Magistrate Seaton's inquiry is brought to some sort of conclusion."

His listeners exchanged startled glances followed by murmurs of assent, to Hugh's and Seaton's relief.

With this announcement, the reality of the death finally sank in, and gloom prevailed. Before, shocking though the death had been, it had not affected any of the guests on a personal level, any more than if it had been merely some titillating gossip about someone else.

"I shall have to write to the women's parish poor committee, for someone else will have to hold the next meeting," Mistress Hodge sighed to her husband, and Mistress Wilmot instructed her son that he would have to beg off from his planned stay with a friend.

A spate of letters was fired off to inform friends that their plans had changed. Though all but the Hodges were related to Keswick, it was too much to hope that none of them would explain why they were staying on.

The adult Hodges were too discreet to reveal it.

They would prefer to let others think it had to do with the reason they had been invited to stay with the earl. Georgina, on the other hand, was thrilled, although her mother or father cast her a minatory glance when she made it too obvious. Cornelius Wilmot managed to preserve a suitable gravity and to spend as much time as possible in her company. But Georgina divided her attentions among the other men, fluttering from Cornelius to Randolph Cuthbert to Stephen Cuthbert and even to Hugh.

The only person apart from the earl who was bothered by the continued presence of the others was Ismay Tate, whose distress had to do with how to provide entertainment for them and the need to order more delicacies for their dinners. Hugh would not have known of it if the earl had not grumbled to Wallace that his cousin was worried over what, to him, seemed trivial.

"As he is not called upon to think of amusements and new dinner menus, of course he regards her concern as female foolishness." Wallace chuckled. "Noblemen seldom allow themselves to be inconvenienced. Now let us turn our minds to the miscreant."

Someone was guilty. Hugh refused to believe it was Eilidh, but if not his old playmate, who had done it and for what reason?

They had already discussed motives, but had they thought of everything? They had not considered jealousy. He only thought of it because he was jealous of Randolph's possession of the woman he himself had wanted to marry. If Lydia had seduced away the husband or sweetheart of one of the guests, that might lead to murder. The thought of rich, lovely Lydia taking Joseph Wilmot or Caleb Hodge to her bed was impossible. If she had, the idea of vague Dorothy Wilmot or plump Joan Hodge murdering the woman and devising a plan to escape from a locked room was ludicrous. Men would fly to the moon on thistledown first. He crossed them off his mental list.

Ismay was a spinster, intelligent, composed, and familiar with Cuthbert Hall. Could the Forsyth woman have toyed with a suitor of hers, destroying a budding romance and perhaps Ismay's last hope of marriage? He could not rule her out. They should find out whether a destroyed courtship was a possibility.

He and Wallace had discussed blackmail as an incitement to murder. Almost anyone might be tempted to do away with a tormentor who knew their guilty or embarrassing secret. Not Mistress Wilmot or Mistress Hodge, eliminated by simple inability. He could perhaps imagine Mistress Georgina tripping someone or giving someone a shove in a fit of pique but not as a cold-blooded killer. If she had killed by accident or impulse, her unfettered tongue would surely convict her before the day was out.

That left the men: Keswick, Randolph and Stephen Cuthbert, Cornelius Wilmot, Joseph Wilmot, and Caleb Hodge. Any of them might have a secret worth killing for, but how could he or Wallace find out, except by making inquiries among their friends and business partners? Almost impossible in the earl's case and difficult even with the commoners. Any investigation should be done in person, which would mean sending someone or several someones, because he could not leave Wallace on his own for long. They would have to manage as best they could until they had a suspect. Then it would be worthwhile to send someone to delve into his background and motive.

Who were the most likely possibilities? Stephen Cuthbert was intelligent and had visited the Hall before. As he lived in London, Wallace's source of information there might be able to learn something discreditable in his life.

Caleb Hodge was a Londoner, born and bred, and if he and Wallace found anything to cast suspicion on him, his secrets would also be found in London.

Could Cornelius or Joseph have any guilty secret? Wallace's friend in London was unlikely to be of assistance there, as the family did not figure even on the fringes of the beau monde. Randolph might have any number of disreputable secrets, though perhaps Hugh's suspicions arose from personal animosity. If there were something to find, perhaps Wallace's magistrate friend would know of it.

****

With the funeral imminent, no one spoke of the event that overshadowed the gathering and there was little else to occupy their minds. Light, witty conversation (not that many of the guests excelled at such) struck all as inappropriate, the sole exception being Georgina Hodge, who prattled on except when her mother aimed a basilisk gaze at her or her father uttered, "Georgina! Enough of your gibble-gabble."

Ismay Tate made a gallant attempt to keep the group from falling silent, and Hodge related items of potential interest from the *Newcastle Courant* and the *Newcastle Journal*, both of which he had arranged to have delivered each week at some expense, Newcastle being the nearest town with a newssheet.

Wallace spoke of local matters in which the earl might take an interest. Cornelius and Cuthbert engaged Georgina Hodge's interest with the praiseworthy goal of keeping her from uttering something ill-suited to the circumstances. Eilidh responded if a remark were addressed to her but initiated no conversation. Joan Hodge inquired about the difficulty of managing so large a household and keeping servants in so rural a place. Stephen asked Caleb Hodge about his many commercial endeavors and listened with apparent interest.

Hugh and Wallace sent for more changes of linen and another suit or two each.

****

The Fifth Day

All gathered in the Great Hall though the earl had not requested their attendance. In some cases, they attended out of good manners only and in others, out of fear of being thought guilty, Hugh suspected. The vicar's intoning of the Order for the Burial of the Dead left even Georgina Hodge solemn and sniffling. At the words "…forasmuch as ye know that your labour is not in vain in the Lord," Hugh hoped his and Wallace's present labor would not be in vain. The listeners stood silent as six footmen stepped forward to bear the coffin to a wagon draped in black for its journey to the Hall's burying ground.

Keswick and Randolph Cuthbert would follow the coffin to hear the reading of the Committal to the grave. Any gentleman among the guests who wished to join them might do so, though the invitation was so grudgingly made that only Hugh and Stephen Cuthbert accepted it. Wallace meant to do so, saying he considered it a duty to the victim. When Hugh whispered to him that surely one magistrate was enough and that Wallace's more pressing duty was to discover the murderer, his cousin agreed reluctantly.

"…in sure and certain hope…"

The plot in which Cuthberts had found their final rest for centuries was some distance from the house, concealed from its sight by well-grown hawthorn and hazel trees. The ruins of a small church stood close by, no part of the remaining walls taller than head height. The effect was uncommonly somber.

The last time Hugh had watched a few clods of earth dropped into a grave, it had held the mortal remains of an abductor who died attempting a murder. This occasion was eerily similar. Only the earl and the grave digger cast a handful of dirt onto the coffin.

Keswick had done his duty by attending the burial of a guest in his home, whatever his opinion of her had been. That no one in near three weeks at Cuthbert Hall had come to like Lydia enough to be even mildly grieved told him something about the woman.

After dinner, a notably subdued meal, Hugh returned to his chamber and after a moment's hesitation, chose his riding coat. He cut some of the threads holding a sleeve button, teased out a few more, and asked the nearest footman where to find Nurse Kettlewell. The man offered to deliver the coat to her with Sir Hugh's instructions.

"I'll take it to her if you'll direct me." The old woman seemed likely to be a rich mine of information about the family. He found her in the sewing room on the second floor of the south wing, darning a hole in a curtain. After begging her pardon for interrupting her work, he asked if she would sew the button back on.

"Reckon I would, sir." She held out her hand, and he handed it over with a sheepish smile.

"I can do it in a trice if you want to wait."

Thank God for old family retainers. The offer was precisely what he had hoped for. At his questioning of Georgina Hodge, he thought the old woman was suppressing a pithy comment or two.

Nurse Kettlewell put aside the curtain and fished in her battered sewing box for thread to match the coat. Her eyes must be as keen as her wits for she threaded the needle without difficulty.

"You've been with his lordship's family a long time, I think?"

Without looking up from her task, she answered, "Since I was a little girl."

Not deaf. "You've seen a great deal, then."

"I have. Might be I've seen some things I oughtn't."

"I'm acting as Mr. Seaton's assistant."

"As I very well know." She frowned, setting a stitch. Hugh did not think the expression was about the sleeve.

"We are all anxious to find the murderer."

" 'Cept the killer himself, I'd say."

"Very true. That's why we need all the help anyone can give us."

"If it's true help, sir."

A warning that some would lie? He had been a magistrate long enough to know that anyone questioned in connection with a misdemeanor or felony might lie, whether or not they were suspects or merely witnesses.

Some prevaricated to avoid embarrassing admissions, some to make trouble for the accused or another witness, others because they never told the truth if they could lie instead. This dispiriting commentary on human nature seemed to suggest there was some truth in the concept of original sin, an article of faith in the Church of England.

"You have sharp eyes and ears and a mind to match, I believe. Anything you can tell me will be of assistance." He waited while the needle ran in and out.

Finally she said, "I can't tell you who the killer is, but I can tell you a few things."

"Please do, Nurse Kettlewell."

She eyed the other buttons, checking for any that were loose. Predictably, she found one and threaded her needle again.

"His lordship, the earl, is good master and a good landlord, even if he's a mite short-tempered at times. Being as he is…" The old woman ran out of words.

Hugh waited through several more careful stitches.

"There's no way to put this without giving offense, but I hope you'll take none."

"I promise I won't."

A nod. "Men mostly don't think much about why folk do what they do or maybe don't pay close attention."

Hugh believed he was reasonably perceptive, or hoped so.

The nurse went on in a seeming non sequitur. "Lord Keswick was mad as fire the day Mr. Cuthbert and his lady arrived."

"Do you know why, mistress?"

"There's often some chafing betwixt a man and his

heir, isn't there? The current Mr. Cuthbert came into the title not long since. He wasn't born to it or raised as heir. I reckon he got a bit puffed up with it. Mr. Cuthbert takes after his grandfather, who was as wild as any man in King Charles II's time, though he isn't so open about it.

"I feel sorry for Mistress Cuthbert, with no new gowns and that maid of hers who was with her the last time they visited. If Mr. Randolph was still a boy and in my charge, I'd box his ears. Men can't help being the way they are, but they should be discreet. Mr. Cornelius is a good, pleasant fellow but bashful. Mr. Stephen, now, he takes after his uncle, though less starchy and with more humor. And there! Your coat's done, sir, and if you have any more mending, I'll be happy to do it."

Hugh pressed a penny into her hand as she passed him his coat, neatly folded. "Might I ask you a question or two, mistress?"

Her withered cheeks creased with a smile. "You may and I might answer."

"Why was Lydia Forsyth here?"

"That one! Not for Mr. Stephen, you can be sure." A decisive nod emphasized the statement.

"Why do you pretend to be hard of hearing?"

Her pale gray eyes twinkled merrily. "I don't. That was some notion the family took years ago. After the boys outgrew the nursery, they weren't so easily managed. Some weren't always on good terms, and there were times his old lordship shouted at Bartie, and Bartie and Abel came to blows now and again. I got in the habit of not seeming to hear things I could do nothing about, being as I wanted to keep my place and I came to find out things I shouldn't have. There are a mort o' secrets in any family, I reckon. His old lordship trained Bartie as best he could and told him the things that were passed down from father to son or heir. Bartie told Simon, the third brother, not knowing I was in earshot, and he maybe passed on some that were meant to be secrets, too. But Bartie died sudden-like not long after he took the title, and so whatever they were can't have been passed on to Abel. Though I think if Bartie had known he was dying and had time to tell Abel, he wouldn't have done it. There was that much ill-feeling betwixt them. Now I've said as much as I should about the Cuthbert family, and you can cross that good Mistress Cuthbert's name off the list of your killers." She tutted. "There's already been talk about the chamber door and windows being latched and foolish speculation about ghosts and devils and sorcery, and Mistress Cuthbert's kerchief."

Hugh returned to his bedchamber and wrote down the chief points of her rambling discourse, feeling that she'd revealed something important. That Nurse Kettlewell did not believe in Eilidh's guilt any more than he himself did was cheering, but on what did she base her conviction? She could not have spent much time with her, as Hugh and Wallace had.

The evening dragged. The men lingered over their port, and the women were hard put to entertain themselves or the men when they finally joined them in the drawing room. Those who played the harpsichord or sang kept to hymns or melancholy music, except for Georgina, who had to be chided for one of her choices. Randolph Cuthbert stood by the harpsichord, turning the pages of the score she was attempting to play with much giggling. Speech over the card table had to do with the game, with no idle chat.

Stephen and Cornelius were playing piquet in one corner. Joan Hodge and Dorothy Wilmot had their heads together, discussing their charitable activities. Ismay and Eilidh were playing cribbage. Keswick had gone off to his study. Joseph Wilmot sat pondering the chess board, the game unfinished when Wallace went up to bed. The last few days had been tiring for one not in good health, and he had been eating very lightly.

Caleb Hodge abandoned his chair near the harpsichord and took the chair closest to Hugh's. Under the sound of the harpsichord he said, "I like music and I love my daughter, but she has no ear for music. She's like her mam that way."

"Girls are expected to acquire some proficiency at a number of things, and few can be accomplished at all of them."

"Very true. She draws prettily enough and embroiders well, and no man marries a female for her accomplishments. Georgina's face, her sprightly ways, and her dowry will get her a husband. I've no objection to a young man of no great expectations but good character like Wilmot. He's not wild and will improve with age. But he should be the one turning her pages, not Cuthbert, though he is an earl's heir. He's the sort to attract an inexperienced miss. Though he can't raise impossible expectations, he could give a girl a longing for something she can't have."

He pondered for a few moments while Hugh wondered what had brought on these confidences.

"Sir Hugh, I'm a forthright man, but I've had few dealings with the nobility or what they call the 'beau monde' except in the commercial way. You are more familiar with them than I and as a magistrate must be of good character and morals, so you are the only man here I can ask: would Mr. Cuthbert attempt to seduce Georgina in his uncle's house? He pays her compliments and banters with her as a man does with a girl he favors."

Clearly Hodge was as unfamiliar with magistrates as with the aristocracy. In his own experience, no class or group were all of one sort. In London, there were "trading magistrates" who made money from the fees they levied, some unjustified. "It would not be the act of a gentleman," Hugh said, reflecting that the baron's behavior to his wife was not gentlemanly. Still, some men were careless of their wives' feelings. "I don't think he would, as Lord Keswick and the rest of the family are hoping for a match between your daughter and his nephew, and to do so would cause a resounding scandal. Furthermore, I'm sure Miss Georgina is well chaperoned."

"There is that," the merchant agreed. "Although I could not help but be concerned, with Georgina full of his fine ways and wit and him being a lord's heir. I wish she might show the same fondness for young Mr. Wilmot's company. I've spoken to my wife, but she sees no harm in it. I'll swear she's half in love with him herself."

"Any young girl might be flattered by attention from a handsome older man." Hugh recalled that much from his own youth. "Or perhaps she hopes to encourage Cornelius Wilmot to be more bold?"

That drew a chuckle from Hodge. "He's a shy lad. If that's what my girl is about, I hope it eggs him on." His amusement faded. "Ladies do love a title."

"He is married. The most romantickal-minded girl could not overlook that fact."

"Thank God."

Judging by Hodge's reaction, having a daughter must be harrowing.

****

The Sixth Day

"We will question everyone again, this time seeking them out for informal conversation. Sometimes that shakes loose a new fact. We'll start with the ones who were most observant." Wallace counted them off on his fingers. "Mistress Tate, Stephen Cuthbert, Cornelius Wilmot, Caleb Hodge, and of course, our Eilidh. You do the ones I interviewed this time, and I'll take yours."

"There's someone you've missed. I want to talk to Nurse Kettlewell again."

"She wasn't present, was she?"

"I don't know. No one spoke of seeing her, but then, she would have been near the home farm and barn, and the guests were unlikely to know who she was. I should have asked her. Even if she wasn't, she may have heard talk among the other servants that would be helpful."

"Very well, then. I'll start with Mistress Tate."

In his bedroom, Hugh unpicked a few inches of stitching from the sleeve of one of his shirts and went to the sewing room.

Nurse Kettlewell's wrinkled face beamed at him. "Another repair to make, sir? Hand it right over."

He thanked her and said, "I'll wait if you don't mind."

She nodded him to the chair he had occupied

before and turned the sleeve inside out.

"I suppose it's usually lonely work, doing the mending."

"You'd be surprised at how many stop in to have me set a few stitches, to ask my advice, or to deliver some bit of news, sir."

So much for the notion the old family retainer was isolated in the sewing room, ignored by all.

"Did you join in the harvest celebration, mistress?"

"I did. I've only missed two in all my years working here, once when Lord Bartholomew was ill, and once when I was a-bed with lung fever."

If he asked a direct question, would she answer? Would she lie? Servants would do so either to protect their master or mistress or because they feared being turned off without a reference. He had no doubt at all that she remembered the day, though it was now a week past. He chose indirection.

"You'll have heard Mr. Seaton and I have asked the guests and anyone who was present near the house about their memories of that afternoon."

"Ay, so I have." She gave him an arrow-sharp glance from under her eyelashes.

"Would you tell me what you observed?"

"What, all of it, sir? I hear you and Mr. Seaton were asking about the early evening of that day. For that's when the mischief began, isn't it?"

Nurse Kettlewell must have been a terror to small boys hoping to mislead her about their activities. "That's true. Were you close enough to observe the guests?" He waited to give her an opportunity to pass on what she knew, or wanted him to know, in her own way.

"Oh, ay. I sat on a bench under a tree far enough not to offend the gentlefolk but near enough to see. If I turned a bit, I could watch some of the contests, too. 'Twas a fine harvest day, with the guests and all." She smiled reminiscently. "There was a mort of folk, though the laborers and servants were mostly at some distance from the house, where the trees gave some shade and the tables of food and drink were there. The lords and ladies and gentry were closer to the house, between the two wings. There were canopies set up over some chairs and tables. Most sat only to eat or rest their feet, between watching the games or taking part in them."

"I suppose the guests came and went from the house."

"A gentleman or lady might go in to the necessary or have some repair made to their hats or gowns. The servants bringing food and drink out or taking the empty dishes in to be washed or refilled were back and forth."

Hugh waited patiently through several backstitches and while Nurse Kettlewell inspected the seam closely.

"Mistress Forsyth died in the evening, seemingly, if what I hear is true about no candles in her chamber being lit."

Servants always knew anything their masters did and sometimes more, as well. An idea occurred to him. "Unless the murderer replaced the burned or partly burned candles to make it appear she died earlier than she did." Lockhart had given an estimate of the time of death which accorded with their theory of the murder occurring between six and half six, but he could be mistaken, or the death might still have fallen within his estimate if it took place not long after dark. The spot of wax on the table supported there having been a lighted candle in the room during the relevant period.

She came to the end of the split in the sleeve and set several more stitches in the fabric before cutting the thread. "Was there wax on the drip pan or on the dressing table?"

"No. But beeswax doesn't drip much unless there's a breeze or the candle is tilted."

"I'd expect some trace of wax if any lit candle was snuffed and removed from the holder by someone who was not in the way of doing it. A servant doesn't pull the burnt one out and jam a fresh one in. There's always bits of wax so you clean the nozzle. If the blow was struck while the candle was lit, I'd look for some drops of wax on the floor or even some sign that the candle had burned something it fell on. Or it might leave fragments if the candle broke."

"You raise very good points," Hugh admitted. "There were no drips, just a broken candle on the floor."

She examined the threads holding the collar button and frowned. "This will soon be off without some help." Her needle was still threaded, and she must have more to say. Kettlewell abandoned the subject of candles. "A few began to go into the house toward evening. I reckon they were tired from the sun and the games. Many went in when it began to be dim. I did, myself. A few stayed out to watch the bonfire, but most had gone in by then."

The murderer would have wanted to be done with his crime before too many returned to the house and he ran the risk of being seen entering or leaving his victim's bedchamber.

Nurse Kettlewell gave him a long, rather troubled look. " 'Tis a dreadful thing to have a murder in this house. The Cuthberts go back a long way. A stubborn bunch they always was, by all accounts. The new parts of the house were built when King Henry with the six wives sat on the throne. The earl then knew something of building, seemingly, and made the plan and oversaw the work himself. He wanted the two wings to look just like the old part." The old woman folded the shirt neatly and handed it to him.

She was not finished with him, however. Taking up a pillow cover from her basket of mending, she remarked, "Families are odd things. The common way of thinking is we love our father and mother and our brothers and sisters or should feel guilty if we don't. Yet we all know families that fight like cats and dogs, or people that don't deserve our love."

He waited for the something else that was coming. It did not, though he sensed she was not done. He asked her opinion on whatever guests and inmates of the Hall she knew, who numbered more than he expected.

"Mistress Hodge's maid brought me a sleeve ruffle of Mistress Georgina's, as she couldn't mend the lace herself. House parties are terrible hard on clothing. That girl's a flibbertigibbet."

"The maid?"

She looked up from under her white eyebrows and said, "The young miss. Flighty as can be. Mr. Cornelius would be a fool to marry her, though it may come to nothing anyway, as now she's met an earl, she dreams of marrying higher than a plain gentleman."

She respected the earl, and though she seldom saw him now, he always had a kind word for her. "I

146

recollect his lordship and his brothers as children, and their half sister, too, o' course. My lord was only the second son and had a good deal of starch in him, right well-behaved. His older brother, Bartholomew, took after their father and grandfather, who were both rakehells, though not bad landlords and masters, except to maids. Bartie was a handful, always popping up here or there. He fair hated Abel for his prim ways, but he got on well with his other brothers. He was closest to Simon, the third brother, who sired Mr. Randolph. Like best friends they were and shared all their secrets. Paul, the fourth brother, was Mr. Stephen's father. With all the bad feeling between Bartie and Abel, I expect Abel felt he'd got his reward when Bartie died a year or two after inheriting without getting an heir."

She did not know Stephen Cuthbert well, but the other servants approved of him.

"That Ismay Tate, now, she needs to marry. She's wasted as a spinster."

Finally, feeling he could learn no more, Hugh thanked her and pressed sixpence into her hand.

"Thank you, sir, but don't be too free with your money. You may need it. But if you should happen to speak with Mistress Cuthbert, you might ask her to visit me. I recall her as a pleasant young lady."

"She was. And is." He should not have said so. No one here but Wallace was aware he and Eilidh had been friends in their youth.

Chapter 10

Stephen Cuthbert was dressed for riding when Hugh found him in the passage leading to the door nearest the stable block.

"May I have a few minutes of your time, Mr. Cuthbert?"

"Of course, Sir Hugh. Here?"

"Somewhere private would be best. The chamber where I spoke with some of the guests when Mr. Seaton and I first arrived is nearby."

"Certainly. My horse isn't expecting me at any particular time," he quipped.

"You gave a statement already, but we wondered if you have remembered anything else or have heard or observed anything odd or unexpected or merely curious since then."

"I don't think I have."

At the faint hesitation in his reply, Hugh raised his eyebrows interrogatively.

"It's not something new, but I didn't mention it earlier because the murder was so startling that it overshadowed everything else."

Hugh nodded encouragement.

"The day I arrived, Lord Keswick was furious with Randolph. He managed to rein in his temper, but he's still cool toward him, and Cuthbert is rather tiptoeing around his uncle." He frowned. "The incident

148

influenced the mood of some, though not everyone seemed to notice."

According to Eilidh, the earl and his heir had had a falling-out on the day they arrived. She had not mentioned any subsequent coolness, but how well did she know Keswick and how often had she seen her husband and his uncle together? "That's interesting, Cuthbert. Have you any idea what may have caused the breach?"

Cuthbert shook his head.

"You know all the other guests, don't you?"

"I met the Hodges for the first time at this curst affair. I can hardly help knowing the rest, with Wilmot, Cuthbert, and Cornelius being my cousins. Ismay is Keswick's cousin of some degree on his mother's side of the family, and I've known her for years. I can't claim to be well acquainted with Mistress Ellen Cuthbert, though I've met her now and again in town."

"And Mistress Forsyth?"

"I've encountered her in London." The colorless statement gave no clue as to how he felt about her.

"As I understand it, this gathering was meant to be an opportunity for Keswick to meet the Hodges and for Cornelius and Miss Georgina to become acquainted. How was Lydia Forsyth involved?"

"Oh, she wasn't. It wouldn't really have been necessary to have another lady to round out the numbers, and if it had been, she was an odd choice. I asked Ismay…mmm, Mistress Tate…the same question as she had sent out the invitations."

"What did she say?"

Stephen Cuthbert flushed slightly. "Keswick told her I should marry, and perhaps Lydia would encourage me to do so. I assume the earl lied to Ismay about that, though I can't think why he should."

"About your needing to marry?" Hugh could readily imagine Keswick would not disclose to Ismay that Stephen wished to make Lydia his mistress. If he did; Randolph Cuthbert had said so, but was he a reliable witness?

"I don't 'need' to marry, certainly not for money. I should like to have a family but under no circumstances would I choose the Forsyth woman."

"May I ask why not?" Hugh added, "It may give me some insight into why someone would want to kill her."

"I want a woman who will be a friend as well as my wife. I don't want a marriage of convenience with a woman who will take lovers and expect to live in London much of the year and spend the summer at house parties. I'd like children. As she has none from her late husband, she may not be fertile or she may have taken steps to avoid them."

That seemed reasonable. "Do you know for a fact she had lovers?"

"She has been—was—coquetting with every man here except my uncle and Cuthbert. Hodge disapproved, Cornelius was terrified, and I suspect my uncle Wilmot did not realize what she was doing. I find it difficult to imagine any of them responding to her lures."

"Did you?"

"I could hardly misunderstand the coy glances, her hand on my arm, and the suggestive comments. What I don't understand is why she bothered unless she was simply in the habit of, ah, fishing without intending to catch anything, as otherwise, why exert herself to enthrall Uncle Wilmot?"

"Yet you say she did not practice her wiles on Earl Keswick and his heir?"

"I don't think my uncle would be taken in by her ways. He wouldn't marry a woman like her. He loved my aunt dearly, all of us could see that, and she was a comfortable woman. Warm, kind, and not capricious."

"What of Cuthbert?"

"Her behavior to him was perfectly appropriate. Mayhap she feared he would accept a seeming invitation and did not wish to offend Keswick by responding to it. I don't know. Cuthbert is my cousin, but we're no more close than casual acquaintances."

"Family," Hugh said with a wry grin. "Wallace Seaton is my cousin and one of my best friends, though we don't see each other often now I live in Northumberland. Yet I hardly know my youngest cousins on my father's side, despite their home being half the distance. However, they're also half my age. There's only five or six years between you and Cuthbert, I think?"

Cuthbert admitted, "That's true, but our interests and tastes are different. One must have something in common beyond blood relationship to make two people friends."

Hugh waited. Silence was useful in questioning suspects. It worked with others, too.

Stephen said, "I don't like him. He's arrogant, irresponsible, and treats his wife badly, from what I've seen." His face hardened. "A good many titled men or their heirs are arrogant. Men of all classes may be irresponsible or bad husbands. I think what bothers me most is that Randolph gets his way by a sort of mental sleight of hand."

"Explain that, please, so I'm sure I understand."

"I never noticed it until we were in school. One of my friends told me something about his older brother, who was in the same form as Randolph. They were assigned an essay to write. I don't recall what it was now or if my friend told me. The brother had given Randolph some informal tutoring once or twice, and on this occasion, Cuthbert claimed he hadn't been able to finish writing his essay because he'd had to do a favor for another friend, so the other boy gave him his own draft as he'd already finished copying it out to turn in, to give Randolph some idea of the key points. Randolph copied it and submitted it as his own. When the headmaster questioned them about it, Randolph claimed he'd written it and let the other student have his draft because the other was 'only a jumped-up Cit's boy.' My friend's brother was expelled because Randolph was an earl's nephew and had been careful to flatter the masters.

"Even now I don't understand how he does it, although I've seen him do it. He befriends or flatters his victim, and if they balk at doing what he wants, he makes them feel guilty. He claims he's their only friend, or that he always defends them when others speak ill of them, or he's done them favors. I think most of them capitulate." Cuthbert shook his head. "I suppose that's why Keswick's anger at him was so unexpected. Randolph's always been careful to keep our uncle's good opinion." Cuthbert could tell him nothing more.

He separated Dorothy Wilmot from Joan Hodge on

the flimsy excuse of asking about Cuthbert Hall. She twittered happily about its history. Most of it he already knew from Nurse Kettlewell, which was Mistress Wilmot's own source for it, he supposed.

"I love the house and had a delightful childhood here, but I do wish Simon hadn't scared me by coming up behind me so suddenly. I never knew where he would turn up next. And then there was the ghost, too."

"A ghost?"

"Oh, yes. I'd wake in the night and there it was! A spectral form, all white and moaning. I screamed and the nursery maid came in, but by then it had vanished. I was sure I saw it, but Nurse dosed me with some remedy before bed every night for weeks. It appeared to me two or three times more and then never again."

****

Seaton had requested that a table large enough to serve as a place to lay out their notes for comparison be brought to the Yellow Parlor, together with two chairs. They had gone through each other's interview accounts soon after the interviews, but in the flurry of activity one or the other might have missed something. Since then, Hugh had written out what he had learned from Nurse Kettlewell.

Caleb Hodge had had little to tell Seaton in the first interview and admitted frankly to Hugh when approached that he did not know what he could contribute this time.

"I am at a loss to understand the nobility and even many of the gentry. I could see that Mistress Forsyth might offend or even anger some, but enough to cause someone to slay her? For that matter, why was she invited? No, you need not answer," he said before Hugh could think of a courteous way of avoiding a reply. "I have heard that a good deal of immorality goes on at these gatherings. Better it involve a widow, I suppose, than a married lady."

Unnecessary to comment, Hugh judged. "I would like to ask you about the harvest festival. You spent much of the day outside, I understand."

"Ay, I did. I'm a townsman and had never seen one before. I am thinking I might have something of the same for half a day in my workshops, or mayhap I might hold it in an assembly room before Christmas. But you wanted to know what I saw." He pursed his lips. "A great deal of informality and merriment among the gentry and laborers. Cornelius Wilmot, both Cuthberts, and other sprigs of the gentry took part in some of the sport. Lord Keswick did not, and I would not expect him to do so. He was always speaking to someone and not just the local gentlefolk, either. Mr. Randolph Cuthbert talked only with the guests, that I saw. He spoke to me, looking for ways to make money, although I doubt he has any to invest. He'll not be as good an earl as his uncle."

Hodge might not understand the nobility, but he understood men. Hugh's own judgement of Cuthbert did not bear close examination. Eilidh deserved better. She should have a husband who loved her too much to let her live apart from him.

He said temperately, "I tend to agree, but is it only because he is too proud to speak to the common people?"

"That's one of the reasons, but it's the symptom as a doctor would call it, not the cause. There's some as are good masters and some not. 'Tis a matter of respect and trust between master and man. I value my workers for their skill and loyalty. A fellow like Cuthbert does not. There's another thing besides. I looked into the Keswicks when my Joan and Mistress Wilmot came up with the notion of marrying our daughter and the Wilmots' son. I like to know who I'm doing business with. I found nothing to distrust in his lordship, though I wouldn't do business with Randolph Cuthbert."

Cornelius Wilmot knew nothing that furthered their proceeding.

"My mind has been on my own affairs." He sighed, adding, "If I had any. My parents' plan will come to naught, and it's as well. Georgina is very young and changeable in her affections. I fear I rate no higher than Stephen and perhaps not as high as Randolph." After a moment, he added, "I was willing to make the attempt as my parents favored it, but Georgina is a very silly girl and I don't think she will grow out of it."

****

Of his own interviews, Wallace remarked, "I don't know how the Hodge chit can run on without stopping for breath. Though it is useful in a witness or deponent. She has added somewhat to her statement as you took it. I now also understand your fondness for Kettlewell's company. She's a long-headed one, I can see it in her eyes."

Hugh read his cousin's notes while they discussed them. His cousin's plain hand, faster for hurried writing, made reading quick. "Cuthbert was with Eilidh when she spilled the ale. Georgina says he followed her into the house."

"To, as she put it, 'be certain she was well,' " Wallace quoted in a high, reedy voice, " 'as he is such a devoted husband.' I asked if Mistress Cuthbert were so affected that she needed the support of his arm. According to Georgina, he was behind her when the footman opened the door. Cuthbert also entered and that confirms what the footman told us. Georgina watched them the entire time."

"Or she watched Cuthbert."

"Ay."

"No one else noticed him go in."

"No one else was interested," Seaton commented acerbically. "The girl is infatuated with the fellow: he's 'ever so charming.' "

Hugh chuckled at his tone. "Girls that age form ridiculous attachments and forget them just as swiftly. My sister certainly did. She ran through four poor devils all in the space of two months."

Wallace snorted with laughter.

"Think it's amusing? You've never been embarrassed by your sister making sheep's eyes at the curate, the doctor, the tenant farmer's son who wrote poetry, and a lieutenant visiting one of our neighbors. Now, about the other interviews..."

Joan Hodge's second interview added nothing. She was appalled that there had been a murder—in an earl's home!—and wished they might have left immediately, except of course, there was Georgina to consider and one would not wish to appear discourteous to one's host. The ingratitude of daughters was a mother's burden to bear, she sighed at one point, though she did not explain the remark. Presumably Georgina was showing too little interest in Cornelius.

Mistress Tate's only new contribution to their little sum of knowledge was that the earl was troubled by the slow progress of their search for the murderer, and his temper was suffering cruelly as a result.

"Which is to say everyone around him is also suffering cruelly," was Wallace's judgement. They themselves had been too busy to spend any time in his company except at meals.

Hugh leaned over to peer at the next sheet. "Here's something interesting. Joseph Wilmot saw Cuthbert bump Eilidh's elbow while she was holding a mug?"

"So he said. What recalled it to his mind was his wife saying something about Eilidh having to change the gown she was wearing because it had been stained and what a pity it was, as it was such a lovely printed calico. But that conversation took place after our initial interviews."

Wallace leaned back in his chair, eyes closed.

"Mayhap you should lie down for a while, Wallace."

The round brown eyes opened. "I'm not tired. I am troubled by Eilidh's lies when I asked her why she had left the festivity early. She claimed the air began to be chilly and she was tired. You must have seen that in my notes."

Hugh taxed his brain and recalled the passage. "Yes." He had made nothing of it at the time.

"Eilidh did not mention Cuthbert accompanying her to her chamber. She lied to me if only by omission. Why did she lie? Georgina Hodge, Wilmot, and the footman at the door all mentioned the incident."

"Eilidh did sometimes have mishaps. She may have preferred not to admit a humiliating accident."

Wallace laughed reminiscently. "Eilidh, bless her, was a calamity with feet. Strange in someone who was

157

also athletic. If she had spilled it all on her own, she might prefer not to say anything about it, but why not place the blame where it was due when someone else caused it?"

"Mayhap because she was drinking ale?" But in the past his old friend had never worried much about lady-like behavior.

"I can't imagine her drinking ale when lemonade, barley water, or wine were available, unless her taste in drink has changed, Hugh."

"Her marriage appears not to be a happy one. I would not like to think it has driven her to drink, but we all know such things happen." He did hope not.

"Yet while we have been here, she has taken no more than a glass of wine or two at dinner and perhaps a glass of sherry at some other time. We will make further inquiries, of course." Wallace slid another sheet over Wilmot's. "Cuthbert claims it was Eilidh's choice to live separately. He agreed because she was jealous and berated him so loudly the servants heard."

"That might be the behavior of a woman who cared about her husband's infidelity. Does she love him? I wouldn't think so, given that they married without any prior acquaintance. As I recall, 'twas a marriage of convenience and she is not happy in it," and preferred to live in Durham, far from London and her husband.

"If he humiliated her, she might revile him. I once heard her flay a man for mistreating his apprentice. 'Twould be a short step from a woman dissatisfied in her marriage and, er, jealous of his attentions to other ladies, to murdering him. I am only arguing this as a jury might reason," Wallace said.

His cousin had heard the note of anger in his voice.

Hugh took a deep breath to calm himself. "Was Lydia his mistress? Even if she were, why would Eilidh kill her? He'd only replace her with another obliging widow or a courtesan."

"We do need to find out whether the victim was Cuthbert's *petite amie* before or whether they only had a liaison here."

Hugh agreed. "I would also like to know why Cuthbert followed Eilidh into the house after spilling ale on her. He hasn't shown much concern for her or even common courtesy. Why go in after her?"

"Did you not ask when you questioned her?"

"I haven't yet spoken with her. I began with the nurse, wrote out her statement, and did not have time after talking with the others to see Eilidh before meeting you."

His cousin stared at him in silence while Hugh studied his notebook, as guilty as if he had failed his schoolmaster.

"Do you fear she killed Lydia, Hugh? I don't believe she would have beaten the woman to death. Do you really think she would have done either of those things?"

"No, of course not."

But he had once seen Eilidh walking a few paces behind her sister's toddling child in the meadow near her house. He had been some distance away when a dog, a shaggy, unkempt gray lurcher, came bounding at them from the spinney. Hugh ran full tilt for them praying he could get between the girls and the beast.

Eilidh sprang in front of the little girl. Somehow she both hunched and made herself seem bigger, the way a cat does when threatened. Later he thought he'd

159

never experience anything half as terrifying, no matter how long he lived.

The lurcher, a poacher's dog used to running down prey, skidded almost to a halt, then spun and fled, tail tucked between its legs while Hugh was still several yards away. "Eilidh," was all he could say on reaching her and her little niece, who was chuckling and babbling some gibberish about the doggie. Without a further word, he picked the child up, said, "We're going back to the house now. I'll tell your fa—your brother-in-law about the dog."

"A very good idea, Hugh," she had said.

Eilidh's father was often described as a good soul. Her sister's husband was more likely to take decisive action to prevent further encounters.

"She certainly would not have left her handkerchief under the body," he added. Too late he realized this did not really address whether he thought she would have done murder.

"You are too close to her to be impartial, Hugh. That is a mistake I can understand because I'm fond of her too. But you know a criminal investigation is no time for delicacy. You question her. If she does not tell you, ask her outright. First, however, we should speak with the other footmen on duty in the house at the time to confirm whether Randolph Cuthbert did go up to her chamber. I should have thought of that sooner. That's my error."

They went through the south wing, beginning from the door into the garden: the estate office and muniment rooms on one side, the two rooms which had been used as ladies' and gentlemen's retiring rooms during the festival on the other, a dog-legged staircase, then to the left a small room empty but for a pair of chairs and a table against one wall, followed by the library and the study. Across the hall on the right were two rooms for storage. Another staircase wound its way up before the door into the Great Hall, and beyond that, the drawing room at the western end of the wing. They saw no footman; perhaps he had been dispatched on some errand for the earl or the steward.

"We'll start with where Cuthbert went as he didn't use the stair near the door."

They entered the medieval part of the house through the door after the second stair. What had once been the family's private living area was now the dining room. They ignored it and strolled into the Great Hall. Not far from the main entrance a footman stood straighter when he saw Hugh and Seaton approach.

"Can you tell me if someone was on duty here during the harvest festival?" Wallace asked.

"Ay, 'twas me, sir."

"I suppose as the day was busy you must have been called away at times."

"Not out o' the hall except to use the privy, and then I called to the man in this end of the south wing." He nodded in the direction from which they'd come.

"Where was he posted?"

"Rufus stood near the stair at this end, in case someone needed assistance."

For which Hugh read "tried to go wandering through the upper floors."

"I took his place a time or two, but I stood just outside the door there so I could hear if anyone come to the entrance here and would still be able to help anyone that come up the passage."

"Did anyone?"

"Not while I was there."

"Did anyone come in the front entrance?" Hugh asked to make sure the man's answer had not referred only to the passage.

"Not a one, sir. There wasn't a body for miles around that wasn't in the garden or on the home farm."

"Your name?"

"Samuel, Your Worship."

"Thank you, Samuel."

Hugh thought of one last question. "Was there a footman in this end of the north wing?"

"No, sir. There wasn't no need. No one but the kitchen could use the door at the end of the wing that day, and there was a man there to open the door for them, but anyone else had to come in by the south wing door. One of us was on duty upstairs in the north wing in case a guest did come in and needed aught. There's two men to a floor at times, like early morning and the evening, but some of us was needed outside that day."

When they were in the passage and out of the footman's hearing, Wallace said, "That was helpful. Wherever Cuthbert went, he did not go through the Great Hall unless Samuel is lying."

They found Rufus off duty in the servants' hall. He confirmed he had stood near the west end of the passage. He had gone to the jakes but before the time in question, and Samuel had covered both posts. During the time he had covered for Samuel, no one had come to the front entrance and only one person had approached his end of the passage, and that was Mistress Cuthbert. She had given him a faint smile and a nod and gone upstairs. No one else had come as far as his end of the passage. He would have heard footfalls, but then, he might not have paid them any heed if they didn't come up to him, what with the coming and going from the retiring rooms. He might not have seen someone who came up the passage farther than that because the staircase blocked his view of part of the corridor.

Asked about the staircase, he was more positive. "I would have heard steps on the stairs and anyway, William was on the first floor, so he'd'a seen anyone as went up."

Out of the man's hearing, Wallace asked, "Could he have climbed the stair without the footman noticing?"

They tested the staircase on their way to speak with William. Seaton stood where Rufus would have been while Hugh climbed it. The treads creaked loudly but the stair was enclosed, which might muffle the sound. But when he emerged on the first floor, William stood nearby, attention on the stair in expectation of an arrival.

"It must be convenient not to be surprised by someone coming up."

"Ay, 'tis, sir." The footman's impassivity turned into amusement for a second.

More footsteps, slower than Hugh's, Wallace following him upstairs. "I heard you going up. No one but a deaf man could have missed it."

William was pleased to be questioned about his long, boring assignment on Michaelmas. He'd hardly seen a face the entire time he was there.

"At which end of the passage did you stand?" Hugh inquired.

"Neither, sir. I stood in the middle. Most times if there was guests there'd be one of us at each end as his lordship likes one of us always nearby. But with Harvest Day, I was the only one."

"I suppose you walked back and forth?"

"I did, Your Worship, as it eases the legs. I'd still have heard someone coming up them stairs or seen him or her."

The earl and Mr. Randolph Cuthbert occupied the suites at each end of the south wing, the earl on the east, the heir on the west. "O' course, they were on duty, like, with the guests and tenants, so they wouldn't leave the festivity." The Wilmots shared a chamber with a small parlor attached. Mistress Wilmot had come up to fetch another handkerchief, something outside having brought on a fit of sneezing, but she'd come up the other stair. He had seen her, being by this stair at the time. She'd been in and out again with no more than a few words to him. A very pleasant lady, the earl's little sister. Mistress Cuthbert was, too. She had come upstairs near the end of the day on her way to the north wing. Like everyone else, she had to enter by the south wing, the north wing door being in use only for the kitchen on Harvest Day. Mistress Forsyth that was killed had come up before her. Seemingly she hadn't been well as she'd passed him without a word or a glance.

Young Mr. Wilmot and Mr. Stephen Cuthbert occupied smaller rooms in the south wing. Neither of them nor Mr. Joseph Wilmot had entered the wing or "…not my floor, anyhow," the man clarified.

Chapter 11

In the Yellow Parlor afterward, Wallace remarked, "From witnesses, we know Cuthbert entered the south wing. Three footmen in the house swear they didn't see him. Could he have got by them all, if one of the footmen was not paying attention, slipped away for a few minutes, or is he lying?"

"I don't see how. Jeremy at the wing's entrance saw him in the passage but was not watching him, so Cuthbert might have gone into one of the rooms after the retiring rooms. I'll lay you a penny loaf to the Bank of England Jeremy was too busy to take note of anything more than he told us."

Wallace objected, "Then the footman at the other end of the passage should have seen him."

"He might not have been visible to Rufus if the stair was between him and whatever room Randolph entered."

"Which rooms could he have gone into?"

Hugh opened the map of the ground floor and passed it to him.

Wallace peered at the map. "Huh. One of the rooms after the retiring rooms is where the tables for rent days, harvest, and other outdoor activities are stored, and the other is for cleaning supplies and linens for upstairs. Then there's the staircase. On the other side of the passage, there's the estate office nearest the south door, then the muniment room. They'd be kept locked, wouldn't they? I'll ask Keswick, but by Jeremy's statement, Randolph was already past them because they're opposite the retiring rooms. Then there's the empty room, the library, and his lordship's study. Rufus should have seen him enter the last two, or Samuel should if Rufus were away."

"That leaves the empty room. Except it's not really empty. A table and chairs are stored there," Hugh said.

Wallace's forefinger traced a straight line from that room to the Great Hall's entrance. "Curse it, part of the staircase is in the way. Depending on where he stood, Rufus might not have been able to see him."

"Or he might not have noticed him if his attention was momentarily diverted."

The door was unlocked, although like the estate office and muniment room, it was fitted with a rim lock. For a chamber not in use, it was well furnished with a threadbare old Turkish carpet and a low footstool with ragged upholstery in addition to the scarred tea table and chairs Hugh remembered from his earlier, cursory glance. No more than ten feet by twelve, it was paneled like all the other chambers.

Unlike the ones on the first and second floors, the window embrasure was fitted with a cabinet up to the level of the sill rather than a seat. Hugh had noticed the same in Keswick's study, though there the cabinets had glazed doors and shelves of books. When they had visited the kitchen, the window embrasures held open shelves for the pots, baking pans, and bowls too big to be hung on the wall or for the smaller shelves and cupboards. Whoever designed the wings evidently thought storage would be more useful than seating in the offices and service areas.

"Well, well," his cousin said, seating himself in one of the chairs. "Comfortable enough to sit here for a while. Cuthbert omitted to say he drank his brandy here rather than in his chamber. I wonder why. I suppose he had a flask in his coat pocket."

The room was not unpleasant. The diamond-paned window gave a view of the grounds, but there was not so much as a pack of cards to entertain someone who spent time here, and yet there was the furniture.

Curious, Hugh opened the cabinet and grinned. "Ha! A bottle of brandy and one of gin, a few old, chipped cups, a pack of cards, dice, and a draughts board and pieces. Proof it's used by someone."

Wallace joined him at the window. "Amusements for idle hours and idle servants. I suspect they've been using this as a parlor while they are supposed to be on duty. I wonder the butler does not know of it. Certainly Keswick cannot or he would have put a stop to its use. I do think we can conclude—pending further investigation—that this is where Randolph went. A little brandy and perhaps a few casts of dice to pass the time. If he told Georgina he meant to be sure Eilidh was all right, 'twas only to conceal his desire for stronger drink than ale or wine."

"Or to seem to be a concerned husband," Hugh retorted.

Wallace pulled the cork out of a spherical bottle with a long neck and sniffed. "An excellent brandy, pilfered from the earl's cellar, no doubt. Just to be certain," he muttered as he removed the stopper from the tall green bottle and inhaled. "Gin it is. If Cuthbert knew of this, no wonder he came here." Receiving no response, he glanced at Hugh.

"Wallace, how did he know there were chairs and drink here?"

"The footmen—I assume it's the footmen because the maids wouldn't sneak away to drink and play cards and draughts, would they?—must all know." He returned the bottles to the cabinet and closed the doors.

"Would the servants let Cuthbert in on a secret that could get them turned off with no character?"

"Perhaps not. Mayhap this room's use is of some years' standing. He might have discovered it as a boy and not spoken of it." Wallace rubbed his chin. "Though I don't think he was here much in his younger days."

The old nurse had said something to the point. "Nurse Kettlewell told me about Lord Keswick and his brothers. Bartholomew was the oldest, followed by Abel, our current earl, then Simon, and Paul was the youngest. Bartholomew and Simon were close but did not get along with Abel." *What was it that did not seem important then, but might be?* Ah, he had it. "Bartholomew and Simon shared secrets. If Bartholomew, who sounds somewhat wild, knew about this, he might have told Simon, who was Randolph's father."

"And?" Seaton asked.

"Did you never tell your boy tales about your youth, Wallace? I recall your father recounting how he and his brother spent the night in an oak tree, pretending to be Charles II and his companion."

"A point. Randolph might have heard of 'the footmen's parlor' from Simon. Or he could have discovered it some other way. It doesn't matter how."

Wallace's contemplation of the window had nothing to do with the view. "We know when Cuthbert entered the house. Jeremy does not recall him leaving the house, and no one on our chart remembers seeing him until shortly before supper. He cannot account for about two hours of the late afternoon and early evening. Did he really spend much of it in here?"

"I doubt it. If he actually spent so long drinking brandy or gin here, he'd have been bowsy when he went in to supper, and no one's mentioned that."

"I may have to beg Eilidh's pardon, if only in my own mind, for thinking she lied to me as it sounds as if he did not visit her. When you speak to her, remember to ask, however."

"I very much doubt she lied." He must have sounded grim or else Wallace knew him too well.

His cousin said, "If Cuthbert intentionally spilled ale on Eilidh, then went into the house to loiter in this room, his behavior is suspicious enough that I think we may consider him a suspect. I admit I'd rather he were guilty. However, it's best to verify everything, especially as he's Keswick's heir."

"Innocent men and women sometimes hang. You know they do, Wallace."

"The law is not perfect. We will do everything we can to see that the real murderer goes to the gallows. With both our fine minds, how can we fail?" The final remark sounded flat. Someone had left Eilidh's handkerchief with the body. If they could not prove she had not committed the murder, they must prove someone else had.

"On my soul, Wallace, if we do fail, I won't let her strangle slowly at the end of a rope."

"I won't, either. I'll be there with you to send her off quickly. But let's make sure we do not come to that pass."

****

Why had Wallace Seaton sent for her again? As the footman opened the door of the Yellow Parlor she said, "Thank you for your escort, Cuthbert," and stepped inside. And why had Cuthbert insisted on accompanying her? Such solicitousness was foreign to their relationship.

He shouldered into the room almost treading on her heels before the footman could close the door.

Wallace, standing by the desk, said, "Mr. Cuthbert, your presence is not required at this interview." His eyes were hard as pebbles. That was surprising in a friend whose gaze had always reminded her of a spaniel's, soft and warm. Hugh's presence by one of the windows also came as a jolt.

"As Mistress Cuthbert's husband, I have a right to be present."

Her old friend raised his brows. "No, my lord, in fact you do not. No one else was present when you were interrogated, and the same courtesy will be extended to Mistress Cuthbert."

"That is different. A man has every right to protect his wife from intimidation—"

The sentiment would sound well if 'twere not for its hypocrisy.

Wallace fixed him with a gaze that would have terrified her. He no longer looked like the dear friend of her girlhood. It penetrated even Cuthbert's arrogance momentarily, causing him to loosen his grip on her arm. Hugh left his place by the window and guided her to an armchair near the fireplace. The day was chill, rendering the fire's warmth welcome.

Cuthbert blustered, "You overreach yourself, Seaton. My uncle will put a stop to your unwarranted interference."

"He will not. I am the king's man, not subject to any lord in the course of my duties. Keswick understands that." He stared at her husband with that unblinking regard that reminded her once again that good-humored Wally Seaton had depths to him not readily apparent.

He added, "I will summon you when I wish to question you."

Randolph hesitated.

"Go, or I shall find you guilty of contempt of court, which I have the right to summarily punish."

"Be damned," Cuthbert snarled, turning on his heel and striding out.

"Eilidh, will you object if I do not remain while Hugh speaks with you? I have questions for someone else."

"I won't keep you from your duty, Wallace. The sooner you and Hugh can find the murderer, the better."

Hugh settled in the other chair, pencil in hand and notebook on his knee. "I apologize if my questions seem intrusive, but you will understand they are necessary."

"Of course, Sir Hugh." She might have called him simply "Hugh" as she had addressed Wallace by his first name, but under the circumstances, formality was best, even though she had slipped and referred to him as Hugh a moment earlier.

"Eilidh, I understand from Wallace that after you

came indoors that day"—no need to specify which—
"you rested until it was time to go down to supper. Was
that all?"

"Not quite. I washed my hands and face and
rubbed a soothing lotion into my face. To prevent
freckles if possible," she added wryly, "though I have
no confidence in its powers. I also changed my gown
and took my shoes off."

"Did you read or sew to occupy the time?"

"Hugh, did you ever know me to set a stitch? I lack
all the feminine accomplishments and always have."

He stared at her until she would have begun to
fidget if she were given to displays of discomfort.
Finally he said, "I knew you dislike sewing, but I never
noticed any deficiency in you."

"You didn't?"

"No."

His steady gaze almost made her wish for
Wallace's presence. Gathering her thoughts, she said, "I
simply sat with my feet up and let my mind wander." It
had roiled with anger and humiliation. She had needed
the time to calm herself and resume the mask she wore
in Cuthbert's proximity.

"No one visited you in your chamber?"

"Kitty, the girl who has been acting as my maid,
came to help me make ready for supper. I had already
changed into a *robe volante*, so I did not need her
assistance for that." Though Kitty had murmured
deprecatingly that the edges were not pinned quite
evenly over the stomacher and had corrected the fault.
Pinning oneself into one's gown was awkward. "She
brushed my hair and put it up again." Eilidh had refused
her suggestion of cosmetics to whiten her face and add

color to her lips. Had she been attending some event in London, she would have had to permit it; Randolph would have stood over her until 'twas done.

"Did Mr. Randolph Cuthbert come to your chamber?"

"Cuthbert?" Why would her husband—? Silence stretched as she realized that in many marriages such an occurrence would not be unusual. "No."

Her cheeks warmed as Hugh studied her face. At least she had not foolishly asked, "Why would you think so?"

He answered it anyway. "I wondered because he might have been worried about you and wished to apologize for jogging your arm and causing you to spill something on your bodice."

Briefly she considered denying he had done so and blaming her own clumsiness. His steady, sympathetic gaze warned her he knew better.

"We have testimony he bumped your arm while you were holding a tankard of ale."

"He asked me to hold it while he retied his hair ribbon."

"I see. Did he do it deliberately?"

She refused to lose his good opinion of her by lying to him. Heaven knew she had lied often enough since marrying Cuthbert. "I know it sounds ridiculous, but I think he did. He kindly refrained from blaming my clumsiness." Which was strange, now she thought about it, almost proof he had intended to spill the ale. "I always was blessed with two left hands as I'm sure you remember."

Unexpectedly, Hugh smiled. "You were growing into your limbs like any young filly. You are graceful enough now."

She nearly missed his next question out of surprise.

"Did you know he followed you into the house?"

"No. Did he? Oh, I suppose to visit the gentlemen's retiring room."

He raised one eyebrow satirically. "That would be a reasonable supposition except that he passed it by. Can you think of anywhere else he might have gone?"

She could. To avoid an outright lie, she said, "Perhaps to his chamber?"

"No matter, though that brings to mind another question. Not all couples choose to share a bedroom, but why is Cuthbert's not at least in the same wing as yours?"

"I don't know how Ismay Tate decided where to put guests." Not quite a lie. Randolph had maneuvered it somehow.

They sat regarding each other. Rather than continuing with another question, he waited for what seemed like minutes but was probably only a few seconds. She gave in.

"Cuthbert requested separate chambers, as I would have done had I been consulted. From something Ismay said on our arrival, she thought I wished to be near the Hodges to get to know them as there was some thought Georgina and Cornelius might make a match. They were lodged in the guests' wing, of course, and so I was also."

"There was no question of Cuthbert moving to the north wing as well? In a chamber separate from yours?"

"As the heir, he is entitled to a suite. The Hodges had one of the two suites in the north wing and Lydia Forsyth had the other. The Wilmots and Stephen

Cuthbert were assigned chambers in the south wing. The single women and I were in the north wing. I did not care where I slept," as long as it was not with Cuthbert.

"The south wing is the family wing?"

"Yes."

"So your husband devised the sleeping arrangements."

"Well…as far as telling Ismay I wanted to be in the same wing as the Hodges, yes."

"I wonder why."

So did she.

"Why would Lydia Forsyth have been given a suite when you, Keswick's heir's wife, were assigned such a small bedchamber?"

Why indeed? She could guess, but why had Ismay gone along with the suggestion? "I really don't know," she said, which was partly true.

"Was the Forsyth woman Cuthbert's mistress?" he asked.

She sighed. "Yes." Foolish to believe Hugh would not work it out even if no one else did.

"Marriages are made every day for purely practical reasons, and yet the couples often get along well enough. How did yours fail to maintain a certain equilibrium, Eilidh?"

She was trying to frame an acceptable answer when Hugh added, "Apart from Cuthbert being an arrogant ass, I mean."

That forced a choke of laughter out of her. Lord, why try to make a diplomatic reply? She had suffered humiliation at her husband's hands their entire marriage, and she had nothing better to expect in the years to come. He certainly would not fail to list all her faults and failings if asked the same question.

"I married him because when we met before the betrothal, he seemed pleasant enough. In exchange for my dowry, I received a connection to an earl's family, about which I did not care, and made my parents happy, which was important to me. After we married, he no longer needed to keep up any pretense."

"Could he not bear to be without the Forsyth woman's charms even for the three weeks of your stay here?"

She could not look at his face. "Apparently not."

In her heart-wrenched silence, Hugh snapped, "The scoundrel."

The furious utterance startled her into raising her eyes to his. They were flinty.

"I guessed he was not kind to you, but for this he deserves a thrashing. How could he—" He shut his lips tight on whatever he meant to say and asked instead, "Did you know Lydia Forsyth in London or elsewhere? Or know of her?"

"Yes. We met occasionally in town."

"Do you know why she was invited here? The pretext, I mean."

"I understood from Ismay Tate that there was some idea she might make a fine wife for Stephen. She was quite wealthy."

"Can you think of any reason someone would wish to murder her?"

"I believe some ladies in town resented her for drawing almost all men's attention to herself, whether she wanted them or not. Enough to murder her? Hardly. I suppose it must have been someone at this party, but I can't imagine who." She bit her lip. "From what you obviously know of my marriage, you might think I would have the most reason to murder Lydia Forsyth. I swear to you, I did not. I was not jealous of her. She was welcome to Cuthbert. Alas, that only men can bring an action for divorce in England while in Scotland, either sex can do so." Not that she would be able to afford it in either place. Their interview ended with a few questions about her home in Durham.

Chapter 12

Hugh had finished writing out his almost verbatim report on his interrogation of Eilidh when Wallace entered. He noted the half dozen sheets of closely written notes and nodded approvingly. "I like detail, Hugh. May I?"

"Certainly. That will give me time to complete it."

They wrote and read in silence until Hugh sprinkled sand on the last page and sat back, waiting for the ink to dry, clenching and unclenching his hand, cramped from gripping the quill. Would writing be more comfortable if the quill were thicker? He poured the used sand back into the shaker as Wallace reached to pull the last sheet over. He read the few lines and added it to the stack.

"She has a motive for murder." Wallace's dispassionate tone made the statement a mere remark rather than an accusation.

"We also have Lydia's lover, a man who entered the house at the relevant time and is of questionable character."

"And we have no means for either. We cannot assume Cuthbert is guilty merely because he treats Eilidh badly and we dislike him."

"I agree, Wallace. But if he went in after Eilidh but did not go to her chamber and yet was apparently out of everyone's sight for so long, where did he go? I refuse

178

to believe he sat swilling brandy in the dubious comfort of the footmen's secret parlor."

"We'd better find out, hadn't we? To that end, I have been talking with Rob." He dragged a wad of folded papers out of his coat pocket and smoothed them on the table.

Wallace's younger groom was staying at Cuthbert Hall to act as their messenger.

"I set him to paying attention to the talk in the servants' hall as soon as he arrived. He has a way with the female servants, and the men like him as he's always willing to lend a hand whether it's his job or not," Wallace said. "He turned up some interesting bits. Hugh, we both thought it strange that neither Lydia nor Eilidh brought a maid. Kitty had to take the place of both abigails and do as much as she could of her own work. The other maids had to do some of her usual tasks, and naturally the house party already made extra work for everyone. Read the second page." He passed the several crumpled sheets to Hugh. "These are what Rob took down from talk in the servants' hall."

"Rob can write?"

"His father saw the value of education and made sure Rob learned. Even Rob's sisters were taught."

"Very advanced views." Hugh turned his attention to the page and read.

Housekeeper says Forsyth being put in one of the best chambers with a dressing room where her woman could sleep made no sense when she did not bring a maid. Says Mistress C should have had it, being the heir's wife.

Edward, footman, says Mistress Tate said Mistress Cuthbert wanted to be near the guests. Another, that's called Owen, laughs and says, "Away from her husband, most like."

Carson the butler told him right sharpish not to be talking about his lordship's family and heir and the quality folk. Owen is a saucy one and shoots back, "Lord Keswick's a good master and Mistress C and Mistress T always have a pleasant word. Cuthbert—"

"That's Mr. Cuthbert to you and mind you remember it," says Carson—but the footman goes on, "Cuthbert can't be pleased, no matter what, and as for vails, he'd sooner dance with the Devil than part with a penny."

The butler had nothing to say to that, it being no secret the heir is close-fisted. He did not bring his valet, making more work for the footmen, and complains about their service.

"Strange that he dispensed with his manservant when he's in a suite that has a dressing room where the fellow could sleep, and when he's particular about his clothing and boots," Hugh said. "A man might do without his man if he weren't finickal."

"I didn't bring my man, and I suspect you haven't one, Hugh. That marks us as shag-bags."

"I have a footman who does well enough. We aren't in line for an earl's title, and Cuthbert fancies himself a beau. I'd think he'd not stir from home without his valet."

Wallace scowled. "I want to question Cuthbert."

"So do I. We'll need to do so by stratagem, I think."

****

Wallace's wrinkled and bow-legged groom who had been with his family since Hugh and Wallace were boys, rode over with several letters that had come for

Seaton and one for Hugh. None of them, unfortunately, with any connection to their inquiries.

"Thanks, Ned."

The man stood there, clutching his billed cap. "Sir, there's talk about Miss Eilidh. Mistress Cuthbert as she is now."

Hugh stiffened.

Wallace set his letters down on one corner of the table. "Oh? What have you heard?"

"They're saying in the alehouse as 'twas her handkerchief that was found bloodstained with the murdered lady."

"That was bound to come out once the design was recognized as an *E*," his cousin said. "To make the connection between it and the one person in the house whose name begins with that letter is hardly an intellectual challenge."

Ned's boots shuffled, a bad sign in a groom who was imperturbable except about injury to horses.

"Is there something more?"

"There's some fools think she murdered the dead lady." Like them, the groom remembered her from childhood.

"Seaton," Hugh began, "while in general I do not believe in discussing details of an investigation in progress…"

"Ay, Montgomery?" His cousin compressed his lips on a smile.

"I think we might trust Ned with one bit of evidence to relieve his mind."

"You're thinking of where that handkerchief was found, I take it?"

"I was."

Wallace's ferocious grin was all he needed to assure Hugh his cousin agreed.

Seaton cleared his throat. "The handkerchief was found under the body, and we are at a loss to explain how it came there when it was used to wipe the candlestick, presumably after the woman had fallen to the floor."

"Like as if 'twas put there, sir?"

"That would seem to be the only explanation."

"Why'd he put it under the body?"

"We don't know, Ned. But it's fortunate he did instead of dropping it in plain sight."

"So's to throw suspicion on our miss."

Hugh said, "That's it, Ned. Now your mind is at rest about Mistress Cuthbert, you'll be wanting a pint to celebrate on the way home." Hugh tossed him a coin.

Ned caught it, stared at it, then up at Hugh. "Thank ye, sir." Grinning, he added, "A nod's as good as a wink to a blind horse." Ned could neither read nor write and had spent his life tending horses and their gear, but his wits were keen.

As he stumped out, Hugh and his cousin exchanged looks. Wallace tutted and sank onto an armchair. "A fine idea, to give Ned enough to treat whoever is in the alehouse. So much for the notion that the lower orders are stupid, not that I ever believed it. Word will spread."

"It will take some suspicion away from Eilidh and may shake something loose. Have you ever looked into any case more complicated than a petty theft, sheep stealing, or an alehouse brawl, Wallace? I haven't. The abduction of Lord Hawkslowe's daughters and the death of their abductor made no work for me as there was no mystery about what happened. All I had to do was hold his coachman and notify the coroner."

"What do you recommend?"

"We've been trying to determine who would want Lydia Forsyth dead. Maybe we should ask, who would want to implicate Eilidh?" *Who would benefit from her death because it would be death if she were found guilty of murder. Dear God, they would hang Eilidh.*

"I agree. A lady's servants, especially her maid, know her better than almost anyone else. We should question Eilidh's servants in Durham." Wallace let out a weary breath. "Or rather, I'd like you to question them. We need to find out as much as we can while we're waiting for replies to my letters."

"Very well." He didn't like to leave Seaton on his own, but there was no choice. A ride of some sixty miles would be too taxing for Wallace in his current impaired health.

"There are questions enough here to keep me busy," his cousin said, half smiling.

"A day and a half to get there and a day and a half to return. With luck I will be back in four or five days. I'd best have a letter from you identifying me as your agent."

"Get one from Eilidh, too."

****

The Sixth and Seventh Days

He set out early the next day and broke his journey at the market town of Barnard Castle, the most likely place to find a bed and a meal for the night. The following midafternoon found him outside a neat but not large or elegant house in an acceptable neighborhood. There was no stabling. He had passed an inn one street away and returned to it to leave his mount at livery.

The maid who opened the door squeaked when Hugh asked for Isobel MacDonald, the housekeeper, Eilidh's former maid. Before he could add that he had a letter for her from her mistress, she left him standing in the narrow passage and scurried toward the rear of the house, darting anxious looks over her shoulder.

The height and breadth of shoulder of the woman who came striding from the back of the house hinted she would be capable of dealing with any problem a butler or footman might face. Her forbidding expression changed as she studied his face, squinting. "Mr. Hugh Montgomery?"

"Mistress, I've a letter for you from Mistress Cuthbert."

Seeing the inscription, she accepted it without hesitation.

"And another from Wallace Seaton, the magistrate at Penrith."

Her eyebrows rose in surprise. Had the news had not yet traveled as far as Durham? She spared Hugh another look.

"When you've read them, we must speak."

With a brusque nod, she led him to the housekeeper's room, half office and half bedchamber. When Hugh was seated in a well-worn armchair, the housekeeper settled herself at a small desk by the room's window to read the letters. He wished he could see her face, but she was half turned away. She stared down at the first for longer than it should have taken to read the few sentences before refolding it and breaking the wafer seal on the second. She read it, then glanced at Hugh.

"You were Miss Eilidh's friend, like Master Wally, that's now a justice of the peace," she said.

He smiled to hear his cousin's old nickname. "We still are her friends, and we need information from you and the other servants here and in London."

"And you're now a baronet and a justice of the peace besides."

No wonder she sounded surprised. Isobel MacDonald remembered him as a gangling lad regularly packed off to stay with his uncle's family to get him out from underfoot at home.

He said, "We know a great deal about the movements of the guests and servants before and during the time the murder took place. We need to know more about the people themselves, including Mistress Cuthbert and Mr. Cuthbert. Neither Seaton nor I regard Mistress Cuthbert as a suspect."

Isobel clicked her tongue. "I should hope not."

Hugh ignored this interjection and continued, "However, we hope her maid, Manon Allard, can be of some assistance."

"She won't be much help. Ask me anything you like, and the others here will talk to you freely as well," as she would no doubt instruct them to do.

"That sly piece is French, or half, anyway," the housekeeper went on, "though to hear her you mightn't think it, and she gives herself airs as if she served a duchess instead of a plain gentleman's lady until he became heir to an earldom. We none of us trust her."

"I understand she did not accompany Mistress Cuthbert because she was unwell, but still, I must question her."

"Her unwell? Not likely. In the letter Cuthbert sent to Miss Eilidh that they would be going to Cuthbert Hall, he told her Allard was not to come because there weren't enough rooms for as many extra servants as were expected. I saw it when my mistress showed it to her, because that woman would not believe she was to be left behind. Allard stood there holding it, struck dumb for once, and I took it from her after she'd read it over enough to have got it by heart. The wench's been idle the entire time my mistress has been away and not on board wages, either."

Cuthbert had lied; Hugh had seen the unused rooms in the attic. For some reason, he had not wanted Manon Allard or his valet present.

He and Wallace had discussed what he would ask Eilidh's household in Durham, and he had thought more about it as he rode. Now something Nurse Kettlewell had told him came to mind. "I know nothing of female attire, but Eilidh did not seem to dress as well as the other ladies. Her gowns were not as fashionable and some that were newer did not become her as the older ones did, or so I was informed."

"The old ones were her bride clothes mostly, though we've made them over to bring them more into the mode. But there's only so much the best seamstress can do to alter an old gown. Color and fabric go out of fashion as styles do. That French jade packed her trunks with the newer clothing that she and Mr. Cuthbert chose. My lady and I left one of those at the top in each of the trunks and portmanteaux and put her re-fashioned gowns underneath."

"Then you'll be happy to hear that a certain hideous red and yellow calico was spoiled when ale was spilled upon it."

That won a smile from Eilidh's former maid. "Good."

Casually he observed, "I am surprised to find Mistress Cuthbert living in such a modest house."

"You might expect her to live in a finer street that isn't home to lower gentry and tradesmen who have a bit of coin. We cut our coat according to our cloth."

"Is Mr. Cuthbert is careless with his money?"

"I don't know about that. You'd have to inquire in London to learn more of his finances. 'Twas he that chose this house, which was prudent if he is short of coin. I'm sorry the maid was the one to answer the door, but this is the footman's half day."

Isobel MacDonald did not give a fig for Cuthbert. Who would, who was fond of Eilidh? Without actually revealing anything detrimental to him, she had made it clear that Cuthbert's finances were not all they should be. The size and location of the house, the lack of both butler and more than one footman told Hugh that much.

"Seaton has written to a friend in town who can provide more information. Letters take time, however." He changed direction. "What can you tell me of Mr. and Mistress Cuthbert's marriage?"

"It was an ill day when Mistress Cuthbert's father betrothed her to him. I never liked him and not because he was clutch-fisted in giving vails. I never trusted the look in his eye or the way he spoke to Miss Eilidh. I could hear the serpent of Eden in his voice, and I'm not a fanciful woman. They'd been married only a year or two when he leased this house, claiming London did not agree with her constitution. That was nonsense. She did not like London"—she raised her brows significantly—"and who would that likes clean air and open spaces? She was glad to leave, though she goes south occasionally. But when he became Earl Keswick's heir a few months since, he said she would have to spend more time there."

"She told me he was ending the lease."

MacDonald nodded, tight-lipped.

"Is there a place I can use to question Allard?"

"Ay, the parlor. The drawing room is furnished to Mr. Randolph's taste." Her tone expressed her judgement of that. Besides, a parlor would be preferable as a more reassuring space.

"Good. Send her to me at once, please." He doubted the others would know as much as Isobel and Manon or reveal it if they did. As he started to rise, she surprised him.

"Who was it that was killed?"

"Didn't Mr. Seaton or Mistress Cuthbert say in their letters?"

"No, sir."

Perhaps Wallace had thought it unimportant because how would Eilidh's housekeeper know aught of a fashionable London lady? Or he might have omitted it in his hurry to send Hugh off to Durham. But why had Eilidh not included the information?

"The victim was Lydia Forsyth, a—"

"That strumpet!"

Her outburst and expression were so fierce Hugh was momentarily silenced.

"You know something of her?"

"That light hussy was Cuthbert's mistress when he married our Eilidh and still was when last we were in London."

"Fourteen years is surely an unusual reign for a light o' love."

"I'd not have expected such constancy from that man. If she'd been a widow at the time, Miss Eilidh might have been spared a deal of unhappiness."

Hugh had intended to take a room at the inn at which he'd stabled his horse. Isobel told him roundly that Miss Eilidh would expect him to stay overnight in her home.

"Not if she were here," she said. "That would set tongues clacking. But as she isn't, you may as well be comfortable where there's clean sheets and good food." She dispatched the squeaking maid to the inn to collect his valise and to inform the ostler Sir Hugh's horse would be staying the night.

The moss-green chairs and settee and the heavy curtains of wheat-colored wool in Eilidh's parlor were clearly her choice. Whatever ladylike talents she might lack, she had always known what hues became her.

Manon Allard entered, as self-possessed as a duchess. "You wished to see me, Sir Hugh?"

"Yes."

She seated herself at his invitation, neither nervous nor curious as far as he could tell. He had asked Isobel not to disclose the reason for his coming.

"You must not be shocked by what I have to show you, for I have to ask about something perhaps relating to a death."

The maid inclined her head regally. "I do not fall into agitation easily."

Shown the stained linen square, she stared at it and uttered a disapproving "Oh là là! I do not think that will come out."

"Do you recognize it?"

"No, sir. It is pretty, but I have not seen it before."

"Are you sure?"

She raised her delicately arched eyebrows. "I would remember the embroidery, which is very fine. The design is like a little garden or bouquet instead of a *monogramme*."

"It belongs to Mistress Cuthbert."

"Does it? I have never seen it."

"Are you not in the least curious to know who died?"

"If you wished me to know, you would tell me." She shrugged, vastly Gallic.

"As you are unlikely to have known her, it is probably not relevant," Hugh said.

Manon's reaction vanished so quickly he was not sure he had seen it. Why would she be surprised? To probe deeper, he said, "The decedent was a lady staying at Cuthbert Hall, a Mistress Lydia Forsyth."

"*Mon Dieu!*" She stared at him, her horror unmistakable. She swallowed convulsively. "I am *étonné*."

He should request a restorative for her or at least a glass of water but preferred not to give her the opportunity to recover. He was already prejudiced against the woman, based on Isobel MacDonald's opinion and on Eilidh's less attractive clothing for which the maid was evidently to blame.

"You know her, then?"

Blinking, she murmured, "But yes, I know…of her. She figures in the beau monde. She has such elegance and is so debonair."

Had he heard the briefest of hesitations in her

reply? Allard stirred restively when he did not speak again at once.

"How long was Lydia Forsyth Cuthbert's mistress?" he rapped out.

"*Un mensonge.*" Then, "One cannot believe three-quarters of what one hears in London."

A lie. Why was she angered by his question, when all knew that some married men had mistresses and widows often took advantage of their freedom? That was an accepted fact. For that matter, why had she lapsed into French? She spoke English fluently, without even an accent, although her phrasing was sometimes not quite English. News of the death of a woman she had only heard of as a luminary among London's elite should not have overset her.

"That was a rumor I heard."

"Rumors, *bah.*"

More peaceably he said, "To determine who killed the poor lady, we must take into account all the evidence and everything we are told about the victim and those around her. Can you think of anyone who might be glad of Mistress Forsyth's death, or benefit by it?"

She lowered her gaze to the hands clenched in her lap.

"Mademoiselle Allard?" he prompted when she did not reply at once, either contemplating *un mensonge* or considering the question.

She let out a long breath. "If, I say *if*, Madame Forsyth had been Randolph Cuthbert's mistress, one might wonder if his wife had avenged herself."

"Certainly that is something to bear in mind."

He thanked her, adding, "I may talk to you again

for I see you're a noticing sort and may have seen or heard something that will be useful, once I know what to ask."

She rose, curtsied, and departed in a whisper of petticoats, without acknowledging the flattery.

Chapter 13

Eilidh found she could bear the presence of others for only so long before she wanted to scream. Except Hugh. She would not mind his company. Joan Hodge's attempt to forget the reason they were still at Cuthbert Hall, Dorothy Wilmot's anxious eyes as she watched Georgina Hodge fluttering from man to man exercising her innocent coquetry, Cornelius's attempt to pretend he did not notice or care about Georgina's behavior, all were hard to bear. Her husband's worried gaze whenever he was in her own presence and the solicitude in his voice chafed her. As she could not air her thoughts at the top of her lungs, she had taken to wandering Cuthbert Hall. Had anyone asked, she would have claimed to be admiring its architecture, or searching for her fan which she had set down and forgotten. She walked in the gardens when no one else was likely to be there or admired the view of the Eden Valley from the Long Gallery. Occasionally she encountered one of the others also seeking solitude. The worst was the afternoon Cuthbert found her in the Great Hall where she had gone to sketch.

She was not fond of drawing though its remaining medieval details were well worth studying as the oldest part of Cuthbert Hall had been intended to impress all with the might of its lord. Its advantage in her eyes was that it was too big and cheerless to attract someone seeking a comfortable place to read or chat with a friend.

Her husband was approaching the window seat before she realized he had entered.

"Ellen."

"Were you looking for me, Cuthbert?" That would be a rarity. She made to stand up, but he caught her wrist.

"Sit with me, please. We must talk."

She sank back onto the seat. He released her wrist and took her hand instead, sighing.

"What did you wish to speak of?" she asked. "I cannot linger here long as I must tidy myself a little before supper."

"My dear, your restlessness and unease do not go unremarked. Even those bucolic king's men must wonder at your behavior."

"Randolph, a woman has been murdered here. Everyone, guests and servants alike, is disquieted, as anyone of sense or decent feeling would be, except Georgina Hodge, who is both a ninny and too young to grasp that someone here is a murderer."

Lines of worry creased her husband's face while his eyes remained empty of any expression. "You seem more frightened than disturbed, however." He released her hand.

If only she had noted the disparity between his expressions and his eyes before she agreed to marry him. Her father would not have insisted in the face of her objection, despite her parents' hope she would marry a man from the aristocracy for the family's good.

He sighed. "I fear your response to the death springs from a more personal source."

"Because she was your mistress?" She laughed, the sound harsh in her own ears.

" 'Tis only a matter of time before they bring their investigation to a conclusion. No one here had any reason to do away with her except you."

"You overrate your importance to me, Randolph. You have never cared for me, and I reciprocate your regard."

"You are mistaken. I did value you until you chilled me with your indifference."

"My only importance to you was my dowry. Once you had it, I ceased to exist for you except as a minor annoyance. I have not forgotten the remarks you made almost from the day of our wedding about my unattractive person." To her surprise, they were quarreling, something they had never done before, perhaps because she was unaccustomed to brangling or had never had the resolve to do so. Or because although she had never realized it before, she feared Randolph. How odd.

"Ellen, your temper will be the end of you," he said. Now he took both her hands in a way which would have been reassuring if he had been someone else, Hugh or Wallace, for instance, and studied her face. "How can Seaton fail to arrest you based on the evidence?"

She tugged her hands free. "I did not kill her." But who in this limited pool of suspects had done so?

"Oh, Ellen, I do hope you are telling the truth." He smiled sadly. "I think we must try to avoid your ending on the gallows. If your arrest seems imminent, I will see to it you escape England. I have already begun some arrangements in case it should be necessary." He patted her hand and left her.

Many minutes passed before her heart ceased its pounding. Did Cuthbert really think her guilty or did he merely hope she was? She was in her chamber making ready for the evening meal when she remembered his offer to help her escape. That had been so unlike everything she knew of his character that she wondered what had prompted it. Granted, having one's wife tried and hanged would be a scandal but wouldn't aiding a fleeing felon or supposed felon be a felony itself? That would be far worse for him. Wouldn't it?

Only later in her bed did she wonder about his lack of feeling at the death of his longtime mistress. If she herself had died, he would have mouthed the expected regrets and displayed the correct expressions. But that he had kept the same lover for so long suggested he felt something for the woman. Otherwise, why not move on to fresh pastures? If he did care for Lydia Forsyth in some way, wouldn't it affect him at least as much as it did the other guests?

****

Mistress MacDonald would have served him supper in the dining room. Hugh declined, preferring to eat in the kitchen. In addition to saving the servants work, he hoped they would become comfortable enough with his presence to make questioning them easier. Seeing Manon's empty chair, he hoped that in her absence the servants would let something slip. He need not have worried. All of them were Eilidh's stout partisans and spoke almost as freely as if he had not been there. Perhaps Isobel had prompted them.

His wishes were fulfilled when he asked, "Does Mistress Cuthbert's maid not eat with you?"

Isobel said, "She claimed she felt unwell and took some bread and butter up to her room."

The housemaid said, "A nine days' wonder. I'd expect her to want it carried up to her. I can't think why you gave her the quince marmalade and a tumbler of your special tonic, Mistress Ellery."

The cook said placidly, "To keep her sweet. Don't you know she bears tales to Mr. Cuthbert?"

"She does," Mistress MacDonald agreed, "but don't you let on you know it."

"I find it strange a lady's maid would tattle to the master about her fellow servants."

Their heads all turned to him as if he had uttered something too foolish to answer.

"That's because you don't know Allard. I'm sure she showed you due respect, Sir Hugh," Isobel stated.

"She did not seem quite like the usual lady's maid, Mistress MacDonald. Perhaps that was because she was distressed to hear of the death at Cuthbert Hall."

The cook sniffed audibly.

He chose his next words with care. Servants knew almost everything about their masters. "No one here is suspected of any connection to the death, but Magistrate Seaton of Penrith wants to know as much as possible about everyone who is present at Cuthbert Hall."

"You needn't suspect my mistress of anything." Mistress MacDonald's stare dared him to disagree.

"I don't. Nevertheless, someone wanted Lydia Forsyth dead or possesses some fact that would explain it. Mayhap it's only some little thing like a rivalry or an action that seemed odd. That's why I've come to question you." Loose talk was helpful if one wished to know a household's secrets.

Eyes shifted all around the table except Isobel MacDonald's. "Sir Hugh was a childhood friend of our mistress as well as being a magistrate now."

The housemaid said, "That Allard thinks herself so fine and calls herself a 'dresser,' though her mistress isn't a credit to her, pleasant as she is."

"Mistress Cuthbert 'isn't a credit to her'?" He was sure the phrase "pleasant as she is" did not apply to Manon.

"Her old gowns and the ones she has made here suit her. The ones Allard chose for her in London don't. You'd think Cuthbert would turn her off for making his lady almost a figure of fun."

"Not he," Isobel said. "Mr. Cuthbert hired her, and he'd not want his judgement called into question."

The sharp-faced girl of fifteen who had admitted Hugh broke the silence. She had recovered from her initial terror. "Don't know if it means much, but Allard fair hates our mistress."

"Jenny," Cook admonished. To Hugh she said, "Jenny is our maid of all work."

"There's no harm in telling him anything that might help," MacDonald said.

"Why do you think so, Jenny?"

"Grew up in t'workhouse, I did. You gets a sense about people there. Like who'll steal from you or carry tales to the master. I knows her cut."

"What is her cut?"

"She's sly and sneaking, I won't say like a cat acos I likes cats. They love you if you feed and pet them. I saw the way she looked at her once, as if she hated her."

"Why would she hate Mistress Cuthbert? Isn't a lady's maid usually her trusty friend?"

"This is the only house I've worked in." The girl shrugged her thin shoulders.

"That's often true," Eilidh's former maid agreed, "but I think she wanted to be in London, serving a lady who attended the most fashionable entertainments."

"Doesn't Mistress Cuthbert do that when she's in town, Mistress MacDonald?"

"She has visited London only a few times since coming here. I misdoubt she cares for what's called the beau monde or for London. Here she attends concerts and small gatherings with sensible people and does charity work. Cuthbert sent for her early this spring. She returned from London in June and was the ghost of herself, the same as she was when she first moved here." Isobel MacDonald added, "She was finally recovering her spirits when her husband wrote that he would be coming to take her to Cuthbert Hall."

The talk turned to the coming change in their lives. They had been informed that Cuthbert was ending the lease, and the mistress would be living in London.

"Mr. Cuthbert won't be taking us with her," the cook said. "Mistress Cuthbert has already given us good characters. Still, 'tis hard to have to go to a new situation."

"As she will be doing herself," Isobel said grimly, "having to live in London all year except when he goes to stay at Cuthbert Hall."

Nods all around.

Hugh listened silently apart from complimenting the cook on the food, root vegetables and bacon cooked together and bread and butter. She had augmented their meal with slices of a rich cake full of currants, brandy, and sweetmeats of orange, citron, and lemon. It was the sort that kept well and that Eilidh could serve her visitors, he supposed. Not something that would form part of the servants' meal as a rule. Perhaps its appearance was in honor of his presence, or else Eilidh's cook felt there was no point in saving it if the house was to be given up.

They had finished eating and Mistress MacDonald began, "Well, we'd best let Jenny get on with the dishes," when the footman spoke.

He had returned from his half day in time for the meal to avoid the storm promised by the gathering clouds. As footmen went, he was not impressive: only of average size and not noticeably muscular or handsome. Not a man for a larger, better-paying house. He had been almost silent throughout the supper.

"Sir, there's something I've been wondering if I should add to what the others told you."

He was better-spoken than Hugh expected. "What's that, Mel? Do I have your name right?"

"Ay, sir. I'm called Mel because no one wants a footman named Melchizedek. My father fancied the name."

"What have you to tell me?"

"I take letters to the receiving office and collect the mail from the postmaster. I pass it out here."

In some homes, the mail would be given to the master. In others, it might carelessly be left on the hall table. As there was neither master nor butler in Eilidh's Durham residence, probably it should have been turned over to her.

Isobel said, "Mistress Cuthbert says it is no

business of hers to know if we receive letters."

That sounded like Eilidh. He nodded his thanks to the housekeeper for explaining. "Go on, please, Mel."

"Some servants get a letter once in a while if they can read and have family or a friend who can write. Manon Allard sent letters pretty regular and received them, too."

"Who did she write to? If you recall," Hugh added tactfully.

"There were two. One was a John Penn, in care of Prince's Coffee House, Covent Garden, and the other was an L. Forsyth, North Audley Street, Grosvenor Square, at the sign of the Heart in Hand."

"That's extremely interesting. Did she not worry you'd wonder about her correspondence?"

"She doesn't take much account of me, and how would I know who her letters came from, with no sender's name on them."

"But you saw the letters she sent, too."

"Only one time, but by then I was curious."

Jenny spoke up. "She come down and told me to send her letters, same as she always did. The day was raining and blowing fierce, and I was hoping it would stop so's I wouldn't get wet. Then Mel said as he'd take them. I thanked him kindly and let him."

"She chose you because you couldn't read?"

"I couldn't, then."

Isobel said, "We don't let on that we've been teaching Jenny."

Everyone around the table smiled, sharing the satisfaction of having hoodwinked the woman. Did Allard keep the letters? He could find out.

"Mistress MacDonald," Hugh said slowly, "I shall

need the use of pen and ink and some paper. Can you oblige me?"

"That I can. I'll show you to the desk in Mistress Cuthbert's private parlor, if you are ready now?"

As he followed her, she asked softly, "Will it help our Miss Eilidh?"

"I don't know yet, mistress. It depends on whether Allard has kept those letters and whether I can find them if she did."

Seated at the desk in a little chamber perhaps meant as a child's bedroom, he had everything he needed except a copy of the manual for justices of the peace. Still, he recalled the fundamentals of the form: date, location, name, assertion of the reason. Wallace's letter would be helpful, as would his own declaration. As justification for taking Allard into custody, he quoted Lord Bacon, who declared in the Countess of Shrewsbury's case in 1612, that "all subjects...owe to the King tribute and service, not only of their deed and hand, but of their knowledge and discovery." The Allard woman had or might have information relevant to the murder.

****

The Eighth Day

Next morning he partook of the cook's excellent breakfast before setting out to tell the ostler his horse would be remaining at least another night. Two hours later, he returned to the house with a constable assigned him by the local magistrate. This time the footman opened the door. Mel's eyes opened wide at the sight of the constable.

"Is Manon Allard here?"

"Ay, sir, in her chamber, though I think she means

to go out soon."

"Take us up to her, please."

"Will you be needing me for anything else, Sir Hugh?"

By then, they stood in the third floor passage, some distance from the door the footman indicated.

Hugh shook his head. Mel gave a little bow and retreated down the stairs. Indicating to the constable he should stand against the wall to the side of the door, Hugh knocked briskly.

The woman opened the door a crack, asking sharply, "What do you want?"

"I have one or two more questions for you."

A martyred sigh. "I will speak with you downstairs in the parlor. It is not appropriate to entertain a man in one's bedchamber."

"There will be no entertaining, I assure you." With his foot between the door and the jamb, he pushed it open, causing Manon to fall back. The constable followed him into the room.

"Get out," she shrilled.

"This here's a warrant for searching this room and the rest o' the house if and as necessary," the court officer said, holding the document up.

"This is an outrage. This man has no authority here."

"Warrant's signed by Peter Patterson, Justice of the Peace, Durham, and permits Sir Hugh and me to search for evidence concerning a murder in the county of Cumberland. That's all the authority needed. Sir Hugh?"

"Constable, you will make sure she does not attempt to hinder me or flee."

The room was well furnished compared to most servants' lodgings and larger, but then, she was Mistress Cuthbert's maid. She had a chest of drawers, a small table and chair, a carpet, and an armchair.

He began with the chest, taking the drawers out one by one and going through their contents before examining the inside of the chest and the underside of each drawer. A mirror hung above the table, which served both as a desk and a dressing table. A box containing various aids to beauty and another with quill, ink, and other appurtenances necessary for writing stood upon it. He felt the underside of the top to no avail. There were still places to search: the bed, armchair, a loose floorboard...the sewing box by the chair. It was a handsome one of a reddish wood inlaid with ivory. Out of the corner of his eye, he saw the maid stiffen.

He set it on the table to open it. Inside was a tray with compartments for needle cases, small tools like a bone awl, and things he could not identify. Under the tray were two pairs of scissors, large and small, a pin-pillow, and winders of thread. Below those and a selection of ribbons and both new and old lace and trim, he found the letters.

Returning the sewing things to the chest, he sat down in the armchair to read.

"How dare you touch my letters? They are private, from my friends."

"Quiet, woman," said the constable.

He skimmed the smaller stack. Eleven were signed with the initials J.P. He glanced through them; they were acknowledgements of her own messages with a few comments and nothing to identify the writer.

The most recent in the thicker stack was addressed in an ornate, feminine hand and dated near the beginning of July.

Ma chère Manon,

Lucky for him Wallace's father insisted both of them learn French. "Greek's no use to a man who's not going into the church, but French will stand him in good stead in our next war with those fellows."

I look forward to your opinion on the latest modes when we return to London. I have no doubt you will rejoice at your release from that dismal place. I hope soon thereafter you will have a position more suitable to your abilities than you have at present with the Bony One. I can scarcely contain my excitement at the prospect of marriage at last to the man I love...

The rest of the sheet contained an account of the events she had attended and the notable persons who had been present. The signature at the bottom was only the name: *Lydia.*

He found one more bit of information in a letter written late in December, and he almost missed that one.

I have deposited my gift in your account at Andres and Barlow. A happy Christmas to you, dear sister.

The final phrase leapt off the sheet. No need to read farther for the moment. He re-tied the letters in their original bundles. Eilidh's maid appeared to relax. He had only skimmed through them; perhaps she assumed he could not interpret them.

"Constable, let us take Mistress Allard before your magistrate. Her cooperation is necessary, but I fear she is likely to flee."

Manon Allard's expression hovered somewhere

between fury and horror.

The constable, a stocky, ruddy-faced man, eyed her disapprovingly. "I'd think you'd be pleased to testify against someone that murdered an earl's friend."

"I am! Of course I am, but to be treated as a criminal myself, that is insulting. Sir Hugh may ask me what he wishes and I will answer."

"Thank you for agreeing so readily. Now let us apply for a warrant for your removal to Penrith." His time writing out the application yesterday would speed matters along today.

Chapter 14

She missed Hugh. Even though they had not spent a great deal of time together at the Hall, his presence had been comforting. He did not appear to believe she had beaten the Forsyth woman to death. Neither did Wallace. The reassurance was welcome as she could not help feeling guilty. There had been moments when Eilidh had wished Lydia dead: of smallpox or crushed by runaway horses, drowned, or indeed by any other illness or accident.

God would not have smitten Lydia Forsyth unto death even if Eilidh had prayed for it, and she had not done so. Could she have caused the death of her husband's mistress by wishing for it? No, that was as foolish as believing in Robin Goodfellow. Her occasional thought that it would satisfying if Lydia died occurred only when the harpy had flaunted her relationship with Cuthbert.

By way of distracting herself from these uncomfortable reflections, she drifted past the Yellow Parlor. The door stood open. Wallace was poring over a large sheet of paper and making notes on a small one. He looked up and smiled.

"Come in, Eilidh, unless you are on your way to somewhere more amusing."

"I'm afraid, Wallace," burst out, taking her by surprise because what had she to fear?

Instead of replying to what must have seemed almost equally startling to him, Wallace stood up and trod quietly to the door. He glanced along the passage to left and right before pulling the door shut.

He invited her to sit as he lowered himself wearily into his chair. "Why, my dear?"

"Not because I'm guilty. I swear I'm not. But I see the others looking at me, and I've caught whispers about Lydia being Cuthbert's mistress."

"There's always talk. Sometimes it's right, and other times it is no more than idle minds inventing titillating fantasies."

Though in fact the rumors about her husband and Lydia were true. "She was, Wallace."

"Was she? That explains some things that puzzled me." He shrugged it off. "As for people looking at you, Eilidh? That may be because you appear tired and worried, and they are concerned for your wellbeing."

She swallowed a sob. "He thinks me guilty."

"Who does?"

"Randolph."

"His own guilty conscience speaking, I expect."

She felt her eyes widen. "Do you mean you think he killed her? Why would he?"

"I meant his guilt at his lack of discretion, which was bad enough as an insult to you. Now his paramour has been murdered, the offense has grown into a scandal."

"He keeps talking about hanging and how dreadful it is."

Her old friend huffed. "Has he ever given you any word of comfort in all the years you've been married?"

She did not need to search her memory. "No."

"Eilidh, he's a scoundrel. Ignore him."

****

Getting the warrant was easy. Peter Patterson, the local magistrate, raised no objection to the prisoner being held at Cuthbert Hall rather than Penrith's bridewell on Hugh's representation that it was small and none too secure. After that, matters grew more complicated. The afternoon was advanced by the time Hugh had arranged for a coach, making it impossible to begin before the next morning. He had hoped to hire the wife of either a constable or a warder at the jail to chaperon the maid and prevent her from escaping during the overnight stop. Here an impediment arose: of the women who assisted when necessary by searching female prisoners, the only one who might have obliged by acting as a guard was far along in pregnancy and could not undertake the duty. He would have to manage on his own.

They returned to Eilidh's home to allow the woman to pack a valise. On hearing of his problem, however, Isobel MacDonald volunteered to do escort duty.

"Cook can manage the household while I'm away," she said. "That sly piece won't get away from me."

He believed her and slept well, his prisoner locked in a spare bedchamber.

****

The Ninth and Tenth Days

He hardly noticed the miles of low, rolling hills between Durham and Penrith as he tried to fit together the things he knew or believed were true.

If a wife cared about her husband, he supposed she might murder his longtime mistress. If she did not care about the man or the betrayal, why bother to do murder?

An unhappy wife might murder her husband if she were in love with another man who would marry her. Had Eilidh met a man in London or in Durham and fallen in love? Surely that was not the case here, judging by what he had learned of Eilidh's activities in Durham. Church on Sunday, a ladies' group that collected food and clothing for the poor, calls upon a few friends, and their calls upon her. No assemblies or any other gathering that would have required a male escort, from what Isobel and the others had spoken of. According to Eilidh and Isobel, Manon was Cuthbert's spy. "John Penn" must be Cuthbert, as from his letters it was clear the maid was informing him of Eilidh's activities.

Beyond those arguments against her guilt, there were others. One might argue Eilidh had sometimes been impulsive in her youth, but she had never been thoughtless. Her action in protecting her niece from the lurcher was quite different from committing murder to free herself from a hateful husband. She was too sensible to have taken a lover and risked giving Cuthbert cause to divorce her, an expensive, scandalous proceeding. Polite society would turn its back on her, and perhaps on her lover as well.

Fashionable London life held no attraction for her. If she were free to marry a man she loved, she would be happy to live in the country, though even there she might suffer the cut direct. Would she care? Having known her from childhood, he suspected she would not. But she would have taken into account that her lover might not be willing to marry her in the wake of a divorce.

In support of Hugh's belief she would have done the sensible thing was her acceptance of her arranged marriage to a man she had scarcely met. She had understood her parents' desire to make sure she and her little sister were provided for once her brother had died without a son, because the property would be lost to their family on her father's death. What a pity he had not investigated Randolph Cuthbert more carefully.

Killing one's husband would not make sense unless one were certain of being able to do so without being suspected and tried. The penalty for a wife's "petty treason" against her husband was to be burned. Thank God, the woman was almost always strangled first, or so he understood.

Killing his mistress would be a clever way of freeing herself if she could cast enough suspicion on Cuthbert to get him hanged. As he was as yet only the heir of a peer, he would not be tried in the House of Lords, where he would almost certainly be acquitted. Ay, that would be a clever way of disposing of a detested husband. If she had killed the woman, she would have wiped the candlestick with one of her husband's handkerchiefs which she could get as easily as someone had got one of hers. It would certainly not have ended up under the body, where any reasonable person would know it could not have come by accident. That all made sense to him.

But why hide it under the body? Doctor Lockhart had immediately understood what it meant: the handkerchief had been placed there.

The answer came to him so suddenly he tensed, the slight pull on the reins bringing his horse to a sudden halt. The coach rolled on. He breathed in air that carried no scent of human habitation and urged his horse forward.

The murderer had hidden it under the body because he had forgotten to leave it behind, which might explain why the blood had not been transferred to the night rail. A man unnerved by killing might have put the handkerchief in his pocket from force of habit. Then when he realized his mistake, he returned to replace it, but by then the murder had been discovered. He had had to wait until the room was empty, then slip in by whatever method he had used to escape from Lydia's chamber. He could not risk simply dropping it on the floor where those who had found the body would have seen it.

****

Excerpts from letters to Wallace Seaton, Magistrate, Penrith, Cumberland:

From the late Lydia Forsyth's attorney:

...Lydia Forsyth's testamentary dispositions apart from small bequests to several old servants, none larger than ten pounds: to Gwendoline Beddoe, daughter of her cousin, widow, of Norbury, Shropshire, one-half of her monies on deposit, one quarter of her investments, and her house on North Audley Street, Grosvenor Square. To her half sister, Mary Allard Briscoe, commonly known as Manon Allard, employed by Mistress Randolph Cuthbert of Durham, County Durham, one-half of her monies on deposit and three quarters of her investments. I am sorry to hear of Mistress Forsyth's death. She was a sensible woman, very easy to deal with. As she contemplated a second marriage, she asked me to find a way of securing all

her assets so that a hypothetical new husband would have no access to them. As a husband myself, I should have been appalled but as a cold-eyed, cautious man of law, I could only applaud her…

From Thomas de Veil, Magistrate, Bow Street:

…Mr. Cuthbert is well known in some circles, though word has not yet spread to the better sort, he always having been scrupulous in paying debts of honor. His other debts are unpaid and believed to amount to about five thousand pounds. Until recently he contrived to pay them all something on account so none had pressed for immediate payment.

Mistress Lydia Forsyth is accepted as Cuthbert's maîtresse-en-titre, *his liaison with her having endured for some years. I suspect, though I cannot confirm, that Mistress Forsyth either gave or lent Cuthbert the coin to pay at least some of his gambling debts. I deduce this from knowledge of the income he inherited from his father. It was enough to live like a gentleman but not enough to support his lavish manner of living and pay all the debts he incurred. He now receives the heir's stipend, but I have heard nothing to indicate he has made more than token payments to anyone. As he is now heir to his uncle, he is not in immediate danger of debtor's prison.*

…As for the others about whom you inquired, Caleb Hodge is reputed to be honest and is scrupulous in church attendance and his civic responsibilities. That is not proof he is not a villain, as we know, but his workers and clerks speak well of him, which is a far better gauge of character.

Stephen Cuthbert is well liked, is not in debt, and in general behaves more like a decent country gentleman than a man on the town, as it is called. He is witty without spite, a welcome guest and a good friend.

I trust this may be of some assistance. I do not envy you your murder. It sounds a pretty puzzle.

Chapter 15

Hugh heaved a sigh of relief when they arrived at Cuthbert Hall after two long days on the road. The evening was too far advanced to begin questioning the maid with Wallace, but he was willing to wait, being too tired himself to attempt an interrogation. Another few hours for the woman to think up lies and to fret would do no harm. A footman directed him to Keswick in his study. After informing the earl that Manon Allard must be confined and that only Isobel MacDonald and Wallace Seaton should have a key to the chamber, he went to find his cousin.

The footman opened the drawing room door and stood back. Hugh found himself the focus of every eye as he entered. Ismay spoke first. "Welcome back, Sir Hugh. May I pour you a cup of tea?"

Wallace rose to his feet. "With apologies, Mistress Tate, I think Sir Hugh and I have things to discuss." He bowed to her and to the company in general, murmuring a perfunctory "By your leave."

Hugh managed his own bow and a wry smile and "Good evening," before Wallace herded him out into the passage.

In the Yellow Parlor, Wallace poured him a brandy and himself a restorative tonic of some sort. "What did you learn?"

At the inn the previous evening, he had read

through all of the letters from the pseudonymous John Penn and Lydia Forsyth and made notes. "Manon Allard and Lydia Forsyth were sisters."

Wallace choked on his cordial and coughed so long that Hugh thumped him on the back.

"Sorry," his cousin gasped at last. He took several breaths before continuing. "That's better. Sisters?"

"Half sisters. I assume Allard was Lydia's father's by-blow. They appear to have known each other since childhood and to be close. Have been close," he amended. He added a few more details, like Manon's bank account.

"That's an odd twist, indeed. She may know a great deal about Lydia's affairs. You brought her here rather than take her deposition?"

"I believe there's a good deal more to be learned from her than she was willing to divulge. There were several passages referring to Lydia's intended marriage to an unnamed man, as soon as, and I'm quoting, '…the Impediment is no more.' Another included a reference to Manon leaving Eilidh for a better position."

"Well, well. No clue to the man's identity?"

"No." Hugh felt certain he must be Cuthbert, but the letters were too discreet to prove it.

"Given that her relationship with Cuthbert was no secret and taken together with your 'John Penn's' letters, I'd say Cuthbert was Lydia's intended groom. Can you think of anyone else who would want reports on Eilidh's activities? I'll read those letters tonight, Hugh."

He pulled the thick packet out of his bulging pocket and passed them over. "Wallace, I'd suggest not leaving them here."

"Don't teach your granny to suck eggs. Did you tell anyone you had the letters?"

"No, though our reluctant witness knows, of course, as do the magistrate and constable in Durham. The earl will allow no one access to Allard except Isobel MacDonald and you and I, of course."

"Good. While I read these in my room with my door locked," Wallace said drolly, "you may wish to read the letters I received to my inquiries and my recent interview with Cuthbert. I took it down verbatim with notes about his demeanor."

"I envy your ability to write so quickly." That was a useful skill he himself did not possess. When he tried, his script came out as pot hooks and mice feet. Then there was the annoyance of having to sprinkle each sheet with pounce and manage to pour it back into its pot without getting it all over the desk.

That reminded Hugh of the thing he had not thought to mention, being almost entirely intent on what he'd learned from the letters. "I believe the killer absentmindedly took the handkerchief away with him and failed to return it to the room until after the murder was discovered but before Lockhart removed the body. He had to conceal it where no one could have seen it during that time. If it had dried, there would be no blood stain on the smock or whatever that garment was. Someone was supposed to be on guard outside the door from the time the boy got in and let the earl in, but 'supposed to be' isn't necessarily 'was.' "

"I'll question the carpenter's boy and the footman who took his place."

"Wallace, we can't assume the murderer simply evaded the footman somehow both in entering and leaving."

"Do you still think there may be a secret entrance?"

"We seem to have proven that's impossible. Yet even with half the number of footmen on the first floor on Michaelmas, how could all of them miss seeing him enter the chamber and then leave it? And not see him the next day, either, when he returned the kerchief?"

"When you put it like that, I have to concur. It would be as easy to believe it done by witchcraft, which would be nonsense. We're missing something, that's all. Maybe one of us will think of the answer overnight."

"I'll walk you up to your bedchamber. Ah…it might be a good idea to sleep with Lydia's and Penn's letters under your pillow."

"You really are uneasy," his cousin observed.

"It may sound ridiculous, but if there is a secret entrance into that suite, why wouldn't there be others, too?"

Hugh read over Wallace's session with Randolph Cuthbert in his chamber by the light of two candles, justifying the extravagance by his need to read quickly and without straining his eyes. It was revealing but not informative. He hoped Wallace was being equally free with Keswick's wax.

Q: How well did you know the victim, Lydia Forsyth?

A: She was invited to many of the same events my wife and I attended in town where her wealth made her acceptable, if not her breeding.

Q: I suppose you knew something of her life and connections from her or from gossip, for there's always talk, isn't there?

A: She was a widow left in good circumstances by her late husband. She was lively and amusing in company. That is the sum of my knowledge of her. *NOTE: I am sure he was not being entirely truthful as he seemed ill at ease.*

Q: As someone previously acquainted with her, if not intimately, which is true of no one else here, can you think of any reason someone would want to murder her?

A: No.

Q: None at all?

A: I have said I do not know.

Q: No scorned lover, jealous wife, heir anxious to inherit from her?

A: *Note: a long hesitation before he spoke.* I don't like to say this, but Mistress Cuthbert is a jealous woman. I have no idea why she thought I was having an affair with Mistress Forsyth. I swear I am not. I will not claim I've never used a courtesan. Men have needs, and Mistress Cuthbert and I live separately for most of the year. Even when we are in the same house, we seldom share a bed by her choice, as is living apart. *Note: much of this speech sounded as stiff and unnatural as many actors' speeches. One might ascribe it to embarrassment at having to make such admissions. I thought he told too much with too little reluctance. I would expect to have to drag each confidence out of him.*

Q: Mr. Cuthbert, at about what time did you enter the south wing?

A: I believe I told your assistant when last I was questioned that I paid no attention to the time.

Q: I do remember that. But do you recall whether it

was before or after Mistress Cuthbert's mishap with the ale?

A: I think it was after that.

Q: What was your purpose in entering the house?

A: Why would anyone have done so who had been drinking ale, except to visit the jakes?

Q: Lydia Forsyth's murderer reached her chamber. Someone must have observed that person going upstairs. Did you see anyone go upstairs?

A: No, I do not recall seeing anyone do so. But there are two staircases in each wing.

Q: A guest could not enter through the french windows between the wings, the door in the east end of either wing, or the front entrance without being seen by the servants. We know the period during which the murder took place. We are interested in anyone who entered around that time.

A: Unless the person was already inside. *Note: He did not expand upon this statement.*

Q: Or unless he or she entered before or shortly after you. How long were you inside?

A: I cannot say as I did not look at my pocket watch.

Q: Surely you have an idea of how long you were in the gentlemen's retiring room? *Note: This question disconcerted him.*

A: I did not go to the retiring room. The sun was hot, and I was finding so much rustic buffoonery tedious. I retreated to an unused room in the south wing to restore my spirits.

Q: With spirits?

A: (Laughing) Yes. A nipperkin of brandy and peace and quiet.

Q: Which one?

A: I beg your pardon?

Q: In which room did you take refuge?

A: Oh. The one after the muniment room. *Note: He hesitated slightly here. I am not sure if it was because he was lying or because he was reluctant to tell me. From your excellent plan, the door to that room would not be visible from the doors at either end of the wing.*

Hugh finished reading the account of Cuthbert's interrogation and set it aside. Tomorrow they would question Manon Allard.

Chapter 16

The Eleventh Day

When Kitty arrived with the wash water in the morning, she overflowed with news. "Such doings last night, Mistress Cuthbert," she whispered as if they might be overheard.

"Whatever happened?" She had heard no disturbance, and the only thing of interest that had occurred yesterday was Hugh's return from Durham while they were drinking tea in the drawing room after supper. He had vanished with Wally Seaton without pausing to do more than bid the company a distracted "good evening."

"I'm that sorry, your ladyship, but your own maid was brought here in chains and locked up in one of the empty rooms for maidservants in this wing. Such a trouble there was over it as Lord Keswick had to send for the carpenter to put on a hasp and staple for a padlock, and lucky he had one or someone would have been sent to wake the smith in Penrith."

"What?" She had often wished Manon at Jericho but in chains and apparently under arrest? That strained her credulity.

"Ay, Sir Hugh Montgomery brought her and a great, fierce Scotswoman to guard her."

Her first reaction had been that this was merely a

misunderstanding blown up out of recognition. But the "fierce Scotswoman" was surely Isobel, so there must be a shred of truth there.

"You say Allard is confined on the second floor?"

"She is. 'Twas Rufus went up with the Scotswoman to take the prisoner's wash water and breakfast and replace the chamber pot."

"How remarkable" was all Eilidh found to say. She wanted to find Hugh or Wallace and learn if Kitty's report was correct. She wanted to go to Isobel and be comforted as her old nurse turned lady's maid turned housekeeper had done when she was younger. She knew she could not seek out her old friends who had been keeping a certain distance from her in public to avoid any accusation of bias. She must be patient until after breakfast when she could find Isobel.

After scrambling into her clothing, distractedly eating something from the dishes set out in the dining room, and drinking a cup of tea, she went in search of reassurance and unquestioning love.

She found Isobel MacDonald by asking Mistress Dankworth, the housekeeper, and stole up the servants' stair. Finding where Manon Allard was being held posed no difficulty: it was the only room with a padlock on the door. The one to the left was Isobel's.

When she saw Eilidh, her old nurse threw her arms around her as though she were still a little girl in need of a hug and pulled her into her chamber.

"Sit down and tell me how it is with you, lass. When Sir Hugh brought us the news, I'd near have sold my soul to come to you, and so I told him when he needed a woman to watch Allard."

"It's been..." How could she describe it without

giving Isobel cause to worry? "It's been horrid. I am sure we all find ourselves looking at each other as we drink our tea and wonder which one of us killed that woman. I don't see how anyone who was not staying in Cuthbert Hall could have got in and found her chamber. I do not believe for a minute that one of the servants did it."

"Then Sir Hugh and Wallace Seaton will find out who she angered enough to provoke her own death. The pair of them had good brains as lads."

"Isobel, what's worrisome to me is that there are not many guests here, and I cannot think of any reason for one of them to want her dead."

"Someone must have, or she wouldn't be dead," her old nurse averred, which was only common sense.

In the magistrates' eyes, the two most likely suspects would be Eilidh and Randolph Cuthbert. Yet she had not cared Randolph spent time with Lydia, indeed welcomed it during the early months of their marriage when they still lived together. Nor could she believe her husband had killed Lydia after fourteen years or more as her lover. Whatever her attraction was seemed not to have waned.

"There are two complications," she admitted, knowing she had to tell her old nurse. "One is that the door was latched and they have not discovered how someone left the room after killing her."

"I suppose some fools are claiming it was by magic or the faeries or such nonsense. That might pass in Scotland where some folk still believe in witchcraft."

"There has been some muttering about that. The other thing is that one of my handkerchiefs was found with the body."

Isobel's placid reply—"Taken from the laundry or delivered to the wrong chamber, I suppose"—warmed Eilidh. Isobel would not suspect her, even after hearing the worst and knowing what she did.

"It was one of the good set my mother made, that I don't use."

"The pretty ones? Then it was stolen."

"Yes, and Hugh and Wallace believe that, as well. But that is the only clue that points at her possible murderer." Her voice broke. "I'm so frightened, Isobel."

"Ay, you're looking drawn and tired. Mark my words, you are fretting without cause. Sir Hugh will make all right. We all know you did not kill that light-skirts."

Who did Isobel's "we all" encompass? Not Randolph Cuthbert. Her husband had no more love for her than she had for him and did not hesitate to say things he must know would wound her, but why did he seem to want her to be guilty? Neither he nor the earl would welcome a scandal like that. Unless Randolph wanted so badly to be rid of her that he did not care about his and the family's reputation.

She squeezed her eyes shut against the tears before admitting to Isobel what she could not bear to tell anyone else.

****

They began questioning Manon Allard at nine of the clock by taking her to the chamber where Lydia Forsyth had died. She walked slowly around the room, studying everything. When she came to the door into the dressing room, she stopped. After a moment, she opened it and stood staring into the narrow little room.

Then she closed it and continued her circuit.

It ended at the place her half sister had fallen, the carpet spotted by a few drops of dried blood. The candlestick, traces of blood visible in the moldings, had been returned to where it had lain with the broken candle. Gazing at the dressing table she said, "*Ma pauvre soeur*. She would have hated such disorder."

Wallace asked about the perfumes.

"She had others and chose the scent best suited to her company. She liked the light perfumes because they contrasted to the heavy ones many ladies wear even during the day." She touched the top of the red bottle with one elegant forefinger. "She said the heavy scents were best kept for seduction."

"Can you tell if anything is missing? Or if something is here you would not expect? You may inspect the contents of the drawer."

She proceeded methodically. "I do not know everything she would have brought," the woman said. "However, she has here the things I know she would need."

"We were told she meant to read a little before retiring for the night. The Cuthbert maid who helped her undress saw a small, red book. Do you know if she owned such a volume?"

"I never saw it though she did tell me of a pretty and amusing little book. She wished she had been given it before her marriage. The title was something about a married lady and her young cousin talking, about the intimacies of the bed, I think."

They watched as she went through the clothes press. "I see nothing I would not expect, and nothing is missing that she should have had with her. I knew she would bring the red brocade robe à l'anglaise and the blue riding habit because she mentioned them in one of her letters. They were favorites and precisely what she would wear at a nobleman's country house."

She was now quite comfortable in their presence.

Before bringing her down to the room, Hugh had moved the armchairs some distance from the table and had a footman bring in a ladderback chair which he placed at the table.

"That is most helpful," Wallace said and asked her to be seated in the armchair facing away from the table. Out of her line of sight, Hugh took his place at the table and opened his notebook. Wallace would ask the questions while Hugh took down the answers, as she was likely to respond better to his cousin's avuncular manner than to him, when she resented Hugh for his treatment of her. They had prepared a list of points beforehand.

"I need a little more information from you in order to find her murderer," Wallace began and asked how long she had served as Mistress Cuthbert's maid. Her answer agreed with what they already knew from Eilidh and Isobel.

He went on to ask how she liked her position.

"My wages are adequate and Mistress Cuthbert is not demanding, though in Durham there is no challenge for my skills. Also it is difficult to make a lady of fashion of one so thin and with such hair and freckles."

"How did she come to employ you?"

"She needed a maid familiar with London fashions. I was recommended to her."

"By whom?" Wallace inquired. "I have often wondered how a lady acquires an experienced maid."

"Mr. Cuthbert," Manon admitted reluctantly.

Wallace waited.

"I suppose some friend of his gave him my name."

"Was it your sister?"

That shook her composure. She had not guessed how much they had gleaned from her letters. Perhaps as Hugh had suspected in Durham, she thought that if they could not read French they would not bother with them.

When she sat silent, Wallace spoke. "Come, the victim calls you her sister in several of her letters. You are her half sister, I assume, her father's by-blow."

"That is correct. What can I say? These embarrassments occur."

"Usually such half siblings never meet, however."

"I lived with my *maman* who had been a lady's maid on my father's property. Her marriage was arranged to his head groom. Lydia had no other sisters. I had no sisters or brothers, and the village children were not kind to me. Lydia and I met by accident as children and became friends."

"Did she give your name to Cuthbert as a suitable maid for his bride?"

"Yes. I was not happy with my place as maid to a Cit's fat, stupid wife."

"Why did Lydia not employ you?"

"That would not have been…" She searched for a word. "*Convenable*. I understood that and agreed."

"She did not want to treat her sister as a servant," Wallace suggested.

"That is it, exactly."

"I am surprised you did not accompany Mistress Cuthbert on her visit here."

"We were told there were not enough rooms for all

the servants who were coming," she replied slowly. "But now I am here, I find that at least two rooms for female servants were available for I am confined in one and the dreadful MacDonald is in another. It must be there was some mistake, or else guests did not after all come who intended to do so."

His cousin pulled his left earlobe, considering how to proceed. "Yet this chamber has a cot in the dressing room," he pointed out. "Though perhaps as Cuthbert was your sister's lover and they were both staying here, it would not be quite, ah, *convenable* to have a maid sleeping there, even if illicit encounters are commonplace at house parties."

Manon made an ineffably French gesture. "That is true," she admitted.

"Still," Wallace continued, "to arrange to have his known *chère amie* installed at a family party and in a better chamber than his wife's is ill-bred."

"What of it? With such a wife as his, what else could he do? She would not live in town except for a month or two now and then, and she was so cold to him, it was like lying with a corpse."

"Well, he would say that, wouldn't he? Unfaithful husbands do try to justify their infidelity. Why did your sister let you toil as a maid instead of acknowledging you?"

Manon's eyebrows rose. "One must be practical. A peer of the realm might do so, but for anyone else, it would be social ruin. She is—was—very kind to me. When I no longer work, I will live comfortably."

"You said earlier your wages are 'adequate.' Mistress Cuthbert's house is in a street I imagine a Frenchman would call bourgeois, with too few servants and shabby furnishings. Mr. Cuthbert chose the house, and as we know he has debts, I doubt he allows much to pay his wife's servants. You could have worked for one of the most fashionable ladies in London. Instead you have wasted your talents on Mistress Cuthbert." Wallace did it well, Hugh having primed him with a detailed description. He smiled inwardly at the charge the maid had wasted her talents on his old friend. True enough, though not because of any flaw in Eilidh. Like some jewels, she shone best in a simple setting.

"Why did you do so, Manon?"

Her lips curled in distaste. "My sister asked it of me. Also she made up the difference between what I could earn in London as dresser to a lady of the beau monde and what Cuthbert would pay."

"Would pay or could pay?"

"What he could afford, I think. He wished always to live *en grand seigneur*. Alas, he was only third in the order of succession when the earl arranged his marriage to an heiress. You are aware Lord Keswick's last son died only half a year since, making Randolph the heir?"

"Ay," said Wallace.

"It is too bad she will be a countess when she lacks the style and desire to be a great lady."

It is too bad Cuthbert is a lout and will be an earl, Hugh thought. He forced down his annoyance as his cousin asked, "What was the marriage Mistress Forsyth anticipated making?"

Faint lines creased her forehead. "That foolishness! I love my sister, but she dreamed of marrying Cuthbert someday. You have read her letters. Of late, she spoke as if it was both certain and imminent. She had convinced herself Mistress Cuthbert's health was so fragile that she would die soon, although I told her I saw no sign of such an occurrence. Her ladyship is as strong as a horse and healthier, for horses are subject to many weaknesses and ailments. This I know for my mother's husband was head groom at the estate of our father."

"So it was only the bad air of London which made it necessary for her to avoid the city?"

"Bah. She did not like London's noise, dirt, and bustle." Manon bit her lip. "I will say also that if a man treated me so slightingly, I would not wish to spend time in his presence. I told Lydia she was not sickly despite her thinness and pallor."

"Yet she was so certain the lady would oblige her by dying that Lydia spoke of your getting a new position soon," Wallace pointed out.

"My sister mistook her hope for fact and would not be convinced. She was in love." She shrugged. "She could have had her choice of many men, but she preferred Cuthbert, I think because they were much alike in many ways."

"Such as?"

Wallace's question perplexed her. When she replied, she seemed to be talking more to herself than to them. "They both knew what they wanted and were determined to have it. If he thought himself a *grand seigneur*, she thought herself a great lady because, although her papa had only a little manor and not much money, her husband's father had been a marquess. Even though Mr. Forsyth had lowered himself by making a fortune in shipping, he was accepted because of his father and therefore so was she. But as the widow of a man in commerce, now with only distant connections to a peer, she no longer possessed the same standing."

"She was rich, beautiful, and very well dressed. I'd think she would have had no difficulty making a second marriage with a titled man," Wallace ventured.

"She could have made a good marriage, if not in the upper nobility, as I pointed out often. A viscount or a baron should have satisfied her. Alas, she had not my mother's practicality. Her heart was engaged. She wanted him and only him, and when he became the earl's heir, she felt fate was making possible a title and marriage to the man she loved."

"That does not sound wholly rational."

"And so I thought as well, Mr. Seaton. But it made her happy, so I gave up arguing with her. He might have been as good a husband as most, and she did know his ways."

Hugh knew the interview was reaching its end when Wallace said, "A lady's maid is often blamed for her mistress's choices. Were you not humiliated to have Mistress Cuthbert appear dressed in clothing that did not flatter her?"

She threw her hands up, palms outward. "That man! One would think he would wish his wife to make as good an appearance as possible whether he loved her or not. But no! He ordered me to make her fashionable. The styles and colors do not suit her." Her sharp eyes narrowed. "Sometimes I have suspected he knew as much, for he was always point-device himself."

"I believe we have no more questions for the moment. Sir Hugh, please ask the footman to summon Mistress MacDonald."

"What do you make of that?" Seaton asked when they were alone.

"I deduce she loved her sister and either the victim loved her, as she claimed, or else Manon was blackmailing her. How many servants have an account at Andres and Barlow or any other bank?"

"A vanishingly small number, I imagine. Still, she answered most of our questions with no hesitation or evasion."

"She was surprisingly cooperative," Hugh agreed. "Especially considering her behavior in Durham."

Wallace chuckled. "How would you react if someone, even a magistrate, demanded to search your home?"

"I'd be furious."

"So would I. Allard's response seems perfectly normal to me."

"Viewed in that light, I suppose it was."

"Hugh, do I recall that when you questioned her there, she accused Eilidh of the murder?"

"What she said amounted to more of a suggestion than an accusation."

"Today she seemed to feel some sympathy for Eilidh even if she still regards her as unattractive."

Hugh's notes were not as detailed as his cousin would have written, but he remembered an impression he had received and made clear in his own cryptic phrases. "She doesn't like Cuthbert."

"No, she doesn't, does she? Is it jealousy of Cuthbert's relationship with Lydia or something else?"

"I would like Cuthbert to be guilty, so I'm inclined to think she is suspicious of him. And we cannot verify he was where he said he was or for how long after he entered the south wing. That reminds me: Lydia's door was guarded from the time the carpenter's assistant entered the room and unlatched it. The earl's first words to him were to stand outside until a footman came to take his place and let no one in. The boy was so proud of having been part of such a thrilling event that when the footman arrived about fifteen minutes later, the lad questioned his right to be in the passage until the man told him he'd been sent by the earl to stand guard."

Wallace chuckled. "Did the footman give him a cuff for impertinence?"

"Ay. The footman swears that while he was there, which was until the body was removed, the only people to go into the room were the earl, you and I, the doctor, and the two footmen who carried the body down to the wagon. I believe him. About halfway through his sentry duty, his need to relieve his bladder became so urgent that he urinated into a vase of flowers on the hall table outside Eilidh's chamber. No one could have entered because he kept looking up and down the passage in terror of being discovered."

Laughing, Wallace agreed that he must be telling the truth.

An hour later, after Hugh viewed the chart showing everyone's actions and the times as best as could be determined, which Wallace had revised in Hugh's absence, they discussed the letters from London.

"There's little we haven't heard hinted at," Wallace said. "De Veil confirms what Eilidh's housekeeper told you, that the Forsyth woman was Cuthbert's mistress for years. Here their conduct would be considered shocking. In London?" He grimaced. "A lady needs an escort, and husbands and wives often do not attend the same events. That was accepted as was her status as his mistress. As Eilidh was living in Durham, many would have considered it not unreasonable."

Cuthbert's discourtesy to his wife, his openly parading his mistress around London, and his failure to pay his debts made him a scoundrel, in Hugh's opinion. Keeping an impartial mind was not easy when the matter concerned Eilidh.

He said, "The attorney's letter seems to rule out inheritance as a motive for murder unless either the first cousin once removed in Shropshire or Manon Allard had an accomplice here."

"Unless the cousin has a family member or friend who is part of this gathering, we can probably acquit her of making away with her aunt. A letter to the magistrate for Norbury may elicit some information about the Beddoes female. More delay." His cousin tutted irritably. "Who would be Allard's accomplice here?"

"Not Eilidh. The Hodges or the Wilmots? Unlikely because what would they have to gain, and what would their connection to Manon be? I can't see what connection Ismay could have to Eilidh's maid, and I can't imagine her wielding a candlestick, can you? Stephen Cuthbert? Almost anyone might do murder under the right circumstances, and he would be familiar with the house. If she were blackmailing him, he would have a motive. Though from de Veil's letter, Stephen does not sound like a man who would have a secret. What about Randolph Cuthbert? Could she have threatened him somehow?"

"She could hardly threaten him that she would tell his wife. About his debts? Those are no secret. Then, too, they'd been lovers for years, and you say Manon Allard believed they loved each other. We must look for someone who hated or feared Lydia."

Wallace was the voice of reason, and he was correct. Hugh could not be so dispassionate about this crime and could not ignore the reason. *What a curst coil!*

"Is it possible that the murderer is among the servants rather than the guests? Someone with a grudge against Lydia for whatever reason? Has she ever been here before? Or could someone who wanted her dead have obtained work here—no, that won't fadge. I beg your pardon, Wallace, I wasn't thinking."

"No, clearly not. You always were Eilidh's best friend, and you're worried for her. I don't believe she's guilty either, but my heart is not engaged. That makes a difference."

Dear Lord. Do I love her? The rational half of his brain told him he did, despite the passage of years and her marriage. "Is it so noticeable?"

"Yes, to someone who knows you well. I don't think Eilidh is aware of your sentiments."

Thank God.

"I want to question Cuthbert again."

They had no obvious cause to suspect the earl's heir except his relationship with the victim, untruths he had told, and his unexplained absence for over an hour. They also had a handful of bits and pieces that had no direct bearing on why Lydia would have been murdered or why Cuthbert might have killed her.

Wallace pointed out that questioning him again was fraught with risks. Pondering their best approach, he said, "I fear Cuthbert will object to more questions and complain to Keswick, who will not understand why 'tis necessary. I shouldn't care to explain our reasons to the earl. If they do not convince him, he may get the wrong idea."

"The wrong idea that his heir is a suspect?" Hugh asked, dry as dust.

"Ay, that wrong idea." Wallace smirked.

"We need a harmless reason to talk to Cuthbert. Telling him we want his opinion about others' motives might work, if he's flattered by our seeking his advice."

"And I'd like to ask how he knew of that room by the muniment room," his cousin admitted. "From what I've seen of him, he'd be more likely to tell the earl and have the room kept locked as the steward's office and the muniment room are."

Their opportunity came before they settled on an approach that would not alarm Cuthbert.

They were crossing the Great Hall when a footman approached to inform them Lord Keswick wished to see them in his study.

"I recall this sensation from my days at school," Wallace remarked. "When the headmaster demanded my presence, you know."

"So do I."

They found him staring out the window, either at the gentle land to the south or at nothing. He turned, hard-faced, as the footman announced them.

He dispensed with even a cursory greeting. "My groom heard talk in Penrith today." He waved them to chairs and dropped into the one behind his desk.

"What kind of talk?" Wallace inquired, his tone unconcerned. Hugh admired his acting ability.

They had heard of the whispers at the alehouse near Cuthbert Hall, where most of the patrons were either servants of, or related to, those who worked for the earl. The ones who weren't knew better than to make an enemy of the nearest nobleman.

"There is a troublesome rumor that Mistress Cuthbert accomplished her rival's death by magical means. Ridiculous, of course, but with a beautiful woman brutally murdered in a locked room and another woman's handkerchief found with the body, would you expect them not to speculate about witchcraft?"

Hugh's sidelong glance at Wallace met his cousin's own oblique look.

"You refer to the way the killer escaped the chamber, I apprehend, my lord."

"Of course that's what I mean, Seaton," he snapped, exasperated. "But some think the whole was carried out the same way, with no person in the room at all, which explains the fact the door was locked. We all know the power of rumor does not depend upon fact or logic."

"That is unsettling, but we cannot let ourselves be influenced by the opinions of the ignorant," Hugh said when Wallace did not speak at once.

"That's all very well, but we cannot ignore it. On the market day after the event, no one but the coroner and a few others would have heard of it," Keswick said. "But Penrith is second only to Carlisle in size. Anyone not stone deaf would have known of it by yesterday's market. By today or tomorrow, the story will be all over the north, spread by those who came to town from some distance."

Hugh could imagine the tidbit figuring in the *Newcastle Courant*. It would not mention sorcery, but there would be no need to do so. The known facts by themselves would suggest it and also Eilidh's guilt, though her name would not be mentioned. In another week, the rest of the country would be chewing over the facts and theorizing.

"Annoying," Wallace conceded. "However, we are all rational men living in an enlightened era." Smiling slightly, he added, "We cannot bring a charge of murder carried out by witchcraft. That would be a crime under the Witchcraft Act of 1735 and would subject us to possible imprisonment. You might escape that fate, being a peer, of course."

Rather than being angered, the earl gave a short laugh. "I'd forgotten the Act. I'd not want to be held as foolish as that Scottish lord who opposed the law." His amusement died a quick death. "But you still have no suspect and no idea how the murderer entered or left the chamber. Meanwhile the damage to my family's reputation grows. Do you have no suspect?"

Wallace glanced at Hugh. "We have a person about whom we have grave suspicions, but we need more proof."

"Damme, surely you can get whatever proof you need and a confession by close interrogation."

"That is not yet likely, my lord. There are difficulties." Like the drawback of Cuthbert being the earl's heir.

Wallace continued, "At present we have no motive. We must have patience and continue building a case that cannot be dismissed or end in the guilty person being found innocent."

Keswick studied his sapphire signet ring. "I would find it easier to wait except that Cuthbert is troubled by it."

"How so?"

The man clenched his fist. "He has confessed to me that his wife is bitterly jealous of any pretty woman to whom he addresses more than a civil greeting."

"Is he accusing her of the murder?" Hugh inquired. He found it a struggle to keep the anger out of his voice.

"No, but he is aware of how those facts would look to others. With the ignorant talk of witchcraft as well, he fears for her."

"Does he?"

Keswick failed to recognize Wallace's skepticism. Hugh heard it only because he knew his cousin.

"Yes. He worries that some bumpkin will try to harm her."

"In Cuthbert Hall?" Wallace asked in polite disbelief.

"When she rides or walks, if she goes beyond the gardens close to the house."

"Then she should be safe enough if she stays inside or near the house." Hugh watched Keswick, sensing he had some other trouble on his mind.

"I do not like to tell you this because I had to pry it out of Cuthbert. He tells me her spirits are so low he fears for her life. I suppose that is understandable if she is guilty and now feels remorse or realizes..." He did not finish the sentence.

Hugh turned to Wallace. "Have you noticed this, Seaton?"

"I have not, Montgomery. My lord, have you seen any sign of melancholia in Mistress Cuthbert?"

"No, but my nephew knows her far better than any of us."

Water from a dry well, was Hugh's opinion.

"I see," Wallace said, a careful reply that neither agreed nor disagreed.

Time was not their friend. Could they turn this meeting to account?

"Your lordship, we would like to ask Mr. Cuthbert a few more questions."

The earl raised his eyebrows inquiringly. "You've questioned all of us more than once without my permission, which I would certainly not withhold if you requested it. Why ask my approval now?"

"Mr. Cuthbert is your heir, my lord."

"And as such deserves special treatment?"

"I wouldn't say he 'deserves' it, Lord Keswick, but we all know that titled men and their families have privileges ordinary commoners do not." Wallace added, "We questioned you only once."

"That's true. I erred in saying otherwise. Why have you not interviewed me again?"

"You were on display continually all day. Everyone we questioned saw you at one time or another, and from the chart we put together of the guests' and your movements, there appeared to be no opportunity for you to be absent during the period Lydia Forsyth was murdered."

"And if I had killed her?"

Hugh responded, knowing he was taking a slight risk, but that it would be greater for his cousin. "If you had, there was only an infinitesimal chance the Lords would bring in a verdict of guilty, so attempting to make a case for your guilt would have been a waste of time. We would have agreed that Mistress Forsyth had been murdered by some unknown person whose identity could not be discovered."

Unexpectedly, the earl grinned. "Just as well I didn't murder the woman, then. Will you tell me why you want to interrogate Cuthbert again?"

They had agreed on their reply should Keswick ask their reason.

"New details have come to our attention which we hope Mr. Cuthbert may be able to confirm or disprove. He was in the south wing during the time the murder occurred or at least part of the time. We hope he may have seen or heard someone else while he was there."

"I suppose most of the men must have been there at some point, and the footman at the door should remember some, at least."

"Unfortunately, although we know when he went in, Cuthbert cannot say how long he was there, nor does the man on duty at the door recall when he came out."

"In the jakes? Not usually a long visit, I'd suppose."

Wallace cleared his throat. "He was not in the, ah, gentlemen's retiring room, sir."

"Then where was he?"

"There is a small chamber beyond the muniment room. He said he wished to get away from the crowd and the sun and have a sip of brandy."

"If he wanted brandy and shade, he could have had them out of doors and he need only have walked a short distance to get away from most of those present."

Hugh began, "He may have chosen to go inside because he could sit down. There are chairs there." He feared he would have to reveal the servants' unauthorized lair.

Keswick contemplated them for a long moment, lips pursed. "And he cannot guess how long he lingered there?"

"No, sir." Wallace's brief reply gave no hint of whether he believed Cuthbert or not.

"I believe I should like to be present when you talk to him," the earl said. "If you have no objections, Seaton? Sir Hugh?"

Only one answer was possible. They both maintained suitably grave faces. *Huzzah!*

When Cuthbert presented himself in response to the earl's summons, he seemed surprised to find Hugh and his cousin there. Keswick tersely explained that they had a few more questions. Hugh and his cousin had been sitting before the desk. Now the earl said, "As there are three of you, you may as well use the chairs by the fireplace," and gestured them toward it.

"I don't know how much more help I can be," Cuthbert said deprecatingly, sauntering in that direction. Wallace flanked him on the left. Reading his intention Hugh went to Cuthbert's right so that his cousin and he sat in the chairs at ninety degree angles to Cuthbert's, whose back was to the desk.

Wallace trotted out their query as to whether he had seen or heard anyone in the passage.

"I think Mr. Simmons came in after I did, Seaton." He smiled guilelessly.

"On his way to the gentlemen's retiring room," Wallace agreed.

"Did you see or hear anyone else on your way to the apartment after the muniment room?"

"No."

"Or after you were in the room?"

"I had closed the door, so naturally I could not see anyone, Montgomery."

"You might have heard someone pass, as the hall floor is uncarpeted."

Cuthbert frowned in thought. "I may have, though the door is thick. I really don't remember."

Wallace commented, "I suppose you relaxed by building a house of cards or casting dice?"

"No, I simply sat and rested my brain. My eyes were smarting from the sun. One's tricorne does little to protect them."

"Ah, of course. When I last talked with you, you spoke as if you had only a slight acquaintance with Lydia Forsyth. We are now aware you had been her lover for many years." Wallace let the statement hang in the air, waiting for Cuthbert's response.

At his desk, the earl was out of Cuthbert's sight. With his head angled slightly to the left toward Cuthbert, Hugh caught Keswick's twitch. Evidently the news came as a surprise to the earl.

"I suppose you listened to my wife, who is given to jealous imaginings."

"We learned of your relationship with the woman from Manon Allard, your mistress's sister. They had an active correspondence."

That shot hit home: Cuthbert's eyes widened for a fleeting moment.

At the periphery of his vision, the earl compressed his lips.

"Well," Cuthbert began, "a gentleman should not speak of such affairs when a lady is involved rather than a courtesan."

"I agree with that sentiment as a general rule, but the investigation of a murder is another matter."

Hugh added helpfully, "Because such a

relationship may lead to murder."

"Are you accusing me of murder?" Cuthbert demanded.

Hugh answered before Wallace could speak, to spare his cousin having to cross his fingers. "I am merely explaining why your relationship with the victim matters."

"I see." The flat statement did not convey relief.

They asked him about his and his wife's living arrangements. The earl furrowed his brow on hearing that Eilidh lived in Durham the majority of the year and had for a dozen years.

Keswick cleared his throat and interrupted for the first time. "Cuthbert, I thought Ellen resided at your country house in Kent when she did not reside in London."

Randolph was discomfited for the first time. He turned in his chair to face his uncle. "Ah…Ellen does not care for it, I am sorry to say. She prefers the more bracing northern climate."

His uncle's brows drew together. "All year?"

"No, indeed, sir. She joins me in London during the spring when London is at its best."

The earl frowned over that. "I do not recall meeting her or hearing of her when I was in town. Though I did not visit London this year because of Arthur's death."

"We travel in less elevated circles than yours, my lord. I was never in the habit of boasting of my relationship to the earldom, and I suppose our family name is not so uncommon that those we know would make that connection."

Keswick appeared to accept this humble speech at face value although he did not look satisfied. Hardly surprising. He would doubtless be speaking with Randolph privately.

With the air of someone making a confession, Cuthbert went on, "Ellen does her best, but she finds the air and noise of London taxing." Cuthbert bit his lip as if reluctant to reveal a detail of his marriage. "I will be frank, sir. My wife dislikes fashionable society, and her health is uneven. Sometimes it makes her queer-tempered. She is almost a recluse in Durham."

"You have stated she is jealous," Wallace said.

"She is." He sighed. "She does not want me in her bed, but begrudged me my liaison with Lydia. Everyone understands that men have needs and sometimes resort to widows or courtesans to satisfy them. Everyone except Ellen, that is. I suppose her upbringing is to blame: a rather countrified family and the taint of trade on her mother's side."

Trade that provided the dowry for which you married her, Hugh thought.

"To which you had no objection when I proposed the match," the earl said.

Another sigh. "No," Cuthbert agreed, "and we would have got along as well as most if she were not full of crotchets and whimsies. I fear this recent unfortunate occurrence has quite disordered her mind."

"In what way?" Hugh inquired, contriving to keep the anger out of his voice.

"I do not, needless to say, suppose Ellen murdered Lydia"—which statement somehow implied the opposite—"but the atmosphere of suspicion and the irresponsible chatter about witchcraft have taken their toll on her spirits. I may not love her, but she is my wife, so I am concerned for her. I would be deeply grieved if it became necessary to confine her for her own good, though that would be preferable to something worse."

"Worse?" Wallace queried gently.

Cuthbert stared down to where one well-manicured white hand rested on the arm of his chair. Three fingers of his right hand were tucked into the space made by leaving open two or three buttons of his waistcoat. This was meant to prevent one looking like a bumpkin with dangling hands when they were not occupied. In this instance, Hugh judged it was to keep from fidgeting.

Another dejected exhalation. "Would felo-de-se not be worse? That is a scandal that damns the unhappy sinner and prevents him—or her—from being buried in consecrated ground."

"Have you seen any indication that she might consider such an act?" Wallace's bland face expressed nothing.

"Only her usual morose manner. Though I have seen her ride in a way that would be reckless in a man and dangerous for a female."

He meant Eilidh's riding at a spanking pace and flying over hedges and walls. She had been a fearless rider in her youth and would not fall behind in a foxhunt. The three of them had careered for miles around the countryside.

They learned nothing more and finally let Cuthbert go.

To Hugh's relief, the earl did not ask if they suspected Cuthbert. Before they could take their leave, he said, "My family's reputation will suffer as a result of this business. Dare I hope the scandal will be minor and quickly forgotten, rather than one that will haunt us for decades?"

"We will hope it is the former, Lord Keswick."

If it gave less reassurance than his lordship wished, he accepted Seaton's answer without comment, perhaps bearing in mind Hugh's threat of involving the Lord Lieutenant.

As Hugh and Wallace rose to leave the study, Hugh paused. "My lord, do you know whether there are any secret passages in Cuthbert Hall?"

The man's surprise was so obvious that Hugh's heart fell. "No," the earl said slowly. Then, "By that I mean I have never heard of any, not that there are none. There may be a plan or plans in the muniment room. You are welcome to study them if you think they will be of assistance. God knows I would far rather have a rational explanation than this nonsense about witchcraft. Although I doubt the plan would show a secret passage."

He scrawled a note for his steward. "Fielding is likely in the estate office. If not, have a footman fetch him. Someone will know where he is."

In the Yellow Parlor, his cousin cast himself into an armchair. The sun shone in, falling across his torso. It glinted on the gilt buttons on his coat and revealed dust motes drifting in the air. A carriage rolled past toward the entrance. Several ladies had made a foray into Penrith and must now be returning.

"Wallace?"

Seaton shook his head. "It's nothing. I just need a moment to collect myself. Do you think that went well?"

"It didn't go badly. The earl learned something about Cuthbert which may make it less of a surprise if he is committed for trial. I'll do anything to assist you, Wallace. You know that." *And to safeguard Eilidh.*

"Yet we have no motive for anyone to have killed the woman and do not know how the killer could have reached her chamber or left it without being seen by any of the footmen we questioned. Is that correct?"

"Ay."

"What evidence can we cite against Cuthbert?"

Hugh counted them off on his fingers. "He entered the house at the relevant time, the gap in his whereabouts that evening, his lie about knowing Lydia only slightly—"

"Which could be dismissed as reluctance to become involved, Hugh."

"It could, but he is a liar in other matters as well. He misled his uncle about his marriage, he lied about Allard being ill and unable to come with Eilidh and about Eilidh wanting to be close to the Hodges rather than share the suite with him. According to Stephen Cuthbert, he claimed another student's work as his own, and Hodge doesn't trust him enough to do business with him if Cuthbert had the money. We know he is in debt. Taken all together, those things cast doubt on his character. As a member of the family, he's more likely than a guest to know of a secret passage. There's also his treatment of Eilidh and his arrogance, though they aren't proof of anything."

"The last two are true of many men who are not murderers. But I find the others convincing though they are circumstantial," Wallace said. "If he is guilty, there's proof of it for us to find."

"He has also attempted to blame Eilidh. Is he really so lacking in discretion as to have announced before everyone that her kerchief was used to wipe the candlestick? You and I and the earl are agreed Eilidh shows no sign of…of…"

His cousin completed the thought. "Being troubled in mind or spirit."

"Ay. Certainly not to the point of taking her own life." Something Stephen had said came back to him. "Stephen Cuthbert told me Randolph played on people's emotions to get what he wanted."

"I recall your account of that interview. I didn't really understand from your notes."

"From what he described, that's what he meant."

"He implied Eilidh was guilty, didn't he? And unbalanced enough to take her own life. But that's not working on Eilidh's emotions, only an attempt to persuade Keswick of her guilt or mental state. Perhaps in the hope the earl will influence me to send her for trial." The sound Wallace made deep in his throat sounded like a growl. His next remark was a non sequitur. "Do you think Manon was correct that Cuthbert loved Lydia Forsyth?"

"She appeared convinced of it, and if he did not, the length of their relationship is yet more remarkable."

Wallace, boneless in his chair and lost in thought, grunted. Hugh forbore to interrupt his reflections.

"One thing puzzles me," Wallace murmured finally, "and pray do not say, 'Only one?' "

This mild display of humor was reassuring. "What is it?"

"Assuming Manon is correct and that our surmises about Eilidh's marriage are true, it seems to me that Lydia Forsyth was the wrong victim."

"Are you suggesting…" Hugh could not force

himself to complete the question.

"That if Cuthbert is the murderer, the logical choice would have been our old friend? Yes."

The idea of Eilidh as the victim was as unthinkable as that of Eilidh hanged. He forced himself to consider it anyway.

For all Cuthbert's protestations of being a concerned husband, dislike of his wife had tainted his words like poison. He had painted her as jealous, reclusive, and hysterical, and implied he thought her guilty. He spoke to her unkindly and had deliberately spilled ale on her. "Hysterical" referred to an ailment of the womb and as Eilidh was without children, many would believe the accusation.

Wallace continued his train of thought. "Perhaps becoming Keswick's heir made him realize he needed a son or two. That might have provided the impetus to rid himself of a wife for whom he has no affection, who has given him no heir, and whose dowry he has already wasted. If he killed Eilidh, he would be suspected as murder of one's husband or wife is not unknown. Arranging an accident or a supposed suicide while she was living apart from him in Durham would be a risk. Either he would have to go there to do the deed or he would have to hire a bravo who might then be tempted to blackmail him."

That made sense. "He may have loved Lydia, but she was about Eilidh's age and had no children." Hugh said slowly, "Lydia was the only one here Eilidh might have a reason to kill. With Lydia dead and Eilidh hanged for her murder, he would be free to marry a younger female more likely to breed."

"And with another dowry," his cousin pointed out.

"Wallace, tomorrow we should question Manon again. Let us give her a night to stew."

Chapter 17

The Thirteenth Day

Hugh and Isobel brought the maid down to the Yellow Parlor, the servant's chamber in which she was being held having no place to sit but one wooden chair and a bed.

Hugh and Wallace had reviewed the notes of Hugh's interrogation in Durham and of their joint questioning of Manon in Lydia's chamber to prepare. Her plain gown and kerchief modestly covering her neck and chest made her the picture of a respectable lady's maid. Hugh was pleased to note she had not regained the confidence lost at the place of her sister's death.

"Please be seated. We have a few more questions for you." Wallace gestured her to the settee.

Hugh murmured to Isobel to sit in the farther window seat, less as chaperon than as a witness. He and Wallace took the armchairs facing Manon.

"About Mistress Forsyth's expectation that Cuthbert would marry her..." His cousin cleared his throat. "Pray, forgive me for an indelicate question, mistress, but would she have been able to give Cuthbert an heir, assuming he was free to marry her?"

"There is no reason she could not do so."

"Your sister had no children with her first husband,

did she?"

"No. He was quite old and they were married only two years." She pursed her lips. "Performance was a difficulty, you understand."

"Was there never a pregnancy during the years she and Cuthbert were intimate?"

Manon Allard opened her eyes wide. "The apothecaries' books contain dozens of remedies for bringing on the courses. To fall enceinte would be inconvenient and not *convenable*."

She succeeded in shocking Wallace though not Hugh, who had heard of such things though not that there were so many. They should have changed the order in which they asked their questions to spare Wallace.

His own turn was next. "Your sister believed Mistress Cuthbert was so sickly she must soon die because Cuthbert told her so. We do not understand why Lydia seems to have been convinced despite your assurance she was healthy. I would think she would trust your judgement in the matter over her lover's, who might have mistaken his desire for fact." *Or been lying.*

Her gaze turned inward, she did not reply at once. "I also have wondered about this, sir. She was sensible, yes, in the management of her money and investments. She did not let anyone impose upon her. But she loved him and perhaps she deceived herself. We women do that, sometimes."

"Even you?"

"No, thank God! I want to be comfortable and not take such risks. Though I will admit my *maman* was happy with Briscoe, my *maman*'s husband, who was good to her and to me. However, I have observed such men are seldom to be found."

"She would have been a desirable bride for Mr. Cuthbert."

"Perhaps, Your Worship. Certainly she thought so."

Catching a note of doubt in her voice, Hugh said, "Did you foresee some problem?"

"I believe he loved her as she loved him. Yet the money might have made a problem."

"How so?"

"He was fond of spending his coin. Lydia also spent, but she was careful, like her late husband. Lydia received a great deal of money every year, but the trust would not pay out more than that sum. This was to protect her from suitors who would waste her entire fortune." Her hands clenched more tightly in her lap.

Someone they had questioned much earlier had stated that the earl had been angry with his heir, and then there were Eilidh's old gowns and meager budget. "We know Cuthbert was in debt."

She wrinkled her nose. "I am not surprised. His wife's household allowance was calculated to the shilling. These northern and Scottish women are thrifty and could manage on it, or we would have lived on oatmeal and turnips. Oats are for horses, not people. Even at the prices of a provincial mantua maker, Mistress Cuthbert could afford no more than a gown each year. She did not always order a new one, to save the money. I pitied her, although the most elegant gown could not give her the grace of movement and so would be wasted. MacDonald and I sewed her night rails, smocks, and under-petticoats. Cuthbert did buy Lydia gifts."

"I suspect you do not care for Mr. Cuthbert."

"He is handsome and often charming, and his taste is exquisite. Nevertheless, one cannot like everyone."

"From what you have said, we understand he and your sister were much alike," Hugh said. "In what way did they differ that made you dislike him?"

She tilted her head. Allard was not pretty, but she had elegant, sharply cut features.

"I will try to explain. Lydia loved me because I was her only sister and friend and because I was never her rival as almost all other women were. We each knew we could trust the other. She was also fond of the daughter of her cousin, who was like a niece to her when we young and still lived in Kent." She gave a delicate shrug accompanied by a tolerant smile. "I do not think there was any person in the world Randolph Cuthbert loved except her. He thought everyone was either like him or else existed to be preyed upon. This does not make a man likeable, and he was often discourteous to anyone he considered beneath him unless he wanted something."

Wallace was stirred to ask, "Even to you, though you were Lydia's sister? Assuming he knew as much?"

His cousin had recalled Cuthbert's reaction to hearing of the women's relationship.

"He knew. That was why he wanted me for his wife's maid."

Then his surprise had been at discovering Wallace and Hugh knew of the relationship or mayhap at learning the two had carried on a correspondence, perhaps sharing secrets? Did he wonder if Lydia had confided her anticipated marriage? Hugh hesitated over the phrasing of his next question.

"Would you trust him if you possessed something he wanted or a secret he did not want known?"

"I cannot be certain, because I do not like him and perhaps I am unfair to him. But then, I am a careful woman, so my trust would be limited."

"Let us say he had to choose between the chance of a fortune and Lydia," Hugh suggested.

"But she had a fortune, and he loved her. I am not mistaken about that, even if I do not like him."

"You have not seen him since Sir Hugh brought you here, I believe," Wallace remarked, "but I have observed no signs of bereavement."

"He would not wear his heart on his sleeve. The English," she murmured deprecatingly.

"Lydia was a very wealthy woman. You have said she was both sensible and in love with Cuthbert. What if he found out he would not control her money?"

Manon Allard bit her lip. "He knew. He did not care; he valued her above wealth and would marry her tomorrow if he could. My poor Lydia was so happy when she told me of their conversation. This was two or three years ago. If he had wanted money, he could have found a mistress who would lavish gifts upon him. There are many wealthy women in town who would be happy to have a handsome, attentive lover, and a gift to a lover is not like paying for his services. I think Lydia did give him gifts sometimes."

"Would she have given him five thousand pounds?"

"Five thousand—?" For once Manon Allard's composure cracked. "*Non.* That is not a gift. That is a small fortune."

"That," said Hugh, "is the current amount of his

debt. More or less."

"Faith! Is it truly so much?"

"It is. I begin to wonder if that was what angered his lordship the day the Cuthberts arrived," Wallace mused. "We believe Cuthbert killed your sister."

"A tale of a cock and a bull, Briscoe would say. To murder the woman he loved? I do not believe it. If Mistress Cuthbert had been killed instead, I could believe him guilty."

"As could I," Hugh agreed. "However, he might be suspected of murdering his wife. If his acknowledged mistress were murdered, throwing the blame on his supposedly jealous wife would be simple. Mistress Cuthbert's blood-stained handkerchief was found with Lydia's body, left there to implicate her. If she is convicted, she will be hanged, and he would be free to marry a well-dowered young lady who would come with fewer hindrances than a Cit's widow whose fortune was safely tied up."

A shadow passed over Manon's face and she shook her head. "No. It cannot be."

To Hugh, it sounded less like a denial than a refusal to believe it could be true. "Cuthbert has already prepared the way by dropping hints about her guilt very subtly. He told us and his uncle that she raged at him in her jealousy and is now overcome by melancholy at what he implies she did."

The woman's eyes widened. "Mistress Cuthbert raged? Did she raise her voice and call him bad names? Throw breakable things at him? That I do not believe at all. She possesses great self-control even when she is most angry. I have seen her furious once, accompanying her to the workhouse. She grew quieter and quieter and when she spoke, her words were sharp like the edge of broken glass. I am very glad her anger was not at me. Nor was it at Cuthbert. The governor of the workhouse slapped a girl for spilling some wash water. Mistress Cuthbert is on a committee that deals with the workhouse, you understand, and she reduced him to a schoolboy fearing punishment. She also took the girl into our house to be our maid of all work." Her dark brows came together. "I would not blame her if she did throw things at Cuthbert."

"Then I am surprised you would think she might bludgeon your sister to death. That seems inconsistent for a lady so controlled."

"Have I not said I do not believe it? Someone killed my sister but not she or Cuthbert, I think."

One more weight on their side of the scale would convince her. Later Hugh described it as divine inspiration, half joking. "Manon, during the period your sister died, Cuthbert disappeared from the harvest festivity. We know when he entered the house. He was not seen again until an hour and a half later. He claims he passed the time in a small room the footmen use occasionally, drinking brandy, resting, and perhaps amusing himself with dice. As they were all busy, none of them happened to visit it so no one can confirm he was there."

"And yet no one can affirm he went to Lydia's chamber?"

"No. The house was almost empty except for the kitchen servants and a footman on each floor. None of them saw him."

"With no one in the house, the footmen may not have been attentive," she pointed out.

"That's true," Wallace conceded, "but we cannot think of a way that he could have evaded two or three footmen on two different floors. He would have had to pass at least one to get up the stairs, and another on the first floor."

Her face became as immovable as if she had been turned to a pillar of salt like Lot's wife. Then she swallowed hard, evidently fighting some overwhelming emotion.

"What do you know, Manon?" Wallace, voice gentle. "Are you willing to aid us for your sister's sake?"

"To avenge my sister? Yes. And also to make some amends to Mistress Cuthbert. I am not trusting, but I believed what Lydia said of his wife. Mistress Cuthbert did not like me, and why should she, when she must have guessed I was there to spy upon her and to insist she clothe herself in his choice of gowns. Tchaa! They would look well on some. They did nothing for her." She bit her lip, vexed.

"You have something more to tell us, I think?"

"You have read the letters from my sister, the ones Sir Hugh found, but there is one more." She slipped her hand into the opening at the side of her skirt and withdrew a folded sheet from the pocket beneath it. "Lydia sent me this before she set out for this place." She held it out to Wallace.

Hugh rose to peer over his shoulder as his cousin opened the sheet.

"I do not mind if Sir Hugh reads aloud, translating it if necessary, Your Worship," she added tartly, "as he obviously understands French. I think Lydia feared her letters falling into some other hands than mine, which is why she wrote in that language. I have kept it between my stays and my stomacher since I first read it, until you sent for me today."

Manon, my dear sister,

Such news! I have been invited to the Earl of Keswick's seat near Penrith in Cumberland. There is to be a gathering of mostly family members in honor of Randolph becoming his heir. Randolph has arranged for me to receive the invitation on some pretext. How amusing that I shall be there among his family and with his wife present! We will of course be under closer scrutiny than at the ordinary sort of house party, but he says it will not affect us. He will appear in my chamber as if by magic as he knows a way of moving through the house like a phantom. We will be quite safe from discovery.

He says also it may not be necessary to put off our marriage until the Boney One's ill health kills her. My dear one has confided that his wife's suffering both physical and mental is become so extreme that he anticipates she will soon make away with herself. It is a pity she will perforce be buried as a suicide, which is a dreadful thought. I am sorry to wish the woman to hasten her own damnation, but I console myself that much of her misery is of her own making. Besides, do not coroners' juries sometimes find that a suicide was the result of a disordered mind? That was the finding when Frances Harrington drowned herself in the Serpentine. You remember her, don't you? Short, plump, flaxen-haired, and in despair because that fellow seduced her and vanished. She wasn't even enceinte, which would have made it more understandable. A foolish girl.

I did remind him that he will not control my money, but he assures me that is no obstacle now he receives the heir's allowance and will have great wealth when he inherits the title. I suppose we must wait at least six months to marry. If the Boney One had given him a child (preferably a daughter), we would be able to avoid so long a mourning because the child would need a mama. But at least it will now take place sooner rather than later. I would write more, but I depart early in the morning.

Your affectionate

Lydia

"Eilidh told me he has been pretending to believe her guilty and pouring poison into her ears," Isobel MacDonald cried in the silence that followed Hugh's translation, "trying to convince her she will be tried for the murder and hang unless she kills herself. She almost believes that everyone suspects her. I have not been able to give her much support."

"Because you have had to guard me," Manon said. "I am sorry for that, too."

"Damnation! Seaton, he intends to make sure of her death."

"If he cannot persuade her to self-murder, he would have to make her death look like suicide," Seaton pointed out.

"That devil gave her a vial of laudanum, saying it would help her sleep!" Isobel's hands clenched in her lap. "She hasn't used it. She said something to me about Greeks and gifts."

"A second death would not pass without question."

"It might, Hugh. He has cast suspicion on her without doing it overtly. 'Tis all how concerned he is about her uneasiness and melancholy, and his hints have made her fearful she will hang for the murder. I am no more perceptive than the ordinary man, but I have noticed she is anxious. He may have given up waiting for Eilidh's arrest."

Hugh had seen it, too, in the shadows under her eyes and her restlessness but had ascribed it to the same concern the rest of the guests and the earl felt at the prolonged uncertainty. He forced down his horror; he needed to use his brain, not his heart and gut. "She wouldn't hang herself to escape hanging. Women seldom know much about firearms and even less often use them to kill. A death by laudanum might appear to be believable."

"Cuthbert might think himself free to court another lady for her dowry. But surely the scandal of the murder and his wife's suicide would make many families hesitate to approve him as a suitor," Wallace objected.

Manon spoke again. "The handsome, debonair heir of an earl? He would be set upon by a pack of mamas anxious to see their daughters a countess."

Hugh left Manon writing her deposition with Wallace making sure all the points they had covered were set forth in logical order to twist a rope for Cuthbert's neck.

Luck was with Hugh. Ten minutes later, the steward was rooting through a file box, saying "When I was hired, the estate's documents were all higgledy-piggledy but for the last fifty years or so. In my spare time, I was able to reduce the chaos somewhat. As I recall, I found this"—he held up a square of yellowed, folded sheets—"among a hundred years' worth of personal correspondence, which strictly speaking should not have been taking up space in the muniment room." He passed the packet to Hugh. "If you wouldn't mind reviewing it here, Sir Hugh? You may use my desk and oil lamp, and I will use the smaller one. I cannot permit anyone to remain here alone."

"Thank you. The light will certainly be better," as the muniment room possessed no windows but did have an oil lamp on the steward's desk.

As he gingerly unfolded the sheets, he hoped they would not be damaged by handling and that the ink would not be too faded: they were two centuries old. Carefully smoothing them on the steward's desk, Hugh's first thought was to admire the draftsmanship and the elegance of the antique hand, hard to read even if it had not been so small. His second was relief that they were on parchment, heavy and durable. The draftsman had meant them to last.

The first sheet showed the house as originally built: a long rectangle consisting of the great hall in the center, with the kitchen on one end and a private living area for the family on the other. The outer walls were thick enough to withstand a siege, he estimated, based on the depth of the window alcoves. With a source of sandstone nearby, walls four or five feet thick had posed no difficulty. A grim existence, with the servants sleeping in the hall and little privacy even in the chambers set apart for the family.

The second sheet was the ground floor with the new wings. They were perfectly proportioned and differed from the original construction only in possessing more windows. Notes in one corner specified wood paneling throughout, an improvement over the old building's bare stone interior.

The next was the first floor. Three of the four suites occupying the east and west ends of the wings were unlabeled. The fourth, on the east end of the south wing, was marked "*My Lord of Keswick*" as indeed it remained to this day. That previous earl, with his talent for architecture, had done a fine job of melding the old fortified manor and the additions.

The third sheet was titled "Penthouse," which would now be called an attic story, where the servants' rooms were. Or where they should be. The title must be a mistake, as it was really the second floor. He had gone through it. Why the confusion? And why accommodate servants on a floor no whit different from the one for the family and guests, except that many of the rooms were smaller? Alterations had been made at some time as originally most of the floor had been dormitories, with small chambers at each end for the most important servants. An annotation instructed that the paneling was to be of suitable wood, not oak. Another addendum by a different hand, undated, directed that the long rooms be divided into apartments for one or two.

The division of the dormitories had been a kindness, giving the maids and footmen more privacy, which they would have cherished. While the rooms were small, they were surely more comfortable than the hall's stone floor had been for their ancestors. Hugh wondered idly who had thought of the change. It could not have been very recent, both because the ink was as faded as that from 1535, the date of the plans. The writing was no more modern, either, so the modification must have been an afterthought no more than a few years later.

Did the architect think another story might be needed some day? If so, servants' rooms could be moved to the real attic and the second floor turned into larger bedchambers by removing some of the rather flimsy partitions between the servants' rooms.

The real attics were shown on the fourth sheet. He shook his head. The steward noticed and asked, "Is something wrong?"

"No, not at all. I was merely so fascinated that I forgot why I was looking at the plans." Now he had been jolted out of his preoccupation, he recalled something about the windows in the servants' rooms. They were the same size as the windows on the lower floors with the same deep embrasures. Servants' attic rooms usually had dormer windows set in the slope of the roof, didn't they? He closed his eyes, remembering his examination of the outside of Cuthbert Hall with its peaked roof. All the windows in the wings were the same size and evenly spaced excepting only in the old part of the house, where they were fewer and smaller.

Had there been windows in the roof? He thought not. He had stood for some minutes studying the north wall for any means someone might have used to gain access either from the ground or upper story. It had quickly been apparent that no one could have done so without using a ladder, as the estate carpenter had done.

"Fielding," he said, "I need to have a look at the outside of the house. I'll be back in a few minutes."

"Certainly, Sir Hugh. The plans and I will await you."

Hugh almost bolted for the main entrance. Outside, he looked up and counted the first floor with the Long

Gallery the length of the old manor house. There was another floor above it, the one with the servants' rooms. The same was true of the rest of the house. His heart beat faster as he returned to the muniment room. There were no dormer windows of any kind in the roof.

"Did you find what you were looking for?" the steward asked.

"I think so."

He bent over the sheets once again to search for further anomalies. The first was that there was no floor plan of the attic, but why would there be if there were no rooms there? There was a careful rendering of the gables from peak to eaves, showing the pitch of the roof and the trusses and crossbeams. Notwithstanding that he was no architect or house carpenter, he found their placement strange.

While he pondered what seemed like a foolish sacrifice of space useful for rooms or storage, he noticed the thickness of the wall under the eaves. Referring to the plans of the ground floor and the two stories, he confirmed that the outer walls of the wings were as thick as the original manor's. It could not be an error in the ground plot because the deep window embrasures that provided comfortable seats and wide window sills proved the thickness of the walls. Such fortress-like construction gave him a moment's pause until he remembered that Cumberland had suffered incursions by reivers as late as the seventeenth century.

He folded the sheets up again and thanked Fielding. He retreated to his chamber to ponder the only facts of which he was certain: Lydia Forsyth was murdered by someone who was able to get into her bedroom and out again though the door was latched.

Therefore a means to do so existed. Then there was Lydia's letter to her sister, saying Cuthbert claimed to be able to pass through the house unseen. Hugh should have taken more account of that boast.

The plans of the Cuthbert Hall addition were exact, with measurements given for each room. He confirmed they were correct by asking the estate carpenter to make measurements in Lydia Forsyth's suite and the adjoining rooms.

Hugh had watched and took down his findings. Then he and the carpenter compared them to the plans in the muniment room.

"There you be, sir, not a speck o' difference," the man said. "A fine job of drawing and figuring, though I'd've made use o' the space under the roof. That was right foolish."

"Even with what appear to be beams in the way, it must be good for storage."

"Not 'less it's things can be got up through a trapdoor," the man said with a grin. He tapped the sheet showing the second floor. "There's no stair going up."

"I must be half-witted not to have seen that."

"Nay, sir, just not used to reading builder's plans. Seeing as the drawing of the attic-story floor is missing if there ever was one, you'd have to study the ceiling of the rooms below to see if there's a hatch."

Hugh thanked him for his time and tipped him tuppence, asking him not to discuss their work. "I'm mum," the carpenter assured him and ambled out with his calipers.

Somehow the killer had escaped from that bedroom. Hugh begged several sheets of foolscap from Fielding and made rather less neat copies of the floor plans but with the proportions as right as he could make them and all dimensions shown. With luck, having his own set of plans and time to mull over them, enlightenment might dawn.

By suppertime, his only insight was that he should examine the walls from the Long Gallery side and from inside Eilidh's bedchamber. He and Wallace had searched for concealed doors, but perhaps the secret entrance would be more easily found from the other side. At any rate, it was all he could think of, and his cousin had nothing else to suggest.

"Mayhap overnight something will shake loose in your head," Wallace said.

"Or yours. I do hope so because I know there is a way into that room. There has to be."

In the middle of the night he woke, remembering one of his talks with Nurse Kettlewell.

"He knew something of building, seemingly, and oversaw the work himself." She had said that of a past earl. And hadn't she had used the word "secrets" several times? He drifted off again, counting the various kinds of family secrets.

****

The Fourteenth Day

He was late in coming down to breakfast and distracted as he ate, several times failing to hear some remark addressed to him by Randolph, who was the only one still at the table. His arrival had been delayed by his having scrutinized the plans once more after dressing. He and Wallace had accumulated a hoard of facts—his brain stuttered in mid-thought. What exactly was a fact? A popular opinion was not. Neither was a conjecture nor a cherished belief.

The witness of several unconnected people might constitute a fact. A bloodied candlestick and clout were physical evidence and therefore facts, but such things could still lie, like the handkerchief found under the corpse. Given its concealment in a place it could not have been dropped or fallen, it had been left as a deceptive clue.

Writing could also lie, as proven by lawsuits for libel. With that and the memory of the nurse's mention of secrets, the murderer's seemingly miraculous exit from his victim's room, and Lydia's final letter, Hugh thought he knew how the trick had been worked. There could be only one way to pass through the house unseen. He ate hurriedly and sought out Nurse Kettlewell.

Chapter 18

Hugh found her in the sewing room, stitching a shirt by the hearth. A small fire burned in it, the morning being cool.

"Mistress, you mentioned secrets in families when we spoke earlier. What are they in this family?" For a moment he feared she would not answer or would give one as obscure as those of the Greeks' Delphic oracle.

"All the usual, sir: adultery and bastards, for certain, and mayhap a trace of madness, though not in his lordship. The worst, I suppose, though 'tis no danger to them now, is that they were staunch Catholics long after King Henry made the new church."

"That was not unusual," Hugh said. "They did not all embrace the Church of England at once or disappear."

"No, sir. And some of them continued to hear the mass in their houses and to shelter priests, even though they appeared to accept the new church."

"Are you saying the Cuthberts did so?"

"Ay, they did. I don't mind admitting the same to a king's man, as they gave it up before I was born. I heard it from my grandam who was a maid here when she was young. The earls of Keswick were mostly good men and charitable, she said, besides being the most important family for many miles around, which must have made the neighborhood overlook any question about their religion. By the time I went into service, everyone hereabout had forgotten."

"Then the family must have had ways of hiding the priests."

"I think they did." She came to the end of her thread and was silent while she threaded her needle again. He held his breath. "I do wonder if there is a way to move through the house rather than just priest hides. There was one time Bartie got himself from his bedchamber to the library and back in less than the time it took me to go to the kitchen to make a special posset for him. He was ill and supposed to stay in bed."

The library was in the south wing adjacent to the earl's study. The kitchen was in the north wing, and the nursery was on the first floor of the old part of the house.

"How do you know he went anywhere, Nurse?"

"There was a book in the library he was hot to read because it was about some voyage to the East Indies. The doctor said he must rest and not tax his eyes and brain, and we had all been warned not to let him have anything to read. Yet when I brought in his posset, there it was before he could hide it under the bedclothes."

"Could he not have simply gone down the stair you did not use?"

"That's what I supposed at first, but the footman in our passage swore he hadn't come out the door."

"Was there no other footman to see him?"

"The old earl saved his coin for his pleasures and didn't keep as many as his lordship now, and he'd taken two or three to London with him. 'Twas the middle of the night, and the house was quiet with him in London and some of the servants given a holiday to visit their families that lived at a distance. Mayhap I should have told you sooner, but I didn't think of it at once, it being so long ago it happened. I was only the nursery maid then and just about fourteen. Old Nurse was busy with one of the younger boys who was sick, too. I never told Nurse for she'd have scolded. That footman was young and sweet on one of the maids, so I guessed he'd sneaked into an empty room to meet her and so would Nurse have thought. If she'd told his lordship, he'd have turned the fellow off."

"I'd like to see—" The sentence died on Hugh's lips. "A secret passage would be dark, if there is one. Did you leave a candle in the boy's room?"

"I'd been sewing by the light of a hanging oil lamp. There were two new candles. I lit one from the lamp and took it with me. He could have lighted the other from the lamp and I didn't think much about how he'd got the book right then, being distracted by finding him with a lighted candle and the bed hangings so near. I put the candle out and made him swallow his drink and after thinking about it I supposed making the posset had taken me longer than I realized. I returned the book to the library and spoke to the footman when Bartie went to sleep. He swore he hadn't left the passage."

"Then either the man lied or your charge used some secret way to make his escape."

"That footman became the butler and served here until he died a few years ago," she said, "and there was never a word against his honesty."

"Ah. Well, I'd prefer a concealed passage myself." It would quell the talk about supernatural crime—he hoped!—and it was more likely Randolph Cuthbert would know of a hidden means of moving through the building than someone not of the family would. The earl knew nothing of it, but the previous earl and Randolph's father had been close. If Randolph's father had learned of the secret passage from Bartolomew, he might have told Randolph.

"There was a bit of beeswax on the table where Mistress Forsyth ate her supper," Hugh mused.

"And none of the candles in the room lit, I've heard." The nurse's intonation was wrong for a question. She had followed his unvoiced thought.

"No. She supped early while there was still daylight. Besides, I've been assured the table was covered by a cloth, which was taken away with the dishes when she was finished. Nothing was left on the table but a bottle of wine"—*and two glasses*, he recalled, more confirmation she expected a guest. The murderer had brought a candle and set it down on the table. Likely the entrance to the passage was close by because why carry it farther than necessary?

"I need to find that passage." He could start with whatever room the young Bartie had occupied and perhaps get an idea of where others would be.

"There were other times as I think on it now. Though it was likely Simon who played ghost a few times."

That sparked a memory. Hadn't Dorothy Wilmot told him she had seen a ghost when she was a child? "Nurse Kettlewell, can you tell me which rooms were Bartie's and Dorothy's? I believe Mistress Wilmot thought she had seen a ghost."

"Easier to show you than to tell you," she said, putting her needle through the linen front to back to front again to leave it ready for her next stitch.

****

Eilidh found herself watching the servants' expressions despite herself. Cuthbert had said, "I am afraid even some of the servants here have begun to suspect you. You will not regard that, I know, as it's all only superstition, that silliness about red hair being one of the signs of a witch."

This would not have bothered her if she had not begun to notice that some of the maids and footmen were watching her. She might have been able to shrug that off, too, if Keswick had not seemed tense after his long meeting with Hugh and Wallace yesterday. Cuthbert had been present for part of it, according to Kitty, who had heard it from one of the footmen.

Two days ago, during a ride to the Penrith Beacon meant to provide some distraction to the guests, she had overheard Georgina's ghastly tale of a witch burnt alive recently. She must have been mistaken as the execution could not have taken place in England, where witches were hanged. Eilidh had not heard of any execution for witchcraft as far back as she could remember, though of course she might not hear of an execution in some other part of the country. Had the Hodges been present on the ride, one of them might have silenced Georgina as they did every time they heard her utter some indiscretion.

Cuthbert, riding beside Eilidh, whispered, "Foolishness. That was in Scotland and was hardly recent, having taken place in 1727."

Thirteen years ago was not yesterday, but neither was it ancient. She made some meaningless answer and wished for comfort. Perhaps Isobel had some to offer or brisk common sense if not reassurance. But much of Isobel's time was taken up with guarding Manon. Hugh or Wallace would have cheered her, but they were maintaining a distance from all the guests, which was only right when they had to appear impartial no matter what they might privately think. She wished she knew what that might be.

Yesterday morning there had been a noose on the threshold of the front entrance. Cuthbert had sought her out to make sure she had heard of it, almost destroying what remained of her composure.

Her husband had heaved a sigh and asked, "What are we to do, my dear? You are the only one with a reason to slay Lydia. The magistrate and his helper must conclude you murdered her in a fit of madness over my having sometimes acted as her escort. Even a rural magistrate will understand it is customary for ladies of our set to be squired to events by male friends when their husbands attend some other entertainment. Some ladies even have recognized cicisbeos."

As some men have recognized mistresses.

Receiving no response, he pressed on. "The chamber door being latched will not stop them charging you as they must arrest someone, and if you are brought to trial, I see no possible result but your being found guilty. It may not come to execution. Some of those awaiting trial at the assizes die of gaol fever or some other ailment. Perhaps a death by illness or one's own choice would be preferable to hanging. But mayhap the female felons are better housed than the men." He had patted her hand while she wanted to recoil from his touch. " 'Tis not a quick end. I have seen hangings. They are quite a spectacle and draw crowds. The condemned man dangles at the rope's end, legs dancing and jerking, losing control of his bowels, for as much as twenty minutes before he dies, while the crowd jeers. Or she dies, as the case may be."

She listened to Randolph frozen-faced. He did not know Hugh and Wallace had been her friends in the past. Unaware of that fact, he assumed they would accept the simplest solution. Why was he attempting to frighten her, cloaking it in the guise of concern? The pose failed to deceive her as he had never shown any concern for her before.

Any curiosity about his thoughts and sentiments had been lost after only a few days of marriage. Her sole value to him had only been her dowry. Once he had secured it, she had ceased to exist except as an occasional nuisance. He had not spoken as much to her in the past two years as he had in the last two weeks.

Did he really believe she had killed Lydia and was taking out his anger by trying to torment her? The woman had been his mistress as long as they'd been married or longer. Unusual devotion to a mistress, surely, but if he were devoted to her, anger would be understandable. But he showed no grief at her death, no sign of anything at all on hearing of her murder.

He was still talking, something about women who murdered or had been murdered or perhaps should have been murdered, she hardly knew and did not care. Thinking back to the morning after the quarter day, she remembered one lightning flash of genuine emotion on his face, and that only because he happened to be facing her. She closed her eyes to envision that moment.

He had been startled, even shocked, and that unguarded instant came after the news of Lydia's death rather than when it was first announced. Someone, she no longer remembered who, informed them the door to

Lydia's suite had been latched, making it necessary for someone to enter through a window.

"I'll leave you to your contemplation, Ellen. A word to the wise, eh?" He rode on ahead as Cornelius Wilmot circled back, evidently with the intention of riding with her. He had been with Georgina but from their postures, she thought they had quarreled. Randolph took his place beside the little ninnyhammer.

Now she had remembered it, she could not forget his expression at the revelation Lydia's door had been latched. The others had been surprised into exclamations at the mystery of it. Randolph had been shocked to speechlessness before pretending to be bored by the talk.

****

The schoolroom, nursery parlor, and children's sleeping rooms, like all the others, were paneled. Hugh and the old nurse walked through all of them before returning to one once occupied by young Bartholomew. His was the last chamber and adjoined the south wing.

"Has anything been altered or moved, Nurse?"

"No, sir. The only changes have been to the bedding, bed hangings, and curtains." She nodded toward the bed, a smaller version of the oak tester bed in his own chamber. "That's too big to move without taking it to pieces. When I was nursery maid, I had a long stick with wool half its length that I used to dust the wall behind the headboard."

He lit the candle and spread the first floor plan out on the bed, orienting it to the room. Being small, the chamber had only one window halfway between the left side of the bed and the wall shared with the room to the north. He began at the left corner and studied every join between the panels, working his way along, tapping and poking until he came to the window embrasure. He lifted the seat. The space under it was empty, its sides and bottom immovable.

"I don't think that can have been the way in," Kettlewell said. "I expect the children always stored toys and little treasures there."

Of course they would. Any pursuivant would surely look for an entry to a priest hide there first. Nurse Kettlewell sat placidly knitting.

He continued on until he reached the bed. Hugh knelt on it to examine that headboard that extended the height of the bed and held up that end of the wooden canopy. He found nothing that suggested a moveable panel that might give access to the wall behind it and moved on to the wall to the right of the bed.

A few inches farther on, only a handspan above the floor, he found a small knot in the wood of one of the panels. The knot looked a bit loose, as the others he had noticed did not. Crouching, he probed it with his forefinger. The knot pressed inward with a faint creaking. He sat back on his heels. The paneling provided nothing to help him pry it open. He pushed, and the panel opened but began to swing back when he removed his hand. The old woman had come to stand behind him. She caught it before it shut.

As he rose, she slipped past him into the dark, rather like a ferret going into a hole. "This is how he did it, the rascal," Nurse Kettlewell said. "Will you hold the candlestick in the passage, sir?"

He held it over her head while she peered to the left.

The panel nearly blocked the way to the right. She

took hold of its edge and pulled it half closed, turning to the right as he maneuvered the candle to give her light. After seeming to stare at something, she ducked out past him. "You'll have a fine time exploring, sir. Mr. Seaton's a mite wide to be comfortable in there. To the right the passage turns. To the left a ladder goes up just inside here."

"Nurse Kettlewell, you are a pearl of great price. If you were a few years younger, I'd be tempted to marry you."

"Go on with you," she cackled.

He slid through the entrance and examined as much as he could see while she held the door open a few inches. He yearned to venture farther in but restrained himself. A lantern would be better than the candlestick. Also he needed to talk to Wallace about the discovery. He ran his hand over the inside of the door and found a latch. It would be used if pursuit was close behind.

Hugh emerged from the passage, letting the door swing shut. The knot in the wood popped back into place as the panel closed.

"I ask that you not mention this to anyone, mistress. I don't want it to come to the murderer's ears."

"I won't speak of it. Now let me dust that great cobweb off you before someone sees you and wonders what you've been about." She had already made herself tidy if she had collected any dust. He pinched out the candle, and they went their ways.

An hour later, Wallace grinned as a tiger might at the sight of a plump...what did tigers prey on? Some East Indian form of a cow or sheep or a villager, perhaps, Hugh supposed. He had waited, almost too restless to sit and write out his findings, for Wallace's return from his manor where he had spent a few hours dealing with estate business and tenants. "Who would have guessed what appeared to be a stone wall five feet thick was hollow?"

"Not I," Hugh said, "until I studied the plans and found that the measurements on the plans matched those of the rooms. There was simply no other place a secret passage could be. Then certain things I'd been told gave me a hint."

"We'll need to search the passage to find the route Cuthbert took. I assume he left from the footmen's parlor?"

"Ay. Now I've discussed it with you, I want to begin. I didn't want to start with no one knowing where I was."

"Sensible of you. Who knows but what you might run into trouble and need to be rescued?"

"I hope to avoid that," Hugh said repressively.

"From what you describe, I'd be no use to you. Take my groom with you. I'll appoint Rob a temporary constable to assist you. After all, magistrates in town have constables; why shouldn't I? I'll have him sent to me after the servants' supper."

Hugh nodded abstractedly. "Yes, best to do it when most of the guests are in the drawing room or in their chambers, or not roaming the halls anyway. We'll need lanterns and spare candles for them."

"Rob can bring those. I assume neither of us wants news of your discovery to get out? Will your helpful nurse hold her tongue?"

"She's a trusty Trojan."

"Good."

"Wallace, will you arrange for Isobel stay with Eilidh at night until we arrest Cuthbert? She fears he will murder Eilidh and make it look like suicide and I agree."

"So do I."

****

The guests had been retiring early, house party amusements having palled in the wake of murder. The only one who seemed not to realize that the killer was in the house was Georgina Hodge. Wallace agreed that ten was late enough for their purpose. One footman would be on duty on the first floor, and another roved the ground floor in case someone should come in the night. Wallace mentioned casually to the butler that he and Hugh would be in the Yellow Parlor conferring until late, and his groom would be present in case Wallace needed to send him off with a letter. Wallace would let him out and bar the north wing door.

When they were ready to begin, Wallace called up to the footman to fetch a flask of barley water to his chamber and leave it on the nightstand as he meant to retire soon. When they heard the man's footsteps retreat on his way to the kitchen in the other wing, they slipped upstairs to Bartie's old room.

Wallace rolled up a towel and wedged it against the bottom of the door. "So no light shows under the door for the footman to see when he passes. Best to keep our discovery of the passage secret for the moment." The window was both shuttered and heavily curtained, so they need not worry about someone outside seeing Wallace's candle. The stable hands and grooms would all have gone to bed anyway. They had to rise early.

Rob had brought two lanterns, one of them a bullseye lantern, and two extra candles apiece. "Good man," Hugh said. The thought of being in the dark if a single lantern suffered an accident was not one he enjoyed. Rob lit the lanterns as Hugh pushed in the knot and entered.

He had not noticed earlier how thick the hinged panel was: almost as thick as the interior wall. Even if they had thought of tapping the walls, they would have heard no difference. Hugh told Rob to hold the door open a few inches while he searched on either side of the opening and on the door itself for the thing he knew must be there. He would really prefer not to find himself unable to get out once the door was closed. He found it in the lower part of the wall where the knot hole was. To his relief, the mechanism was simple: when the knot outside was depressed, it pushed in a spring attached to a thin metal bar, allowing the door to be opened. From inside, pulling a knob on the bar allowed the door to be opened.

Holding the panel ajar, Wallace asked, "What are you looking for?" when Hugh continued his examination after he had proven the device worked.

"There has to be a way to see if anyone is in the room. Without that, someone in the passage might blunder into an occupied room."

He found it several feet above the floor, under the eye level of anyone but a child. It gave only a limited view, and on looking for more, he found a series of almost invisible gaps between the panels. He and Rob exchanged grins. "Found it," he murmured to his cousin, and turned to the left.

As Nurse Kettlewell had observed, a ladder leaned

at a gentle slant against the left half of the stone wall that appeared to end the passage. He raised the lantern.

The stone wall must surround and support the window. The top of the ladder disappeared through an opening in the ceiling, no doubt to a bridge over the window. Presumably another ladder led down on the other side.

Rob eyed the walls and ceiling. "I hope there's no attercop webs in this ginnel," Rob said and sneezed as dust rose, stirred by their footfalls.

"We'll try the other direction first," Hugh said.

The space being a little less than three feet wide, they flattened themselves against opposite walls so Hugh could squeeze past to take the lead. Turning the corner, he swept a trailing cobweb out of the way.

Now they were in the south wing. Ten or twelve feet along they came to another wall. This time, instead of one ladder, there were two, one leading down, the other up. Of course, because the old manor's walls were solid, only its new upper stories had concealed passages, while the wings had them on all floors.

"We'll climb down. It's the ground floor we want anyway," he whispered to Rob.

The ladder's thick slats looked sturdy, but Hugh tested each rung before trusting himself to it. The crosspieces took his full weight without protest, and Rob was shorter and lighter than he. Both lanterns had been fitted with a short chain and a loop so they could be hung from a hook or over their wrists, making it possible to use both hands. When his foot found a solid surface he stepped off and held the lantern up to look around. One ladder on each end of the platform went up to the first floor, the other two went down, to the cellar, he supposed.

"Come on down, Rob."

They crossed the ground floor window and continued in the confining darkness. A few feet farther on, Hugh estimated they were passing the storeroom. Then came the retiring rooms. More windows to climb over. If he or the windows had been an inch taller, his head would have scraped the underside of the floor above. They came to a right turn Hugh knew was the end of the wing, and another ladder almost at once.

"This one has to lead over the door and the windows on either side of it," he muttered over his shoulder. Past that stretch and around another corner, they were into the south wall.

"Rob, look for knobs."

"I been doing so the whole way, sir."

By counting the windows they had clambered over, Hugh calculated they had reached the room where Cuthbert claimed to have taken refuge. A pace farther on, he saw a door pull.

"Here, let's look in this one." He crouched to peer through the narrow slot. The chamber was dark. Pulling the door open, he held up his lantern. The golden light illuminated enough to prove this was where Cuthbert had lingered for some unspecified length of time with no one to see or hear him. He closed the panel gently and moved on. A moment later, the groom exhaled sharply and stopped.

"What is it?" Hugh demanded.

"I stepped on something, sir." He was bent over, staring at an object on the floor. Picking it up, he displayed it to Hugh.

"A clothes brush." Hugh brought his own lantern

closer to look for some identifying mark. There was no monogram or crest. "I think we can guess how it got here."

"Here's another thing." This time Rob held up a lantern.

"Set them back on the floor as near as can be to where you found them in case their owner returns before we're ready to take him."

At the next window, they climbed to the first floor as Cuthbert must have done and worked their way along the first floor zig-zagging up and over the windows. Cuthbert Hall's wings contained many windows. Many, many windows.

There was one benefit to the unaccustomed exertion, so different from riding. Aching muscles took his mind off the impenetrable darkness confined in the narrow space. "Wouldn't be fast to go any distance what with having to go over or under the windows," Rob muttered. "No webs, anyways. Mr. Cuthbert must have got them all."

"That's true, but that would not have been a consideration when it was built to hide a priest. Once he was in the wall, he would be safe and could take his time getting to wherever he was going." Somewhere there would be a little room or more than one where he could be comfortable while sitting out the search by the Crown's pursuivants, even if it lasted for days. Probably there were hides in the cellar and in the attic story. Their limbs were going to ache after they completed their search of the first story. However, the difficulty would account for Cuthbert's disappearance for well over an hour.

A lifetime later or perhaps only half an hour, Rob

spoke close to his ear. "The north wing is right ahead. We passed four windows, that was the front of the south wing, and now we've passed seven windows and that's all but one of the main section. Up the next, come down the other side, and a few paces will take us into the north wing."

Hugh had lost count while peeking through the spy slits at intervals. Thank God for an observant helper. "Thanks."

After clearing the eighth window, he mumbled, "I never want to see another ladder."

Rob expelled a soft "Heh!"

Some fifteen feet from the wall supporting the window, Hugh found the metal bar, tugged it, and pulled the panel open. He stepped into the suite with Rob on his heels. The bed was before them, the table where Lydia had eaten her last meal several feet to their left.

"This would have been the nearest place to set down his lantern. If he had to replace the candle, a drop of wax might easily fall."

Hugh let out a long breath. Now they knew how the crime had been accomplished. "We are done for the night." He contemplated the return journey over multiple windows with no enthusiasm.

Wallace's groom cleared his throat. "By your leave, sir, and if you don't mind me saying…"

"Out with it, man," Hugh said, clapping him on the shoulder. "You've made suggestions already tonight."

"It's only, we're right near where we want to go, if we could go to it direct. We come past the Long Gallery which is beyond that wall." He jerked his head back toward the way they'd come. "There's a door into the gallery from the passage."

"Then we could cut across the hall to Bartie's door if there's no footman in sight or hearing. But as there's only the one man on duty at night, he must walk back and forth between the wings."

"Mayhap he does, Sir Hugh…once in a while. Likely there's a chair or a bench where he sits between times. In the gallery, we can listen for him and cross the hall when he's farther away. And if he does see us, you've only to say you're investigating and he's to keep silent about it."

"Rob, I fear you've the makings of a rogue."

After making their way over only two windows and finding the hidden panel, they listened by the Long Gallery's door, before tiptoeing across the hall to Bartie's room. Hugh opened the door cautiously.

His cousin sprang up from his chair. As soon as they were inside and the door closed, he exclaimed, "Thank God! I was beginning to worry, you'd been gone so long."

****

The Fifteenth Day

Neither of them was bright-eyed in the morning even after several cups of strong tea, although they had postponed Hugh's account of his and Rob's exploration until after breakfast. Their silence over the meal went unmarked as both Keswick and Caleb Hodge were reading the most recent newssheets and Ismay Tate was lost in her own thoughts and sometimes appeared to be counting on her fingers. She must be rehearsing her hostess duties or plans for the day. Georgina was mourning over the activities she was missing at home. Stephen had little to say, but his gaze wandered often to

Ismay while Cornelius was sitting as far as possible from Georgina. He avoided looking in her direction. Eilidh did not look rested. Like Wallace, she had chosen to have a bowl of caudle, though she had also taken an oatcake still warm from the griddle. Comfort food. Once when she raised her eyes, he smiled and gave her a small, reassuring nod. She failed to understand it for the trouble did not leave her face. He would find an opportunity to speak with her privately.

In the Yellow Parlor, Hugh described their adventure, ending, "I think there's no doubt both wings are encircled by passages, and that the old part of the house is, also, above the ground floor. We saw ladders going down from the ground floor in the wings so there are entrances into the cellar where it would be easier to hide a room or several, though I don't imagine they'd be comfortable."

"No more uncomfortable than their occupants would be in the Tower under a charge of treason," Wallace objected. "No need to spend more time creeping around in the dark, I think."

"No wonder Cuthbert was vague about how long he spent in the house that afternoon. While it would have taken him less time to get from that room in the south wing to Lydia's chamber than it took us beginning from the nursery, he could not have made the journey there and back quickly. He used the brush Rob found to tidy himself before leaving the passage. A certain disarray would pass unnoticed as he'd been taking part in some of the contests, but dust and cobwebs would have been noticed."

"He didn't bring his valet, who might have noted his comings and goings, and kept Lydia from bringing her maid for the same reason," Wallace remarked. "Eilidh was told not to bring her maid who might have provided an alibi, so implicating her was planned."

"Or mayhap Manon was left at home because she might have suspected him," Hugh replied. "We should ask whether he might have been aware of her opinion of him. His only mistakes were that he did not realize the door was latched and forgot to leave Eilidh's handkerchief. He thought that was easy to fix, as he had only to use the passage between his suite and hers. Will you question whichever footman has been filling in for his valet in case there may have been some traces left on his clothing?"

"Yes. I'll have to ask discreetly or perhaps Rob can do it. Asking some of the servants if it's possible to start as a footman and work up to becoming a valet."

"They'll never believe he'd be asking on his own account."

"No. Too short though he's got the brain for it. No doubt he has a cousin with aspirations for whom he's inquiring."

"Should we tell the earl, Wallace?"

A shake of the head. "Not until I have set out our reasons for suspecting Cuthbert and listed our evidence, including your declaration about the passages. Help Rob with his statement. Most witnesses have no notion of what's important to put in. I hope we may be able to convince the earl. I'll arrest Cuthbert anyway, but it would be less awkward with Keswick's support."

"I think I have a plan that will secure it," Hugh said, "if we make the bait tempting enough. We can begin by speaking with Keswick."

Chapter 19

"Our inquiry is nearly complete, my lord," Wallace announced as the footman closed the door. "I am confident we will be making an arrest within a day or two at the most."

The earl cut him off. "Are you going to arrest my heir's wife?"

Cuthbert must have been poisoning the earl's mind as well as Eilidh's.

"Not at this time. We will begin by questioning Mistress Cuthbert again. And Mr. Cuthbert, too," he added as an afterthought.

"We now have both motive and method," Hugh said, and hoped the man would not inquire about the latter.

"Then why not make your arrest now and get your proof through questioning? The woman is already terrified and will confess at once. I have no doubt she will be relieved to be done with this ordeal."

"We need certain physical evidence that will lead…someone…to the gallows. Be patient, Lord Keswick. Justice will be done. The mills of the gods grind slowly, but they grind small."

Hugh had never before seen anyone actually gnash his teeth. Keswick ground out, "My guests feel like caged animals, I anticipate that printers in London are already producing satiric prints of this outrage, and your own reputation will be affected by the length of time you are taking to find the Forsyth woman's murderer."

"That cannot be helped if we are to do our duty without fear or favor."

Those who did not know Wallace well underestimated his backbone of steel.

"Now if you will excuse us, my lord, we will be about our business. We will question Mistress Cuthbert before supper and Mr. Cuthbert afterward. "

The earl compressed his lips. His patience was worn thin. "Very well. Do what you must."

Chapter 20

The urgent request to speak with Sir Hugh, actually an order, was not a good sign. Could he or Wallace really believe she had murdered Lydia? She hesitated at her mirror to attempt an unruffled expression. The glass showed her a pale countenance with shadows under her eyes: the face of someone facing the gallows.

When he told her she might go, Hugh took her hand. How different that sensation was from Cuthbert's touch. "This is almost at an end. Can you be strong?"

"If I must."

She entered the drawing room before supper, having paused only to wash her hands and tidy a few strands of hair escaped from their pins. The others could not fail to be aware of her long interview with Hugh. She answered their careful, neutral questions almost at random.

At table, she picked at her food, too filled with apprehension to have room for anything else. Everyone in the house, guests and servants alike, must guess at the interview's significance. Some around her tried to conceal their conclusions. A few stole sympathetic glances at her. Keswick displayed no emotion though his eyes were stony. Hugh and Wallace revealed nothing except a certain grimness around the eyes and mouth. Randolph gazed at her mournfully until he seemed to recall he should pretend nothing was wrong, but his eyes glinted with satisfaction. At first Eilidh had attempted to school her own expression, only to realize there was no need: she was terrified.

The men did not linger long over their port before joining the ladies in the drawing room for tea where young Georgina was tattling on about nothing. Ismay Tate's attempt to give the gathering a more ordinary tone was a forlorn hope. Either Hugh or Wallace kept a not quite inconspicuous eye on Eilidh at all times.

Her opportunity came when all the conversations ceased at the same time as will sometimes occur in the most convivial group, which this was not. She placed her tea bowl and saucer on the table by her chair and tottered to her feet. "If you will excuse me, I have the headache a little and will retire." Hugh and Wallace rose a second later, exchanging a glance. She managed a curtsy in the company's direction.

Wallace approached the footman. His order, "Send for Isobel MacDonald to attend her in her chamber to bring headache powders or some soothing drink as quick as she can and then return to her charge," was presumably meant to be inaudible to the rest of the room.

"Permit me to escort you, ma'am," Hugh said, offering his arm.

"Thank you, sir. I own I feel somewhat unsteady."

The footman had relayed Wallace's message to the man on duty in the passage post-haste. Isobel was hurrying toward them as they reached Eilidh's chamber. She had been waiting for the summons.

Chapter 21

Hugh bade her a dispassionate good night as she and Isobel entered her bedroom. She heard him mutter to the footman on duty in the passage, "Mistress MacDonald will come out shortly. The maid may go in with wash water and to light the fire. No one else is to enter or leave the room. If you go off duty before morning, impart that instruction to the man who replaces you."

Once they were inside, Isobel hugged her and whispered, "All will be well. Now, we will change your gown and stays."

Dressed in jumps, her casaquin, and plain petticoat, she waited in the armchair she had turned to face the outer wall. If she had been able to read or write a letter or even do some simple needlework, the time would go faster. Under the circumstances, she could not imagine being able to pay attention to any of those things. She wanted it to be over. How long would it take?

Probably it was no more than half an hour before she heard the faintest sound from the wall between the right corner and the window as a section of the carved paneling began to vanish and Hugh appeared in its place. She almost ran to him before he stepped into her bedchamber and went to stand by the bed.

"Isobel did an excellent piece of work," he said, his voice low. "I left Cuthbert playing piquet with Hodge.

You won't be very comfortable, I fear, but I doubt we will have to wait long."

Even if the rest of the night was still to come, the battle was joined, an oddly military description of a deadly game.

"Come." Hugh took her hand and led her to the opening in the wall. A lantern on its floor illuminated a narrow corridor. Another military term, meaning a path around a fortification, as she recalled from her brother's youthful fascination with warfare.

"You go up the ladder first and wait for me at the top."

"In case you have to catch me?" she inquired wryly.

"No. I remember how you climbed trees. But I'm carrying the lantern. You can get off the ladder at the top?"

She suppressed some amusement at the sudden doubt in his voice. "I have gone up ladders when harvesting Ribston Pippins." She had not had to climb off except when descending, but how hard could it be? "I admit I may be rather awkward." She would be lucky to show no more than her ankles. Her heart had lifted at the badinage and the prospect of action. She set one foot on the first rung.

Earlier he had assured her they would not have far to go. Hugh had spoken nothing but the truth: once on the second floor and over the barrier of the next window, he halted a few paces along to pull a panel open and lead her into a box-like servant's room. "We were lucky," he said, pulling the hidden door closed. He kept his voice low. "Not only that this chamber is unused but that the only occupied rooms are all at the other end."

At the door, he paused to slide the cover across the front of the dark lantern, before whispering close by her ear, "We must be quiet now. Take hold of my coat's skirt."

She groped hesitantly and found the rear side seam where pleats were set in from waist level to hem. Then they shuffled along in darkness, which would have bothered her had she been alone. With Hugh, she felt no more qualms than the enjoyable excitement she remembered from adventuring with the boys…except that holding onto his clothing, her hand so near his hip, was strangely intimate. She tried to keep her mind on the faint sound of his left hand brushing along the wall. In the dark, sound acquired greater importance.

He came to a stop. A door handle moved, causing her fingers to twitch. They grazed his hip, though only through his many layers of clothing. Still, she jerked back. "Come," he said close by her ear. The door opened, and he moved forward with Eilidh clinging to his coat.

"Stand still." The door closed, and the latch dropped into place. A moment later, the lantern's light revealed a thin mattress covered with a blanket or two, a basket, an armchair, and a chamber pot.

"We would not have had to risk being seen by a servant if we had made use of the other room," Eilidh said.

"There's no opening from the passage in this one. I did not want to take even the remote chance that something would go wrong and he would escape me. If he had fled up here and found you when he emerged…"

"He might kill me, even if it did him no good?"

"I had to consider it. Now, there's a bottle of barley water, an apple, some cheese, bread and butter, and sweetmeats in the basket. Isobel thought you might not eat much at supper."

She found she now had the beginnings of an appetite. "When I'm worried or overset, I don't."

He took a small candle holder and several short candles out of the basket, fitted one into the holder, then lit it from the lantern's candle. "I don't think anyone will be awake up here to see the light under the door. Will you be all right?"

"I will, Hugh."

"Good. Wallace or I or Rob will come for you when it's done."

A rogue impulse made her wish he would kiss her. Staring into his eyes, she almost thought he felt it, too. It would be so easy. She looked away; she was still another man's wife, however unworthy he was.

He must have understood, for he said, "If it does not happen tonight, I'll come for you at first light. The danger will be past for the time being, but we may have to do this again tomorrow night."

"Then I will pray it is tonight."

"So will I." He seized her hand and brought it to his lips. The murmured "I love you, Eilidh," struck her speechless. Hugh was gone before she could reply.

****

The Sixteenth Day

In the blackness, the scent of rosewater teased Hugh, reminding him of Eilidh. The simple fragrance was so often used in wash water, soap, lotions, and on handkerchiefs and gloves that it might easily be missed. Having stood inches away from her recently, he noticed it. He banished the memory as a distraction he could not afford.

The door in the paneling was near the one window. That Eilidh had been given so small a bedchamber, the sort one might give a lady's companion or an unwelcome visitor, was an insult. The well-cushioned window bench did make a convenient place to await events, however.

Randolph was unlikely to act until most of the others had retired. When he came, it would be through the panel. He himself had latched the door when he came for Eilidh because if they caught Cuthbert entering by the door, he could claim he had gone to his wife's chamber to make sure she did not need a physician or a dose of laudanum to help her sleep.

When the curst fellow was in Eilidh's bedroom, Hugh would have him. The man was soft from town life and too little vigorous exercise: riding in London and playing at bowls or archery were not enough to overcome heavy meals and perhaps nights spent drinking and carousing. Hugh hoped his expeditions in the passages had been exhausting. He must have been stiff and sore after he slew Lydia. If it had showed, he could have blamed the harvest festival activities.

His use of the passage and Lydia Forsyth's letters to Manon had to be enough to hang him, though Hugh would wait until Cuthbert made his move. He was almost certain Eilidh's murderous husband meant to tip a bottle of laudanum down her throat, then hold her still and silent until it took effect. All would assume she had taken her life because she was guilty of Lydia's murder and feared the gallows.

How long had he been sitting? He estimated he had

now been up for sixteen hours after a night with only about four hours of sleep. But there were few stimulants as efficacious as anger, though the thought of having Eilidh in his arms was also bracing. His longing for something he might never have was too hard to think about now, however.

He wished he had his hands around Cuthbert's throat. Even once that scoundrel was charged, months would pass before his trial. Carlisle's assizes were held only in the summer because of the difficulty of winter travel in the north, so Randolph Cuthbert would wait eight months or more before his trial and—Hugh devoutly hoped—his death on Gallows Hill in Harraby, near Carlisle. That was assuming he survived the winter in a cold, damp, possibly crowded cell. In such conditions, prisoners could die of lung fever, jail fever, or other illnesses before they made their final journey. If he did not survive to be hanged, so much the better.

Hugh pitied felons who stole to feed their families, though instead they should have gone to a workhouse. Not an easy choice when those places separated men from women and women from their children, but the woman and her children would either starve or end up in the workhouse anyway if her husband died or was transported.

He felt no sympathy for most murderers, and none at all for those who killed with malice aforethought. As for Cuthbert, who had treated Eilidh without the barest civility, he would like to—A faint creaking banished the savage fancy. Hugh waited motionless, mouth dry, as a vertical strip of pale light appeared and increased several feet to his right. The glow fell upon the bed as Hugh waited, heart pounding. A slight metallic sound reached his ears followed by the appearance of booted legs. The intruder had set the lantern on the passage floor to keep the panel open. The body above was invisible but for a white sleeve and a hint of the same at the neck. Cuthbert had left off his coat as Hugh had done though he had retained his waistcoat. The shirt at least made him easier to see in dim light.

The bed, its head against the right wall, was directly in front of the figure. He approached it cautiously. Hugh's every instinct prompted him to spring upon the man. He held back.

With the man's body between the lantern and the bed, only the sleeper's white frilly night cap, a bit of the night rail's collar, and a deathly pale blur of a face were visible.

At the bed he paused and fumbled in his pocket. Hugh could not see what it was or what he was doing with it. A heartbeat later, he heard a faint sound: something had fallen to the floor and rolled. Almost certainly a cork. The man took one more step and bent over the bed, suddenly pulling the sleeper's head up.

Hugh was already on his feet when a hoarse cry was cut off. Two long steps brought him close enough to plant a wide-swinging left-handed punch to Cuthbert's temple, sending him sprawling against the wall. A quick examination proved him to be insensible. On the bed, Rob hunched over spitting into his handkerchief. "Waited too long to be sure. Smelled like laudanum," he mumbled.

"How much got in?"

"Most." The groom disentangled himself from the rest of the bedcovers. "I'll try to spew into the pot."

Hugh pulled the lantern from inside the passage

and allowed the door to swing shut before snatching the coil of rope from under the pillow to bind his prisoner's hands and feet. Not a neat job, but it would keep him from trying to escape when he came to himself again. With Cuthbert bound, he lit the bedside candle, then used it to light the five-armed candle-branch on the wash stand. Rob sat on the edge of the bed in shirt and breeches now that he had peeled off Isobel's night rail. Still wearing the night cap and the heavy white powder Eilidh had supplied from her cosmetic case, he would look ridiculous if he had not appeared shaken.

"How are you?"

"All right, Sir Hugh. I'm all right."

"You did good work tonight."

Leaving the groom to wipe his face with a towel, Hugh let himself out of the room. The night footman stood halfway down the wing, gazing blankly at the wall, so lost in his own thoughts that he failed to hear Hugh's soft-footed approach until Hugh addressed him. "I need Magistrate Seaton and Lord Keswick, Seaton first." The man jumped and turned, beginning to stammer an apology.

Hugh cut him off. "Once you've roused them, send for Dr. Lockhart."

"Sir...it's near two o'clock. His lordship won't be pleased to be waked at this hour."

His wrath would fall on the footman.

"You may tell him we have the murderer, caught attempting a second murder."

"Yes, sir! At once, sir."

The identity of the killer would come as a shock to the earl. Would he want the matter covered up, Cuthbert perhaps consigned to a discreet private madhouse? Wallace would not agree, and Hugh would have no hesitation about informing the Lord Lieutenant if the earl persisted.

What did they know about Lord Keswick? He had wanted the murder solved as soon as possible, had conceded the necessity to question his guests, and was concerned about the gossip the murder and the rumors of witchcraft might be spawning. Keswick's tenants and servants were contented, which meant he was a good landlord and master. The footman's hesitation to wake him at this hour was reasonable. Anyone would object to being roused out of sleep in the middle of the night.

The earl had believed some, if not all, of his nephew's lies. In Hugh's experience, honest people expect honesty from their family and friends. On the other hand, his nephew's interview in his presence had tarnished Randolph's image somewhat. The earl was proud of his family's history, and propriety mattered to him, though not more than truth, Hugh hoped.

Cuthbert was still lying insensate on the other side of the bed. Rob was standing by the bed, recovered, his unsuitable head-gear cast aside. He had got almost all of the powder off.

"Sir, I found the bottle." His voice was level, but his eyes were alive with excitement.

"Did you? Excellent. I confess I had forgot it for the moment."

"So had I, Sir Hugh. It was in the bedclothes. And before I put on my shoes, my foot came down on the stopper. They're both there." He jerked his thumb toward the bed.

A cylindrical green glass bottle about four inches long lay in a reddish-brown stain on the coverlet.

Leaning over the bed, Hugh sniffed. "That's laudanum, if we needed more proof." He stoppered it and dropped it in his pocket. "Still a few drops inside. I'll want the coverlet as well. Help me lift it. We'll drape it over the chair to let it dry before folding it up."

Should he send Rob to fetch Eilidh? She might have fallen asleep. He hoped so; from the blue circles under her eyes, she must have lain awake for the last few nights. Or she might be wakeful, waiting for word the trap had been sprung. In either case, better to let her be, as Keswick and Wallace should soon be here. Once the explanations were made and Randolph Cuthbert was confined, Hugh would go up to her. By then, a different chamber could be ready for her. The air here reeked of vomit and laudanum.

His cousin, rumpled from napping in his clothes, arrived. He viewed the prisoner, the laudanum bottle, and coverlet with approval. "I'll write to reconvene the coroner's jury as soon as I can get to pen and paper," he was saying when the earl strode in. He was as untidy as Wallace, having thrown on yesterday's clothing rather than wait for his valet to be wakened. His waistcoat was half-buttoned, his cravat tied with a simple loop. His head was covered only with short gray stubble. He had not paused to put on his wig.

Keswick did not acknowledge Hugh's and Wallace's brief greetings or notice Rob's bow. His first words as he glanced around the room were "You have the murderer?"

"Yes, my lord. He's here, behind the bed."

"Good God!" He stared down at Randolph. "Is he dead?"

"No. I had to knock him senseless as he was

pouring laudanum down his victim's throat."

The earl swept the bedchamber with his eyes. "Where is Ellen?"

"Safe elsewhere," Wallace said.

Hugh took advantage of the moment to tell Rob, now recovered, to let Eilidh know she was safe.

"He murdered the Forsyth woman?" his lordship was saying as Rob hastened out the door.

"Ay," Hugh stated, voice flat. "His intention was to cast as much suspicion as possible on his wife, then convince her she was certain to be charged. He killed his mistress in order to free himself to marry another heiress. I believe you already know he was in debt, my lord. From a magistrate in London, we understand it amounts to about five thousand pounds."

"I do. But he told me…" The earl's lips turned down. "He spun me a tale out of the whole cloth, didn't he? I saw him seldom before he became my heir. From his answers when you questioned him, he showed himself to be a liar at least in some things. Mayhap the untruths were only to save appearances, as you have said is common, Sir Hugh. But my brother, Simon, was a reprobate, hand in glove with my older brother whom I disliked for his libertine ways. He returned the favor and called me a precisian, foolishly straitlaced. When I inherited the title, I thanked God Bartholomew was scrupulous at least in his care for the lands." After a slight hesitation, he continued, "If Randolph takes after them, I cannot deny he would be capable of murder." The earl gave his head a shake, trying to clear it. "How did you guess he would come here?"

Wallace answered. "We anticipated he would make an attempt on her life as he had been hinting to you and others he feared she would kill herself and suggesting to her that felo-de-se would be preferable to hanging. Yesterday evening I announced I would arrest the murderer today, as it was too late to go through the formalities and convey the prisoner to the Penrith bridewell. We expected Randolph to take the opportunity to arrange Mistress Cuthbert's supposed suicide."

"Surely that was a risk for him as well as Ellen. Why not wait for justice to run its course unless he wished to avoid a public scandal?"

"Eilidh's—Ellen's—immediate death would greatly shorten his wait before courting and marrying another heiress." Hugh bit off the words. "And there was not much risk to him. His late lordship and Simon were close. At some point I believe he shared with Simon a secret passed down to him as the eldest son: the secret of passages in the outer walls. Simon must have told his son. That was how he entered and left Lydia Forsyth's chamber, and how he entered this one." Hugh stooped to find a knot in the paneling by the lantern's light. He pushed it in, shoved the panel open, and replaced the lantern as Randolph had left it.

"Uncle?" Randolph Cuthbert croaked. How much had he heard before he came to himself? Did he understand he had no way to escape trial and execution?

Keswick passed his nephew without a word or a glance and peered into the narrow corridor. "That's why you asked about secret passages. How did you know?"

"There was no other way into or out of Mistress Forsyth's suite with the latch down, and we learned that she herself had latched it behind the maid, Kitty. Your sister, Mistress Wilcox, had spoken of a supposed ghost she had seen in her bedchamber as a child, and Nurse Kettlewell told me of an occasion when as a boy Lord Bartholomew made a sally from his sickroom to the library and back without being seen by any servant. It's my understanding, too, that your ancestors had a reputation for hiding Jesuit priests. When I studied the plan of the house with the new wings and saw the new walls were as thick as the old ones, I finally realized they were the only place a passage could be concealed."

"Good God," Keswick repeated. Once he had recovered from his surprise he had more questions. Hugh and Wallace were still answering them when Eilidh appeared in the doorway.

The earl saw her first. "Ellen, you've been informed?"

"Yes. If you'll pardon me, I won't come in. I think I need to be alone for a little while. The room next door is vacant, and I will compose myself there."

"I understand. This has been a terrible experience. Shall I send for your old nurse?"

"Thank you, but she is already on her way." She nodded, her eyes meeting Hugh's briefly, and drifted away.

"I am heartily sorry I ever suspected her or believed anything Randolph said of her." Noticing his nephew again, he said, "I suppose the doctor has been sent for? Perhaps Randolph should be laid on the bed."

The fellow could lie on the floor and rot for all Hugh cared. Wallace addressed Rob, still standing by the door, bidding him to fetch the nearest footman, just as Dr. Lockhart shouldered past him. "Where is he?"

The earl gestured at the floor.

"Then let's get him up on the bed. Why the devil hasn't someone done that already?"

Hugh said, "Rob. Let's oblige the doctor."

Keswick stood aside to let Hugh and Rob heave Cuthbert onto the bed. His eyes were closed and his body limp. Pretending to have fainted to avoid questioning, no doubt.

Lockhart set his case down on the other side of the bed and glanced from Hugh to Wallace. "How was he injured? And why is he tied up?

Replying to the second question first, Hugh said, "He killed Lydia Forsyth, and we stopped him attempting to kill another who he thought was his wife. I hit him in the side of the head to stop him."

"So he's the one. Well, I'll need him untied."

While waiting for Rob to free their prisoner's hands and feet at Hugh's nod, the doctor studied the bruise forming on Cuthbert's temple. With Cuthbert freed from his bonds, Lockhart removed his neckcloth, unbuttoned the neck of his shirt, and removed the linked buttons that fastened his cuffs. He felt for a pulse. "How long ago was he injured?"

Hugh pulled his watch from his waistcoat pocket.

"About an hour and a half since. 'Tis almost four of the clock now."

"Hmmm," the doctor muttered. "How long was he in a swoon?"

"He spoke a little while ago and then only to call me 'uncle,'" Keswick said. "I did not mark the time." Neither had Hugh or Wallace. "He has not spoken again. Should he have fainted again?"

"There's very little 'should' about the human body,

my lord, or indeed in medicine and surgery. 'Tis not like cookery, in which certain quantities of flour, sugar, and egg well mixed and baked will always be biscuits or little cakes."

"Might bleeding him be of use?"

"I do not advocate it." He gave Cuthbert's shoulders a gentle shake and thumped on his chest. "Mr. Cuthbert!" On receiving no response, he went to his case and brought out a vial.

"Sal volatile."

The pungent odor under Cuthbert's nose provoked a response. His eyes blinked though without seeming to focus on anything. "Uh?"

"I'll send for brandy to revive him," the earl said.

"No spirits," the doctor and Hugh chorused. "I don't like the effect on head injuries," Dr. Lockhart stated. From experience, Hugh expected nothing useful from someone whose wits were scrambled by strong drink.

Keswick began, "Cuthbert," then ran out of words. Hugh would have liked to say a great deal but had to yield the honor to his cousin.

Wallace stepped forward to stand beside the earl. "Randolph Cuthbert, you are under arrest for the murder of Lydia Forsyth and the attempted murder of another person, one Robert Liddell, whom you mistook for your wife." Wallace turned to Keswick. "I trust that meets with your approval, my lord."

Whatever his lordship might once have felt for his heir, he was left with no alternative but to accept it. His objection would have made no difference. Wallace's groom, as the one attacked, could bring the charge. Manon Allard would surely be delighted to charge

Cuthbert with her sister's death.

Randolph turned toward Wallace's voice and blinked in evident bewilderment. "What has happened? Why does my head ache?"

"You suffered a blow to the head," his uncle said when he realized neither Wallace nor Hugh meant to answer.

Their prisoner, raising himself on his elbows, closed his eyes and mumbled, "I'm dizzy."

"We'll need a place to hold him until the coroner's court convenes and writes up their findings for the indictment and we can transport him to Carlisle. I believe we could make use of the room Allard is occupying. I have no doubt she will be happy to remain to testify," Wallace said.

Chapter 22

Randolph Cuthbert had been removed to the padlocked room on the north wing's second floor. Hugh could have appreciated the irony that it was only two doors from the chamber in which Eilidh had passed most of an uncomfortable night, if only he had not been so tired. Isobel MacDonald had overseen the transfer of Manon's belongings to the one between Eilidh's hiding place and the cell while a footman moved furnishings for the maid from a storeroom. The doctor lingered to see Cuthbert settled in the narrow cot and left instructions for his care.

"He was insensible longer than I like, but now that he's awake, I see nothing but what I would expect from even a mild head injury: an aching head, some memory loss, dizziness, and confusion. He should be kept quiet and given a light diet, as sometimes there is nausea also. Have someone look in on him every two or three hours."

"How soon can he be questioned?"

Dr. Lockhart snorted. "He doesn't remember how he was injured or what he did that led up to that point."

"Is he telling the truth?"

"Memory loss is to be expected with a blow to the head. He may or may not ever remember."

If he recalled events before the evening, they might at least confirm why he had murdered Lydia although

311

they did not need it. They had Hugh's and Rob's testimony, the letters, and the little red book, which had been found in his chamber. No wonder Cuthbert had taken it after killing Lydia. The title page inscribed *To my lovely Lydia for her bedtime enjoyment from her Randy* won a reluctant grin from Hugh. He had heard of the salacious *Dialogue Between A Married Lady And A Maid*. The coroner's court would bind Cuthbert over for the Carlisle assizes.

Wallace, who had been able to doze for a few hours, had written out a warrant to search Cuthbert's room and a letter to the coroner. Hugh arranged for the chamber to which Eilidh had retreated to be provided with a truckle bed for Isobel MacDonald. Manon would have a room nearby.

He left a hastily summoned footman to stand guard at Eilidh's old room to prevent the housemaid from entering to light the fire and the chambermaid from cleaning, and to admit no one except Wallace Seaton or himself.

"But if his lordship orders—"

Hugh cut him off. "You may tell him it's by order of Wallace Seaton, magistrate." The stained coverlet was folded over Hugh's arm to deliver to Wallace on his way to his own bedchamber.

He wanted to see Eilidh. Isobel would say she needed her sleep, and she was correct. So did Hugh, for that matter. He had still to write out his description of the capture, though he had jotted a list for Rob of what should go in his own.

As he turned toward his chamber, Isobel emerged from Eilidh's door. She stopped when she saw him, pulled the door shut gently and stood waiting his approach, hands clasped at her waist.

"How is she?" he asked when he was near enough to be heard while keeping his voice low.

"Much as you might expect." Her dry tone gave him to understand she thought little of his common sense.

"I do realize she must be appalled to think of her husband"—*damn him*—"not only murdering Lydia Forsyth but attempting to kill her as well."

Isobel raised her eyebrows. "Yon sneckin' loun—" Her forehead wrinkled, perhaps at her lapse into the Lallans Scots dialect. "—could not surprise my mistress by anything he did. I'll dance a jig the day he hangs. It's the relief she feels and the fear he'll be let off for being Keswick's heir."

Would the earl intervene on Randolph's behalf? From his sense of the man's character, Hugh thought not. He chose to say, "He may die while waiting to come to trial. That would be the most satisfactory conclusion to this terrible matter." Though Hugh would like to see him hang, a death before trial would save his lordship some embarrassment. "Is there anything Mistress Cuthbert would like or anything I can do to reassure her?"

"I am on my way to ask Cook to send up a posset or caudle for her and perhaps a bun or some bread and butter. I'm sure she would enjoy seeing you for a few moments. If you will wait briefly, I'll tell the footman to send word to the kitchen."

The man at the far end of the passage could leave his post long enough to hasten down one flight to relay the message to the man outside the kitchen. Then Hugh waited for Isobel to speak briefly with Eilidh before she ushered him in.

She started up from the window seat when she saw him and hurried forward. Her hands trembled when he took them in his own. Isobel, seated by the hearth almost with her back to them, was knitting one of the flat Scots bonnets, though in black rather than the blue favored in the Highlands.

He stood awkwardly until Eilidh tugged him toward the window seat, its width making it possible to sit with a decent space between them.

"I am sorry I could not come to tell you myself."

"I knew you were busy."

"Will you be able to eat something and sleep now?" He wanted to know, of course, but this was not the conversation he yearned to have with the woman he had missed for years.

"I think I can manage something light. Last night I had no appetite."

He nodded, satisfied she was not overcome. "Good. The case will be referred to the assizes. I only wish they might be held sooner."

Even without as tolerant a chaperon as he suspected Isobel was, the words he longed to say must be deferred until Cuthbert was dead. Would she feel she had to go into mourning for him? Did society require that pretense for a man who had attempted to murder her? Hugh hoped not.

"So do I. It's as if I am looking forward to being released from prison. I comfort myself that it will happen eventually."

"My dear, I hope then you will have the chance for happiness you should have had years ago." Wallace would keep him informed about the case when he returned to Northumberland. Too, he would have to appear as a witness at trial. Wallace would let him know how Eilidh did. "Do you mean to keep the lease on the Durham house now?"

"I don't know if I can. Will his man of business allow me to do so? I suppose I must write, and soon, for even if I cannot extend the lease, I will need some money on which to live."

Given Cuthbert's debts, would there be any money? Eilidh's jointure would not be available to her until she was a widow. He hoped Cuthbert had not somehow got his hands on it already. "Surely Lord Keswick will offer you a home here or in Keswick House in London if you prefer. Though I do not imagine you would choose London." He did not add, "Even without Randolph Cuthbert," though that was certainly in his mind. So were other things of which he could not yet speak.

"I've missed the freedom of the countryside ever since my marriage. Living in Durham was better than London, but it's still a town. I want to be able to walk without a companion or footman and ride at a gallop if I choose."

"I would like to see that, Eilidh. I'd like to be at your side when you do."

She blushed and looked away, but she smiled, too.

Chapter 23

What does he mean by that? Is he only remembering how we used to ride and walk with no one worrying about a chaperon?

Those questions lingered after he took his leave and Isobel set about tidying the clothing hastily put away in the clothes press. She should be thinking of where and how they would live. Cuthbert had been secretive about their finances, but he was deep in debt, and it took no great financial acumen to guess her dowry was gone. She would be surprised indeed if her jointure were intact. If her father had a fault it was that he was too trusting. Her mother had sometimes chided him for it. Would the earl feel obligated to house the wife of his murderous nephew?

At a tap at the door, Isobel abandoned her task. She opened it, saying, "That will be your breakfast," followed by "you," in a tone of loathing.

Manon Allard stood there holding the tray. "I asked to be the one to bring up Madame's meal because I wish to apologize to her. I owe her that. And to you, as well."

Isobel looked to Eilidh, for once uncertain.

"I understand you are willing to testify against my husband," she said.

Isobel took the tray, set it on the tea table, and glared at the woman.

316

"I have already written out my affidavit and will answer any questions the coroner or jury wish to ask. May I confess my foolishness to you while you eat? The caudle is best drunk while warm."

"Isobel, why don't you go down and eat your own breakfast?"

Without replying, Isobel stared at Allard. "This may be a trick."

Her old nurse had always made her feel safe. Here, she thought her suspicion misplaced. "Isobel, what could she gain from doing me harm? I think Manon would prefer to speak to me in privacy."

"If you harm my mistress, I will wring your neck like a chicken's."

Stiletto thin and six inches shorter than Eilidh's old nurse, the maid met her eyes. "I have no doubt you would. I wish her no ill now, having been deceived by my poor Lydia's good opinion of that man."

"Isobel?"

"Very well, then, Miss Eilidh." Having reduced her mistress to the nursery with that reply, Isobel marched out.

"Is Madame aware I am Lydia Forsyth's half sister?"

"Mr. Seaton and Sir Hugh have told me nothing of their investigation." She understood the need for discretion, but she might have worried less if one of them had at least hinted she had nothing to fear. Perhaps they really had considered her a suspect.

"Men." Manon's disdainful sniff made her opinion of the sex plain. "My sister and I were close from childhood and trusted each other."

Listening, Eilidh understood the affection between

Manon and Lydia. She had been close to her own sisters, though she had seldom seen them since her marriage.

"She was beguiled by him. From what she told me, I took him at first for someone worthy of her. Because I knew she was sensible, like me, I trusted her judgement and everything she claimed about you. I knew he was a spendthrift, but many gentlemen are. If I had seen him more often and for more than a few minutes, I might not have been gulled. I did not begin to wonder about him until my sister's last letter, and then I did not know how to let her know of my doubts or what to do. When Sir Hugh told me Lydia had been murdered—" She blinked rapidly and did not continue the sentence. "I am more sorry than I can say that I treated you and also MacDonald badly. I put my trust in lies, and you resented my being forced upon you. It is no wonder we could not deal well together. I will be present when he hangs, if I am able."

"Thank you for telling me, Manon." Did the woman hope to be kept on? If her own finances were not in doubt, Eilidh would almost be willing to keep her on or at least pension her. "I do not know if I will be able to afford to employ you beyond the next quarter day. I fear Cuthbert's finances…" She gave helpless shrug. "I will give you a good reference, however, and as I mean to remain here in the north, your skills would be wasted. They always have been, in Durham, as you know. You would do better in London."

"I have some savings from gifts my sister has given me, and she told me she would leave me enough in her will to make me comfortable. Either I will seek another position in town or else I will hire seamstresses and set up as a mantua-maker."

After she departed, Eilidh finished her caudle, now only lukewarm but still delicious, and ate a slice of bread and butter while considering how much lighter her heart felt this morning. Part of it was the prospect of being free of her husband, except that she could not be glad of the method, now she could imagine too clearly the horrors of death by hanging. She could not think about the other component of her improved mood yet.

****

Hugh found Wallace in the dining room. Breakfast was on the sideboard, and both the adult Hodges as well as Ismay Tate were present. The hour was unusually early for Mistress Hodge.

"Did something happen?" Hodge asked. "I thought I heard activity in the middle of the night."

Surprisingly, the servants who knew must have decided to keep the matter to themselves, unless Keswick had terrified them to silence.

"I don't think I've been awake before dawn since the children were still in the nursery," his wife chirped.

"A problem arose with one of the rooms, making it necessary to prepare another." Wallace took a fortifying sip of tea and addressed himself to his eggs.

Joan Hodge clapped one hand over the portion of her bodice that might be supposed to lie over her heart. "Thank God it was nothing worse!" The avidity in her eyes was unmistakable.

Both Hugh and Wallace ignored it. Word would leak out soon enough, or Keswick would reveal it.

Hugh drank a cup of coffee with some mutton ham and excused himself. Speaking softly in Wallace's ear as he left the table, he said, "I'll write my statement, but then I mean to sleep for a bit. Shall I have a footman deliver it to you?"

"No need. I've summarized our evidence. Your statement will keep for the coroner's court. We will both be testifying anyway."

"Good." He would write it out after he had slept.

****

Some stimulus convulsed his body. His mind, jarred awake, took longer to react. Blinking, he found his cousin standing by the foot of his bed, chagrined.

"I knocked," he said. "When you didn't answer, I came in and spoke your name without any response, so I gave you a tap on your shin. I'll swear you jumped a foot into the air while reclining. If you can do that at will, you might make your fortune at fairs."

Hugh squinted at his pocket watch on the bedside stand as his heart slowed. "Damme, Wallace. I hope your errand is important. I've been sleeping hardly more than an hour."

"It is."

Hugh's heart began to beat a tattoo. "What's happened?"

"When the footman looked in on Cuthbert for the second time, the room was empty."

"Damnation! I never thought—" The next moment, he was putting on his shoes.

"Neither did I," Wallace said grimly. "That room served to confine Manon, and his wits were scrambled, after all."

"Is Eilidh safe?" Hugh threw on his waistcoat, snatched up his pocket watch and coat and strode for the door.

"As soon as I heard, I sent a footman to find and

stay with her as a precaution, and Isobel MacDonald was with her as well. I don't think she is in any danger. He'll be trying to get away. I've summoned Rob and informed the earl myself. The footmen on duty have been told he's free—"

"Shutting the stable door after the horse is gone." Hugh was forced to slow his pace for his cousin.

"He can't have got far."

"We don't know that, Wallace. We never searched the passages after we traced his steps, except to make sure the servant's room we moved Eilidh to had no entrance to the passage. Mayhap there's a way to leave the house."

Wallace said, "What we do know is that he escaped after dressing, but without his wig, as he wasn't wearing it when we arrested him. He had no money in his pockets, for I searched them at the time. Keswick has dispatched grooms to the village to ask if he has been seen, and also to Penrith. He could have walked there, if he's recovered from the blow to his head, but what's he to do with no coin?"

"He could steal a horse or get a ride in a farmer's cart or wagon. How long has he been gone?" Hugh suppressed a curse, battling with waistcoat buttons and fingers grown uncooperative.

"The footman opened the door half an hour ago. Cuthbert was still disoriented when Lockhart left him four hours before that, and I don't think he could have deceived the good doctor, do you? Where are we going, Hugh?"

He started up the servants' stair. "I want to see the room. Maybe it will tell us something."

Wallace puffed up the stair after him.

"Wallace, you've been ill. It's best you conserve your strength." Hugh mounted the last step and waited. His cousin was three steps behind him and already pulling the key out of his pocket. The footman, still on duty outside the door, stood as tense as if he expected blame for losing the prisoner.

"My fault for failing to think there might be another way out," Hugh told the man.

As Wallace opened the door, he said, "Our fault but mine most of all. You were exhausted."

Manon had not bothered to close the shutters at night. In the light from the window, Hugh surveyed the room: bedclothes half off the cot, a neckcloth on the floor, and the chamber pot pulled out from under the bed.

"Wallace, you were here when Cuthbert was brought in. How many candles were there?"

"Just one. I brought a candlestick with several branches and took it away when we left Cuthbert," he added. They exchanged looks.

Hugh voiced the conclusion. "He's gone into the passages with that candle for light." To the footman, he said, "Fetch me Rob, Magistrate Seaton's groom, and have him bring two lanterns and spare candles."

The man bowed and reached the head of the staircase when Wallace called after him, "Warn Lord Keswick his heir is loose, and that he may be in danger. He must either keep to company or have a footman with him at all times until Cuthbert is secured."

"Yes, sir!" The footman clattered down the steps as if the devil were on his tail.

"…because if Keswick dies with no witness to Cuthbert killing him, there would be no chance of bringing him to justice for Lydia or his attempt on Eilidh." Completing the thought Wallace had not spoken, Hugh began to search for the movable panel, a simple task now he knew what to look for.

The cheaper wood used in the servants' rooms had more knots than the oak but he had a fair notion of where to look for the one he wanted. "Here it is." Now all he needed was Rob and lanterns.

Feet pounded up the stair heralding Rob's arrival with lanterns. Hugh swore softly as the tinder resisted catching for a few heartbeats. As he lit them, his cousin spoke.

"Hugh, two of you following him into the passages unarmed is not sensible."

"He has no weapon either and there was nothing here he could have used for one, was there?"

"No," Wallace said, though with a faint note of hesitance.

Rob said, "Sir, by your leave, we won't be unarmed." He withdrew a leather shot flask from each of his pockets and offered one to Hugh, who hefted it by its long neck and found it as full of lead shot as it would hold. "You'd make an excellent constable," he said, dropping it into his pocket.

Stepping inside the passage, Hugh let the panel close partway, one foot keeping it from swinging shut, so he could look the other way as well.

"I hoped to find him fainted just inside," he explained. "I can't credit he would be fully recovered when his brain was thoroughly rattled so recently. Wallace, perhaps it would be well for you to make sure Keswick does not go about unattended."

"I will, and I've had footmen or grooms posted at

all the outer doors.

****

Hugh sent Rob east, the shorter distance. If Randolph Cuthbert had gone that way, he would likely attempt to get out through the door near the kitchen where he would be seen by at least one of the servants who were always busy there. With luck, a footman or kitchen porter would stop him. "If you have no luck, Rob, start from the east end of the south wing. Perhaps we can catch him between us.

He himself would go west and down to Cuthbert's suite where the man might pause to collect whatever money he kept there, his wig, and perhaps a valise with a change of clothing, before slipping out through the door by the estate office, if he could, unless he knew of a concealed way out. Or he might be hiding in one of any number of unused rooms, waiting for an opportunity to escape during the night.

The narrow passage seemed more oppressive than it had when he and the groom had explored the hidden way to Lydia's chamber or when he had escorted Eilidh to safety on the second story. Darkness and still, dusty air blanketed him.

A disquieting thought occurred to him: they knew Cuthbert had been unarmed when they took him, but he might have a pistol in his bedchamber. Wallace had made out a search warrant, but he, Hugh, or perhaps Rob were the only ones who could execute it. Seaton would not trust it to anyone else. Had there been time to go through Randolph's possessions? Neither Hugh nor Rob had been sufficiently alert to do it.

They should have given the order to check all the chambers. Too late for regrets; he must simply hope the scoundrel made straight for an outer door, probably the one in the south wing. Would there be two footmen on duty in the hall as there were for rent day? There might only be one, halfway along the wing. He might have been sent on an errand by the earl, if his lordship was in his study or the library, or the fellow might not be looking in the direction of the door when Cuthbert emerged, probably from the footmen's parlor. That would be his most likely way out.

He remembered that coming from the south, the panel to Cuthbert's suite was the last one before the wing ended and they had entered the first floor over the old house, passing the Long Gallery. This time the suite's panel would be the first after the Long Gallery ended. He found it without difficulty but paused to take out the leather shot flask before pulling the panel open. Cuthbert's suite was identical to Lydia's, and it appeared empty. The housemaid, either unaware of the excitement overnight or acting from force of habit, had opened the shutters, providing plenty of light. Setting down the lantern, he approached the dressing room first. It held a cot for a servant, trunks, valises, hooks on the walls for clothing, and shelves, but no Cuthbert.

If he had stopped here on his way to freedom, the one thing Hugh was certain he would take was coin. At home, he kept money in a desk drawer. When traveling, he usually put it in the cabinet by the bed. If he were staying in someone's home, he might trust it to a dresser drawer. Here, he got no farther than the bedside stand. The top drawer contained a handkerchief and a tinder box. The second drawer was not pushed all the way in. A penny lay inside. A sixpence had fallen to the floor. Cuthbert had been here and grabbed up whatever rhino he had.

Hugh had been moving quickly, but his quarry might be two hours ahead of him or only thirty minutes. Would Cuthbert be warned by the lantern light? The intermittent barriers created by the windows meant he would have comparatively short notice of his pursuit.

At the next window, he went down to the ground floor, where Cuthbert must go to escape the house. Up another ladder and down the other side. Was Eilidh's husband—blast the man!—already out of Cuthbert Hall? The ground on the east side was open with little cover to conceal him. He could not go to the stables where the stable hands and grooms must all have been informed of his flight. Assuming he did get away, where could he go? Scotland was near, of course, from which it might be difficult to retrieve him.

Another few paces. He set a foot on the bottom rung of the next ladder and started up with a wince. His muscles were still complaining from last night's exertions. How long could Cuthbert survive on whatever he had in his purse? Hugh set the lantern down on the floor to the left at the top of the ladder. With his feet on the next to highest crossbar, steadying himself with his right hand on the sidepiece that protruded above the edge, he planted his left foot on the platform and stepped up. As he did so, something moved at the other end of the platform on the diagonal from his own position.

By pure instinct, he threw himself down and twisted away from the near edge. A weight hit his shoulder as someone grunted and stumbled over him—

—and down, in a series of bumps followed by a heavy weight hitting something solid. He rolled and raised himself to hands and knees. Thank God his lantern hadn't fallen. He crept to the edge, reached for the lantern, and peered down. Nothing lay on the floor below. He strained to see down the opening to the lower floor.

Chapter 24

Minutes later, lying flat on the floor by the opening to the cellar and dangling the lantern over the edge, he could make out something lying on the brick floor. "Cuthbert," he called. He could neither see any movement nor hear any sound.

He found Randolph Cuthbert sprawled, his head at an impossible angle. Hugh felt for a pulse in the neck: none. Cuthbert had had a more merciful death than the hempen rope gave, sparing Eilidh months of anxiety and his uncle embarrassment. Thank God! Cuthbert, his wits still scrambled, must have dropped the candle. Without a tinderbox, he could not rekindle the flame. Perhaps half-blinded by the lantern's light or disoriented, his charge at Hugh had carried him over the edge of the platform. Now Hugh had only to return to the ground floor and locate the nearest access into the wing.

Later, with the corpse laid on a table in one of the storerooms and Dr. Lockhart sent for to note the injuries, Hugh sent word to the footmen near the outer doors to watch for Rob and let him know the search was over. He was found before the earl, Wallace, Eilidh, Isobel, and Manon had all arrived in the Yellow Parlor to be apprised of the investigation's end.

Afterward, Keswick observed, "I won't pretend this is not the best result for all concerned. Seaton, I

328

trust the coroner will convene an inquest as soon as possible so we may put this all behind us with as little notoriety as may be. I am sure you and Montgomery will be glad to leave once it's done. Ellen, what are your plans?"

She flushed. "The Durham house lease runs until December. By then, I hope to know whether I still have a jointure."

The earl winced, almost invisibly. "If not, you are welcome to live here. We can discuss alternate arrangements after we have heard from Cuthbert's man of business."

Wallace had finished composing his letter to the coroner regarding the inquest before the gathering broke up. As they filed out, Hugh murmured to Eilidh, "May I have a word with you? Perhaps in the garden at the back of the house. There should be some shade. If you wouldn't mind?"

She wouldn't. She would love to be able to speak with Hugh without the weeks-long burden of fear and worry. His face revealed misgivings. She would like to smooth them away. "I would enjoy a walk in the garden." She said, "Isobel, perhaps you could see if the laundry maid could dye one of my newer gowns black? The red and yellow chintz, I think, as it's spoiled anyway."

"The very one," Isobel agreed with something like a grin, and bustled away.

Outside, Hugh took her arm and linked it through his own. "Things will be better shortly, Eilidh."

"They're already much improved. I'm free." He would not expect her to mince words and pretend to sorrow.

"Ay, but I mean, don't worry about your future. I wouldn't speak of this now, but I don't want uncertainty about your finances to trouble you."

"I have to think about them," she pointed out, reasonably, she thought.

He came to a stop by a well-grown rhododendron and glanced around.

"Is something wrong, Hugh?"

He smiled down at her. "Not at all. Come." He led her around the shrub, really almost a tree in size and halted again.

"I merely need to talk to you about your situation before you leave for Durham, as I expect you intend to do after the inquest."

"Well, yes, and I have to assume I won't be able to extend the lease, and I don't really want to. I'll have to see about whether I can find a new home or must accept Keswick's offer, and packing."

"I love that about you, my girl. You don't stand shilly-shally about decisions."

Eilidh savored the compliment which was all the more precious because it wasn't Spanish money, empty flattery.

"Society would insist that I should not speak to you until your first mourning, at the very least, was past. We've lost too many years already and given the circumstances, I think we could dispense with strict mourning. That cur tried to murder you and that was only the last of his sins against you, and you may be facing poverty. To indulge in a display of grief for form's sake would be nonsense."

"Yes, it would. I won't do it though I will put on black for the inquest." She admired his square jaw. He was more muscular than he had been years ago, and it lent him gravity.

He went on without seeming to hear. "I never married because no lady I met could hold a candle to you. If I acted as your outrider when you return to Durham, we could arrange to have the banns read there and in Rochester. We could be married in a month."

Dreamily she sighed, "I agree, Hugh."

"I realize it seems hasty, but—what?"

"Yes. I'll marry you. What society thinks doesn't greatly matter to me. Most of us here in the north are practical people. You and I both were when we accepted that I should marry Randolph. But that's not why I'll marry you. When I saw you again, all my old dreams came back from the dead. I love you. I never should have agreed to my parents' plan for me, but they were my parents, I loved them, and I didn't want to disappoint them."

He wrapped his arms around her and found her lips. How convenient that he did not have to hunch over to kiss her. So much more comfortable for him. Could they be seen from the house? Perhaps that was why they had stopped on this side of the rhododendron. Now she understood why women sometimes cried at weddings: it was a new beginning. Then coherent thought ceased, and she lost herself in delight.

A word about the author…

Kathleen Buckley has loved writing ever since she learned to read. After a varied career, she began to write as a second career, rather than as a hobby. Her first historical romance was penned (well, wordprocessed) in the manner of Georgette Heyer's Georgian/Regency romances. She is now the author of eleven published Georgian historical novels, each with a romance subplot.

Because historical fiction so often revolves around the famous and/or titled people, her characters often are neither, and ballrooms are in short supply.

http://18thcenturyromance.wordpress.com

Thank you for purchasing
this publication of The Wild Rose Press, Inc.

For questions or more information
contact us at
info@thewildrosepress.com.

The Wild Rose Press, Inc.
www.thewildrosepress.com